Molly:
Enjoy this!
— Chris McG.

ONCE THESE HILLS

D1596035

ONCE THESE HILLS

by Chris McGinley

"'Once these hills had everything people needed, he said. Once.' But now the community of Black Boar is being terrorized by three escaped convicts. Thankfully what they still have is Lydia King, an Appalachian Katniss Everdeen as fierce as Ron Rash's Serena. And thankfully what we have is *Once These Hills*, Chris McGinley's brutally beautiful tale of violence and redemption, a page-turner with genuine depth."

—**Mark Powell**, author of *Lioness*

"*Once These Hills* quickly unspools as an engaging tale of murder and justice, an appealing mix of history, suspense, and folklore backdropped by the creeping threat of modern industrial development. You'll fall in love with Lydia, a canny huntress who seems to acquire from a long-dead predecessor almost mythic powers of fortitude, prowess, and vengeance. This is a fast-paced but layered story about the passing of a particular American way of life, about women and women's pain, and about fear and the power that lies in overcoming it."

—**Julia Franks**, author of *Over the Plain Houses*

"In *Once These Hills*, McGinley thrills us with the voices of our ancestors, the strong men and women of Kentucky who knew the old ways of the land, people who survived against all odds. Lydia King is a marvelous and unforgettable heroine, tough and wise, always observant and respectful of nature, carrying her tragic lessons in her body. McGinley is a literary descendant of Elizabeth Maddox Roberts, in love with the landscape, ever respectful of the hard work of making an honest living. He knows the joy of a good meal with the neighbors followed by a slug of corn liquor, and he knows the bittersweet tang of revenge."

—**Bonnie Jo Campbell**, author of *Once Upon a River*

"Chris McGinley's *Once These Hills* is an Appalachian novel rooted in tradition but shot through with its own contemporary sensibility. The story is everything we want to see from those writers who chronicle the truth of a time and place that is both mythic and immediate. Those who admire McGinley's great Appalachian forbears like Ron Rash and John Ehle will find much to admire in this novel."

—**Charles Dodd White**, author of *How Fire Runs*

"*Once These Hills* is a dauntless tale of tough characters made tougher in the hardscrabble landscape of the Kentucky mountains. In a story fraught with violence and desperation, McGinley's lean prose cuts like a hawkbill knife, exposing the darkest depths of the human condition. This novel will leave its mark in the grit-lit genre, and it's one I won't soon forget."

—**Scott Blackburn**, author of *It Dies With You*

Chris McGinley

ONCE THESE HILLS

a novel

2023

ONCE THESE HILLS
Text copyright © 2023 Chris McGinley

Published by **Shotgun Honey Books**

215 Loma Road
Charleston, WV 25314
www.ShotgunHoney.com

Cover Design by Ron Earl Phillips.

First Printing 2023.

ISBN-10: 1-956957-24-3
ISBN-13: 978-1-956957-24-2

9 8 7 6 5 4 3 2 1   23 22 21 20 19 18

For Scott Lucero.
Rest, brother.

ONCE

THESE

HILLS

1898

BLACK BOAR MOUNTAIN

Eastern Kentucky
(Lydia, age 10)

Lydia was just ten when the bog woman entered her life. She and her father had been gathering moss for a bed tick when they came across something strange—an oval depression in the earth, roughly rimmed by a set of heavy stones. Her father decided to take a closer look. He cut away a dense layer of moss. The sweet smell of the wet soil underneath filled the air. Then he began to wrangle the stones. For just a moment, he and Lydia thrilled over what they might find. "Maybe it's buried treasure," Lydia said. She worked the dark soil with her little hands.

Her father laughed. "Maybe, Lyddie girl. Maybe."

But there would be no treasure.

The hand appeared first, the dark fingers and knuckles. It startled Lydia's father, and he ordered the girl to move back, to wait on him over by the bog's edge. When she lingered, he got firm with her. "Now, I said!"

His first impulse was to sweep the earth into the hole, to set the stones back in place and leave. But then he began to wonder about things. Why was a body buried here, in the bog? And in so shallow a grave with no real marker? Maybe someone's lost kin is in the ground right in front of him, someone killed and buried far away from his homeplace. His mind raced. In the end he decided he'd remove the earth and see what lie beneath. Maybe he would solve the mystery of a missing loved one.

It wasn't long before Lydia had crept near again. Her father poked around the edges of the corpse. And though he told her twice to stay back, the girl simply wouldn't listen. She could see it now from where she stood, the shape of a body in the shallow grave covered in fragrant black earth, the hands and arms visible on top of the chest. And then her father swept away the dirt from the face.

It was a woman.

Like her father, Lydia wondered who she was, this person up on the bog where no family plot could ever sit, where no cabin could be built. And a thought came to her then, a feeling as much as a thought, really. Maybe the dead woman was *outside* of people. Maybe she was of the woods, of the trees and streams, and of the creatures who lived here. It was just a feeling, more than anything.

"You shouldn't see such things, Lydia," her father said.

"I seen a dead body before," she said. "Papaw King, remember?" She sat on her haunches and watched her father remove the earth by the handful. Eventually she began to scoop out little mounds of dirt around the form.

Her father shook his head, but he let her be. This was his doing anyway. He was the one who had decided to remove the earth, to look for the buried treasure of his daughter's imagination. He was the one who had taken her along to collect moss and to check the traps, to do men's things, and to take her away from her mother and from work around the cabin. And it wasn't the first time either. If Lydia was more boy than girl, it was his doing. He wasn't sorry for this, but at times he wondered if he had made a mistake in making a ten year old girl his companion in the woods. She had a fondness for the trees and the animals now, for the rocks and the streams, for the cool, thin air, and for the smell of the forest earth. It was the same with him when he was her age.

Such things could not be undone.

But nor could the bog grave be undone. Not now. And there was something else in there, too. Not exactly the buried treasure they had imagined, but something precious even so. Her eyes wide, Lydia lifted a stone hand axe from the grave. She ran her finger along the edge of it, and as she held it her father poured water from a gourd and washed away the dirt. She could see how the blade had been hafted with rawhide around a hole where it fit into a piece of hardwood, dark and smooth from use. Hickory maybe, she thought. She would ask her father, but not now. The water had cleared away the dirt to reveal the tool, and how finely it was made, how perfectly weighted it felt even in her small hands. The axe was more than what it appeared to the eye, she realized. Words could wait. She ran her finger along the edge again and then touched the piece that protruded through the hole. "The poll's just as sharp as the blade," she said.

Her father took Lydia's hands in his own, and together they held the axe. "It's pretty, isn't it?" he said.

She placed the stone head in the flat of her little palm and felt the coolness there, and the surprising smoothness. "This is lighter than our axe," she said, lifting it up and down. "And smaller, too."

"Heavy enough to do damage, by God."

She looked up at her father. "Maybe it was made for a woman," she said.

"Maybe."

She drew the head flat across her forearm. "I wonder what an axe like this was used on."

"Likely used on all sorts of things. To make other tools, I reckon. Just to do every-day work."

She swept the hair from her face and left a black smudge on her forehead. "Do you think it was used on people?" she asked him. "Like a weapon."

"It's untelling. I'm not even sure how old it is."

At first her father figured the body had been recently buried and hadn't yet decomposed. But the skin was tawny and stretched taut over the high cheekbones. There were age lines above the lips and at the sides of the eyes. The fingers, too, showed the lines on the knuckles and on the back of the hands. It looked preserved more than anything. Dark from the bog but still intact, not decayed. The soil must have something to do with it, he figured, but he wasn't exactly sure. The clothes, too, were from another time, from before his parents' people, even. Buckskin breeches and a tunic with a belt of sinew. A Cherokee maybe, or someone before the Cherokee, he thought. The face appeared to be a woman's, but the axe and the breeches made him wonder. The hair was long, but that didn't rule out a man.

"It looks like a woman, but I wonder if it's a man," he said. "Got breeches on, and there's an axe. That's a man's tool."

Lydia stared at him.

"Well, don't you think that's odd, girl?" he said.

"Daddy, it's a woman."

Carefully she swept the muddy strands of hair from the face. When she touched the high cheekbone with the tips of her fingers, something happened, something she was never able to describe, not truly, at least. Even years later when she had the experience to understand so many different things. She only knew it was something feminine. She *felt* that part of it, but it wasn't a feeling she knew. Not like a mother's love or a friend's. It spread up through her fingertips and arms, and then down into her chest, this feeling, this feminine, wild sense.

She placed the axe on the dead woman's chest. "You might need this," she thought to herself.

Before they set to covering the body, her father thought to peek inside the breeches to check on the sex once and for all. He set his hand there, on the buckskin waist at the top of the breeches. But it was a violation he wasn't ready to make. And there was another reason he didn't check. To do so, he thought, would have unnerved Lydia, who believed without a doubt the body was that of a woman. Whatever governed him, he was glad he didn't do anything.

As it was, the story worried his wife when he told her later. "You dug up a grave, Preston King?" she said. "By God, why?"

For the third time he said, "Inez, we didn't *know* it was a grave until we got down in there." And again, he explained his worry about the would-be missing person, the murdered kinsman … or kinswoman. He even made a case for the buried treasure. "And what if *that* was true?" he said. "I bet then you wouldn't scold me. Not if we came back with gold coins, now."

She shook her head mournfully, throwing her snap beans into the bowl, one after the other. And she refused to let Lydia help her, a sure sign she was upset. At length she spoke again. "It's bad luck is what it is. Bad luck and there ain't no way around it. Law, Press. A grave! Sometimes you have no sense. And you, Lydia, what in God's good name were you thinking?" Preston and Lydia knew it was best to say nothing at such moments. They treaded lightly in the coming days, and there was no talk of revisiting the bog.

When it would get the better of her, and when she could hardly bear to be quiet any longer, Lydia's mother would ask about the grave. "Now, did you *touch* the body, Preston? Were you careful when you placed the earth back on top?" It was concern for her family that drove her to ask. She worried about what her husband and daughter might have unleashed. There was danger in a "defilement," she said. Everyone knew this.

But months later, when it finally seemed possible that no curse would be visited upon them, she had come around to asking more questions about the bog body. It was for her, too, a true mystery, something otherworldly that had touched their lives. "Lydia, dear," she said, "are you *sure* it was a woman? I don't know of a woman buried in breeches, or with an axe, by God. It's not *normal*."

"It's a woman up there, Momma," Lydia said.

Whoever was buried in the bog, and whatever defiling there might have been, what soon happened convinced the settlers up on Black Boar Mountain—at least for now--that none of the King family had been cursed, nor anyone else. It happened on a late afternoon in May, when the mountain air was still cool, and smoke rose in thin purls from the cabins set about the hillside on land the homesteaders had cleared themselves. Years ago, the first families up on Black Boar had girded and felled trees, burned slash and cleared stumps on the uneven land. And they were still doing it. They were small farmers and drovers who sold their crops and stock to the merchants down in the valley, in the little town of Queen's Tooth.

Black Boar was the only world Lydia had ever known.

On this day she stood under the old oak tree, close enough to see the vibration in the breast of the screech owl that sat in a hollow up the trunk. She tried to predict the timing of the bird's eerie call, to sing out just as the owl did. Soon her mother would light the fire in the cabin and call Lydia to help out. Lydia hoped the owl would fly off before she was summoned. To watch such a thing thrilled her, and she willed the bird to take flight. One time, a year or so earlier, she watched the owl dive for a squirrel, though she turned away when it returned with its kill. Lydia knew she couldn't have witnessed the bird tear apart the little creature. Maybe someday she could, she thought. For now, though, she was content to see the owl take flight and soar above her, to watch it glide and tilt its wide wings against the grey sky and the dark hillsides.

But the owl hadn't flown by the time her mother called her, and Lydia coaxed the bird. "Come on now," she said, "spread your wings, Mr. Owl." Still, the bird remained in its hollow. It sang out a few more times before Lydia's mother called again, and now she knew she had better get home. "Goodbye then, Mr. Owl," she finally said. She ran off toward the cabin.

The supper was a disappointment. Soup beans with the morning's half-stale cornbread and the tart blackberries that tortured Lydia with their thorns at harvest. "These berries aren't as good as the ones Mr. McNeely grows on them poles," she said.

"Well, I'm sorry about that, your highness," her mother said, "but those berries don't come in for some time. And those we have to trade for, and he wants too much for them anyhow. These berries grow wild. Now you know this much, Lydia. Why do you worry me about berries?" Her mother plunked down a mug on the table and filled it halfway with milk. The sound startled the girl.

"I didn't mean it mean, Momma," Lydia said.

"Well think before you speak. Last thing I need is a lippy ten-year-old around here. Your father's doing the best he can, we all are, but there's not much beyond squirrels and birds can anybody find right now. And even they're hard to get, seems like."

She rattled the logs with the poker and sparks flew onto the puncheon floor. "It's that railroad work that's run off the animals," she said.

Her mother swept the hair from her face and Lydia noticed then that she seemed tired, frail even. Small circles had formed beneath her eyes. She watched her mother as she worked the fire. Her frame had shrunk in recent months, and the task seemed a real chore for her. The domestic energy she had, before the game had begun to go scarce, had left her. Lydia knew that meat had been harder to come by recently, but she also wondered if it was the *kind* of work that wore so deeply on her mother. Work around the cabin seemed to tire out a person more than checking traps, Lydia felt, more than hauling wood even. For Lydia, there was a fatigue and a boredom that came with cabin work, with boiling shirts, with cleaning and cooking, even if the work itself seemed less demanding than clearing brush, say, or digging a fire pit. Part of her wanted to help her mother, to lessen the burden, but it wasn't in her to feel good about it. Truth be told, she begrudged cabin work, and she often had to be told to help out.

Lydia forced herself to eat the pone of cornbread and then she began work on the bitter berries. Her mother sat down beside her and Lydia noticed that her wedding band no longer fit so snugly. She reached over and took her hand, and when her mother asked about the owl near the stream she knew that their brief quarrel had ended.

"It's beautiful," Lydia said. "I wonder if it's a male or a female."

"I don't know. Maybe we could find out. Ask Hez, maybe. He studies on that kind of thing."

"I sure would like to know."

It was then that they heard men's voices outside. "Lord," Lydia's mother said when she looked out the cabin door. Lydia rose and joined her. A group of men were gathered alongside Hez Coombs' wagon which had stopped near the pathway that led down to the barn. The men were too far away for Lydia to see what was in

9

the wagon, but she could hear them plainly. There was an energy that lifted their voices on the air. She heard laughter, too, and the sound of a heavy chain being dragged. A few women had come out of their cabins. Lydia and her mother joined them and headed toward the wagon.

Her mother yelled up ahead, "What do they have, ladies?" But the answer was lost in the men's loud voices.

"What's happening, Momma?" Lydia said.

"I don't know, dear. I just don't know. We'll find out."

A group of men bustled around the wagon hitched to Hez's mule, some carrying guns and knives. A few had already headed down the steep incline toward the two-stall barn and the oak tree near the stream. Their strides seemed long and quick to Lydia. Something important was happening, she could tell. As men moved off toward the barn, the women circled the wagon. Lydia stood on her toes, but she still couldn't see what was in the bed. She shouldered her way through finally, ducking and sliding sideways until she stood right up alongside the wagon.

Then she saw it.

A dead black bear lay in the bed of the wagon, its legs secured around a birch trunk roughly cut at the ends. The bear's head was turned in her direction and the mouth lay open. She stared wide-eyed at the fang-like canines and the large, tan muzzle. And at once a great sorrow for the huge animal swept over her. Instantly she sensed that this was different than chickens or squirrels. Those were animals that fled, or worse, animals who never even sensed they were hunted. A bear was a rare creature, nothing like those others. Nothing like deer, even. It was more wild than these animals, more terrifying. She stared at the huge body, lifeless on the wagon bed, and it came to her that maybe this was wrong, that the bear should have been spared. And yet, part of her knew that the animal would provide for everyone there, her mother included. She stood and thought about it, her hands on the wagon bed, with the body of the bear just a few feet away.

She studied its jaw with its long canines open in a silent howl, a reminder of the fearsomeness that once was, just hours ago.

The women started asking questions, all at one time it seemed like to Lydia.

"Who claimed it?" a neighbor woman asked.

"Is it a sow?"

"Naw, that one's a boar," someone said.

A neighbor woman named Clytie Noe set her hands on Lydia's shoulders and said to her, "Well, little lady, what do you think of this here?"

Lydia saw that the animal had been field dressed. With her eyes she followed the wide cut that ran from chest to groin. A layer of white fat beneath the fur showed at the edges and the hair along the cut had been matted with blood. She stretched her hand out and touched the animal's paw, gingerly at first. She felt the leathery pads on the bottom and fingered the smooth, dark claws. The bear's legs were cinched tightly around the pole, and though she knew the animal was dead, she thought it looked painful. She ran her fingers through the thick fur, and traces of dirt and blood soiled her hands.

Men circled around and began to direct the women. "Watch out, ladies," one of them said.

"Move away now. This is men's work."

People laughed when Clytie said, "Well, which among you men is gonna *cook* that meat, is what I'd like to know. It's untelling how many ways a man could muss that up."

"Maybe so," a man with a knife said. "Anyhow, Hez said to tell you get the cauldron. He plans to cook that meat right here. And we need whiskey, too. Don't be stingy. If your man has a bottle, go fetch it." He smiled when he said, "And don't fuss about it neither. Not today."

Clytie pulled a small bottle of whiskey from a pocket in her dress. "I got my own jug, thank you." She took a sip and sang out, "Eye-God! Tastes good to a woman!"

Those around her laughed, and someone said, "Clytie knows her way around that old cauldron, don't you, woman?"

Clytie took another sip from the bottle and offered it to a thin, young wife with a baby on her hip who shook her head in amazement. Still, the woman smiled and took a tiny sip before she passed the bottle on.

"I'm like a witch at that pot if there's meat enough to go into it," Clytie said. "Come on and help me ladies. That pot's heavy like to killed you."

"Eunice and me'll haul the firewood," one of the women said.

"I've got fat enough from that hog."

Lydia watched the women walk off to the different cabins as the men moved in on the wagon. She hoped her mother wouldn't drag her along with the other women, and she ducked behind the wagon wheel hoping to stay out of sight. From there she could see her mother looking for her, but she soon gave up and headed off with the others. Lydia pulled herself up on top of the wagon with the men who were ready to maneuver the animal off the bed. More than anything, Lydia didn't want to be shooed away, and she determined that she would be useful. She would help.

A young man with a thick beard sheathed a long knife and said to Lydia, "Watch out now, girl. This is dangerous work."

Lydia eyed him briefly and then crouched down low so as to get her shoulder under the birch trunk. She heaved with all her might when the men began to lift the pole. The man shook his head, but he didn't scold her. Once the animal came off the wagon, Lydia could no longer reach the pole, even with her arms fully extended, but she walked with them down toward the oak, her hand on the bear's flank.

"I'll steady it so it don't swing," she said.

The musky odor was different than that of other animals she had been around. She pressed her cheek into its fur and breathed in its scent as they walked down to the tree.

"Law, I can't believe the size of him!" one of the men said.

"Four hundred pounds at least."

At the oak tree, Lydia was relieved to see the young man with the beard and knife cut the rope that lashed the animal to the pole. The bear was freed now. Still dead, she knew, but ready to be cut up, ready to give over what it possessed. She watched them strain the tackle block to get the bear high enough for Hez Coombs to go to work on him with his long knife. The different cuts were removed and given over to a man who had set up a makeshift butcher's table on two saw horses and boards from inside the small barn. The man cut away the remaining fat and grizzle from the pieces Hez had butchered and reduced the cuts to smaller pieces for cooking. These he set out on a piece of pine board.

It was a real labor for Lydia to carry it, but she relayed the meat up to the women by the cauldron. She slid the irony cuts onto the table where her mother and another woman coated them in herbs and set the pieces into the fat of the giant iron pot where they began to sizzle. The meat smelled stronger than deer meat, Lydia thought, stronger than squirrel or chicken. It was different, and she wondered if maybe the bear would provide something more for the people than those other animals.

At the cauldron, Clytie worked to brown the pieces before she added hambone stock and the vegetables the other women arrived with. It would be a burgoo. In a loud voice, a thick, wide woman talked with Clytie about temperatures, about the addition of water and seasonings, about when to add what and how to know when the burgoo was done.

Some of the men couldn't wait, though, and fished out hunks of the meat for sampling. The hot pieces singed their hands and they cursed out loud in front of Lydia and the other children who had gathered around. "Wait 'til I've cooked it proper, boys," Clytie yelled. But the men tore into the meat, their hands and beards a mess of grease and blood.

"Oh Clytie, you are good," one of them said through a mouthful of bear meat.

"Wait 'til it's cooked proper," Clytie said again, running a man off with the tobacco stake she used to stir the cauldron.

More vegetables were added, and someone had brought canned summer tomatoes that were thrown in, too. Lydia savored the smell, and soon most everyone had gathered by the cauldron to watch Clytie and the women. Now it was they who directed things, the women who held sway. "Richard, go get that cornbread," one of them directed her husband.

"And find some salt. It's in there by the pot," another one said. "Go on, now."

Clytie hollered, "Stand back, everyone. I can't work with you crowding me."

"Nor can I tend the fire with you all worryin' me," the friend said. "And I need more wood, Abe. Go fetch more firewood."

For a little while, Lydia stirred the cauldron under the direction of Clytie and the other women. And though she loved the smell of the meat and vegetables as they bubbled and mingled, the effort itself drained her. As she worked the tobacco stake, she stared off in the direction of the oak tree, below where the men worked. It seemed like the burgoo would never be done, and it was all she could do not to run off. Her mother noticed her restlessness and finally said, "Go on down there, Lyddie." Lydia handed her the tobacco stake.

When he saw her approach, Hez called Lydia to the oak tree where he coiled his ropes. "Everybody left me, Lydia," he laughed. Can you help me here, girl?" Lydia set to work at the little tasks Hez gave her, some of which she knew he could have done on his own, work he intended for her so that she could be a part of it all. She liked him for this.

"Now I hear there's a screech owl down here, a friend of yours, right?" Hez asked her.

"Yessir, he sets in that little hollow up there." Hez looked up to the hollow but the owl was gone.

"All this commotion must have scared him off."

"I bet," Lydia said. "We was wondering if it was a male or female. Is there a way to tell?"

"Not always," Hez said. "The males do more of the hunting, especially if the females are nesting. The females are bigger, though, and they can kill, too. They ain't as fast as the males, though."

Hez cleaned up the last of his knives and placed it a leather sheath. "You know, there's a bald eagle around here, Lydia. A big one, a male I think. I seen it myself."

"Really, Hez? An eagle?"

"Yes. There's men timberin' over there, up on Rusty Mountain. And that brung out the bird, I figure. I talked to one of them woodhicks. He said he seen it fly."

"Well, I hope they don't take down his nest."

Hez said, "Can't see any way around it, sweetheart. They ain't gonna spare a tree just for a bird, even an eagle." Lydia looked at him as if she weren't sure if he were joking. She wanted to see it. An eagle was much more than just a bird, more even than the owl she so loved. It was like the bear in this way, greater than the animals around it. And she didn't like to think that the eagle might be chased from its nest. How would it survive, she wondered?

Hez touched her elbow and said, "Come on now, let's go and see how that food's coming along. That eagle will make another nest somewheres else. Don't worry about him any."

She hoped he was right.

In the gloaming, the cauldron fire cast an orange glow on the men gathered around. Lydia watched them eat from bowls they held close to their faces while others waited their turn, sipping whiskey from the bottles passed about. Some of the women drank, too, and moved close against their husbands. A few couples kissed openly on the lips, and older siblings were given charge of the little ones. Lydia spotted her mother and father in the rear of the circle. In the light of the fire they came into view but receded just as quickly. In one hand her father held a whiskey bottle. His arm was cinched tightly around her mother's waist. There was blood on her mother's apron under her breast and across the stomach, but whether from working with the bear meat or from her father's hands she didn't know. When the orange light revealed them again, they were walking off toward the cabin, her mother's arm wound tightly around her father's back.

Eventually, Lydia pushed her way to the cauldron and was served some burgoo. She put her face over the steaming bowl and took in the scent of the herbs and the rich, fatty meat. She went at it then, devouring it quickly. A boy she had noticed before, Cole his name was, saw her wipe the fat from her lips with her sleeve, something she saw one of the men do. He smiled at her and laughed. She would have been embarrassed, but something about his manner made her laugh, too. Someone drew a bow across a fiddle and music filled the air. Lydia knew by heart all the songs and she joined in, too. A few couples set to dancing. She watched it all and it filled her with an energy and a gladsomeness.

At some point, one of the neighbor women at the cauldron called out for Lydia's mother, "Where's that Inez?"

"Off to ruttin' with that husband," Clytie said as she gave the pot a stir. "Like the others, I suppose." A swell of laughter rose. Lydia knew the word, but she had considered it only in relation to animals in the woods. Still, it was true that several of the couples had walked off to their cabins, their arms around one another in tight embraces.

Later that night, when Lydia lay in bed in the loft, she heard the sounds from her parents down below. She had heard them before, late at night when they thought she had fallen asleep. She had wrapped her quilt around her ears then. But now she listened, forcing herself to hear the primal sounds, what seemed to her like both pleasure and pain. Her skin became so warm she kicked her quilt to the floor. She let it all run around in her mind now. The coupling, the killing, the drinking and carrying on. She tried to think about it more deeply, to figure it all out. She tried to think about the boy Cole and whether or not he would like her, whether or not she would ever be liked someday, by anyone. With her stomach full, though, and her body so warm, she could stay awake no longer.

Lydia rose early the next day and walked down to the oak tree. A few bottles lay about on the ground and a heavy fog covered the hilltops. Down by the oak tree a male grey fox moved toward the stream. It turned its head when it sensed Lydia's presence, though she caused no alarm, and the animal stood still even as Lydia approached. Not until she was almost on top of him did he finally move on. And then at the stream bank she spotted a doe and a buck dipping their heads for a drink. They, too, seemed not to notice.

Vibrating and making its shrill call, the owl had returned to the oak. Lydia moved close to the tree, but the bird kept to its hollow, calling and thrumming. She knew exactly when it would sound, irregular as this was. She felt alive with it then, a part of the living things around her, and also a part of the adults who slept now in their cabins, full and sated. Just then the screech owl lifted from the hollow, rising high and circling. Lydia scanned the stream bank and saw what the bird had seen, a small woodchuck grubbing for food. The owl flew toward it, and Lydia hoped that it would return to the tree with its kill. She knew now that she could bear the scene. Today she would watch the owl tear up the animal. Then out of the dense fog, she saw another bird come into view above the trees. It glided above, floating almost, its wings a giant silhouette against the gray sky, much larger than the owl.

The eagle.

As the owl dove for the woodchuck, so did the eagle. It would be a close race, Lydia thought, and she yelled out to the owl, "Go get it, Mr. Owl!" But it would be no race.

When she thought of it later, even years later, she would swear that she *felt* the strike, physically, as if the violence of the impact had somehow traveled through the air and met her below. A mass of feathers swirled above her and fell to the ground. The owl let out a single, high-pitched squeal, nothing like its call from the oak hollow, and the eagle flew away toward Rusty Mountain, the bird in its talons.

Lydia watched them go.

The owl was forever gone, the oak hollow empty. It pained her, but she never cried. Instead, she stooped and collected a single feather. Later that night she would cut a hole through the shaft and thread some elm bark cord through it. It was a necklace, the vane absurdly long on her small frame. But she would wear it, even if others teased her for it.

She was never sure if the feather belonged to the owl or the eagle. But this didn't matter. In the end, she was glad not to know.

Long, Long Ago

BLACK BOAR MOUNTAIN

T he woman wore a deerskin dress belted with woven hemp and cinched at the neck with a bone pin. She climbed up a sandstone boulder that opened above a stand of ash trees. Like she hoped, several deer grazed with their noses to the ground. It would be a long shot, but she knew it would be too much of a risk to climb down the sheer face of the boulder to get any closer. If they sensed her, the deer would bolt.

Her hickory bow was hard to pull, though she had practiced much of late. She nocked an arrow she had fletched herself, with horned owl feathers, and let fly. It found a large buck, but not where she had hoped. The arrow hit just in front of the rear haunch and the animal leapt off into a laurel patch. When she climbed down the boulder the other deer loped off.

On a patch of briars, she saw some blood and hoped that the deer would be slowed down in the thick brush. But it had quickly changed direction, she saw from a trail that moved along the floor of the forest, and it had descended a small gulley. She leaned into the mountainside and made her way down, slipping and falling here and there, but without real injury. When she hit flatter ground, she spotted the trail. In time she heard rustling and she could tell that the animal had slowed. When she came upon it, she could see that it was still alive. With its shiny black eye, the buck spotted her. Twice it reared up. She could just wait, but she didn't like it that way. Her axe was sharp and light—her husband had made it so--and she could use it just like any knife she had ever held. She buried the blade behind the buck's ear. But before she gutted him, she poured a little water from a gourd into its mouth.

BLACK BOAR MOUNTAIN

(Lydia, age 13)

The granny woman told it this way. She said Lydia was borned all wrong, and that's why Inez could never bear another child. Something about not sitting upright after the baby came, and about the direction Inez should have lain because of a near full moon. She was supposed to be with her feet facing south, but she wasn't, the granny woman later learned, and this was the problem. There wasn't any way to fix it either, she said. No tokens or spells would work now, even if the granny woman herself had sworn them. The old woman shook her head when she told the story. "It's more than catching a baby that's the work of a granny woman," she said. "It's much more. Now you know as much."

Still, some thought the old woman might have cursed Inez for spite because Inez hadn't called for her, because she called on Clytie Noe for help when the baby came. Others thought it was just something that happened in childbirth, not as horrible as the death of the mother--which was common enough with or without a granny woman--but more like damage to the feminine parts. No one could say for sure, and only one thing was certain:

Inez had not conceived since Lydia's birth. Whatever the reason, no one spoke openly against the granny woman, neither then nor now.

Inez taught her daughter much about the life of a mountain woman, about work in and around the cabin, about the skills one needed to live in a place like Black Boar. Lydia listened. She helped her mother run things around the cabin, though she hated it, and longed to be free of it. And because Inez felt her own guilt like a daily weight, she relented. Inez would never give her husband a son, she knew, and so the girl had become her father's companion in the woods. It was there that Lydia thrived anyway. Yes, she would help with the washing and with the other duties around the cabin, but often as not, her mother freed her to her father and to the woods, and even to the masculine work outside the cabin to which the girl seemed more suited. And though she surely could have used the help, Inez figured that this was best for all, for Preston as much as Lydia. And if it helped her to lessen the weight of her own guilt, well then, why shouldn't that figure in too, she reckoned.

By the time she was thirteen, Lydia could trap and hunt as well as any of the boys on the mountain.

It was on a cold fall morning she and her father saw something that would change things for Lydia. They headed out to check their traps and see what they might kill. By late afternoon Lydia had taken a snowshoe hare and a squirrel. She dressed them both and wrapped the meat in some pawpaw leaves she carried in a feed sack bag. Later she would clean the rabbit pelt and see what it might fetch down in the valley. If the traps yielded anything, she would harvest those hides, too, whatever they were.

Her father was empty handed.

Nowadays, they avoided the bog as a rule, though neither of them mentioned this fact aloud, preferring to range around clearings and laurel slicks where rabbits hid, in amongst the trees that yielded mast for the animals. They walked across a bald near the top of the mountain now, a place where they doubted, they'd find anything to kill, but with a view that Lydia never tired of. From the overlook, Rusty Mountain was visible, but there were large patches that had been timbered, shorn down to tree crowns and slash. It was a despoiling the young girl had witnessed in just a few years' time. Still, the full view was something to behold, especially in the crisp air that replenished the lungs after the steep climb of the last quarter mile. The hills spread out in the distance, with one ridge dropping in behind the next in a pattern that stretched as far as Lydia could see. And the trees gave them color--different shades of brown, yellow, and red that reminded Lydia of a painting she once saw in Queen's Tooth. She loved the colorful canvas at the time, and wanted badly to try her hand at such a thing, but the paints were expensive and hard to come by, her mother told her. Lydia wondered now if the artist had stood in this very spot when he painted it. She thought that if she could paint the view from the bald, she would fill in the places where the timbermen had been, where the trees had been taken and the slash now lay. She would guess what colors to use based on what she saw in front of her. She would fill in the gaps. She thought also that she would need a canvas much wider than the one she saw in town that day. In her painting, she would capture the hills that spanned the full horizon. The canvas would be a long rectangle, not a square. But she knew, too, that the painting would be no substitute for the view, and that the vista itself, with the climb and the anticipation, was greater than any painting could be.

Lydia's dress was red around the hips with animal blood, her hands, too. Her father noticed but said nothing about it, not while they admired the view. When they stopped at one of their empty traps on the return hike, he said, "Maybe we can trade clothes. I can wear that dress and your mother will think I'm a good provider." Lydia looked concerned for a moment, but her father's broad smile told her it was just a joke. He laughed and said, "You're good, Lyddie. You need to teach me how you do it one of these days."

"Come on, now," she said. "You're teasin' me."

He smiled and said, "Well, maybe. But you *are* good. Good with a bow, too. I mean it."

Lydia tied the sack to the gun and carried it on her shoulder, like her father did sometimes, so that they could hold hands. The two walked on, only talking when one or the other identified a bird call, or stopped to listen and whisper when something rustled somewhere. They crossed a stream where a doe and two fawns bolted from the bank and startled them. The splash they made crossing the stream roused a coopers hawk whose violent flight sent orange and red leaves down to the stream in a slow fall. Lydia and her father were disappointed to miss a chance at the deer but they watched the leaves float on the air and then on the current that carried them out of sight. Some of the mossy rocks slowed the fallen leaves, and Lydia stopped to pick one from the water. A large oak leaf, still green at the main vein, but changing to yellow and then orange and then red at the deep lobes and tip. She twirled it by the stem in her finger and thumb and thought again about how she would fill in the painting of the vista where the timber men had been. She dropped the leaf in the stream and watched it spin and float away.

In time they reached their traps. A squirrel lay dead in one of them at the trunk of a beech tree. Lydia decided to gut it later, tossing it in the sack for now. Several other traps lay bare, the bait untouched. Lydia's father stopped to examine one of them and said, "It's that Railroad work that's doing this. Those explosions scare hell out of the animals. And those wood hicks, those timber men. They run everything off." He shook his head.

"Then how come that preacher says the Rail is a good thing for us," Lydia asked.

Her father sighed. "I don't know for sure," he said. "Sometimes I think he might be right. It brings business. It makes it easier for people up here to bring their stock and harvest to trade down in town. To sell it. Mostly whenever they want. And the Rail brings people from outside, too. And visitors, they need food and a place to stay. They spend money down in town. That's good for us, for the things we sell down there."

"Well .... that's all good, right?" Lydia said.

"Yes, but *not* good in a way. Too many hunters, too many farmers ... that can be bad. Truth be told, too many *people* can change a place for the worse in lots of ways." He set his hand on her shoulder. "Once these hills had everything people needed. Once. It was never easy for them folks, my momma and daddy, and them before. And it ain't easy for us, either. But you could get everything you needed ... once. Things are changing fast, with the Rail and such. People are changing. It's getting harder. But once these hills were enough, Lyddie dear." Eventually they came to their last trap.

What they saw stilled them.

In the trap was the hind leg of a bobcat. There was a little blood on the fallen leaves nearby and a few drops on the trap itself. But it was the detached leg that concerned Lydia. There was a patch of blood at the place where the animal had chewed itself free, though the rest of the leg was intact, the fur free of debris and the paw neat and clean, almost like it wasn't real. She imagined the three-legged animal hobbling off, likely to hide and die somewhere. She looked around for a three-footed track, though what she would do if she found it, she didn't know.

Her father said, "I don't like to see this."

Lydia said, "No, Daddy."

"If I had it my way," he said, "I'd not trap at all. Just hunt. But that goddamn Railroad and the timber men make it hell on us up here." He threw down a piece of sassafras root he'd been chewing and kneeled to remove the leg and re-bait the trap. "Hell, that must've been painful."

"There's no way it will survive, is there?" Lydia asked.

Lydia's father looked up at her. She was still looking for the cat. "I don't know," he said. "This ain't the first time I seen it. And some folks say they've seen such animals in the woods, three-legged things, hobbling around. So, maybe it will be alright."

"How will it hunt, Daddy?"

"Don't know, little girl. But I know this much. It must really want to live. If there's a three-legged cat that might survive up here, it's this one."

Lydia had seen a bobcat only once before, early one morning when she snuck off on a hike without her mother's knowledge. From a sandstone perch she never told anyone about, she heard the feminine cry, but she knew the cat would sense her if she tried to seek it out, and so she contented herself with listening to the eerie wailing. The cat finally crept out down below, without a sound, not twenty feet from her. She watched it clamber up on a fallen log and scan the trees for birds and squirrels. The cat looked at Lydia but paid her no mind. Lydia could see the lean muscle move beneath the skin at the haunch as it stood with one rear leg forward of the other. Its tufted ears twitched above the above the thick, grey ruff, and it opened its jaws wide in a yawn. Lydia saw the sharp canines and incisors. Eventually, it dropped from the log and loped off into a stand of sycamores. Lydia's heart raced. She could never tell it, though, because of the deception with her mother. But then maybe it was better this way, she thought. A secret. Only the cat knew about her presence and she surely wasn't going to tattle.

Lydia hoped the bobcat caught in the trap today was a different animal, but if it was the same cat, she hoped it would survive. Lydia also knew she would go back to the sandstone perch and look for it. She didn't need her mother's permission anymore.

Her father ran his thumb over the soft fur atop the claws and shook his head again. "Damn, he said." He drew his hand back to toss the leg far from the trap.

"Wait, Daddy."

"What?"

"I'll take it. I'll keep it."

"This will rot in the cabin, Lydia. It'll raise up a stink, dear."

"You think I don't know as much as that? There are ways to keep it, though, like a rabbit's foot. And I know how to do it. At least I know someone who can do it."

"Why do you want it, Lydia? It's not gonna bring any kind of luck." He looked at the severed leg he held. "Might even bring *bad* luck."

Lydia had set her gun and bag down. She said, "That leg is a good token, Daddy. You said it yourself. The leg tells us about the cat and how it didn't want to die."

"Who's gonna make it nice for you?"

"That boy, Cole. He knows how to do these things. So do others, but he won't laugh at me like others might."

Her father raised his eyebrows at this. Then he said, "Open your bag. I'll put it in there."

Clytie pulled a poker from a nail on the wall and said to her husband, "You ain't got enough air goin' through there, Corny." She adjusted the logs in the fireplace and the flames rose, throwing an orange light on everyone. "That's how it works, husband," she said.

Cornelius shook his head and said with mock disgust, "Well, I can't do nothin' right, I don't guess, except maybe pass this bottle to my lovely wife. Maybe that I can do right."

Clytie winked at him and accepted the bottle. When she took a sip she handed it back and said, "Have you a sup, Corny. It's good." He smiled and took a small sip, offering it then to Inez, who refused, and then to Preston who took a tiny sip.

"I reckon Lydia is old enough for a small sup, right?" Cornelius said.

Inez snapped, "No, she ain't. Put that up now, you."

But she saw that Cornelius was smiling, and that he had already plugged the bottle. Lydia saw it, too. Both he and Clytie were lively that way, always playing a joke. And they enjoyed having Lydia around, unlike some of the other adults on the mountain who thought children got underfoot. The couple had no children of their own. No one was sure if it was Cornelius or Clytie who was at fault, but for their part, they never despaired over it. Their way was to celebrate life, never to gossip meanly or mourn the way of things. For this Inez and Preston loved them dearly, and so did Lydia, who especially liked how Clytie teased her, and how she joked and laughed where other women would have hushed up around menfolk.

She loved to hear Clytie tell a story, even if she stretched the truth. Sometimes Clytie would wink at Lydia when she told one of her tales, a little sign between them that maybe what Clytie said wasn't exactly the truth, but that it was worth telling anyway, and that maybe the story was better than the truth because of the way she told it, because of the salt she added.

Clytie was never daunted by men. She spoke whenever and wherever. Nor did Cornelius ever hush her, as far as Lydia could tell. Lydia didn't know if this was because Cornelius loved Clytie for the way she was, or because he was scared to counter her. Maybe both. Of course, Clytie was thoughty, too, and she looked out for Lydia's mother and father, and for all of her neighbors on Black Boar. She never put herself first when it was the welfare of the people at stake. But at the same time, she didn't lack for confidence, and often Clytie herself was the subject of her own stories—how she settled a disagreement once and for all, or how she saved the day way back when. Sometimes the stories were funny, and Clytie would laugh, but often they were serious, about life and death circumstances. One thing Lydia noticed was that Inez, and other women, too, seemed to gain confidence in the presence of Clytie. They might chime up where they normally wouldn't, or say something to surprise their own husbands, Lydia noticed. When Clytie talked in the presence of men, Lydia thought, the women around her straightened up slightly, pushed back their shoulders. She was drawn to this part of Clytie. She thought of this now and smiled as she watched the fire and listened to the sparks pop, contented to sit in her good neighbor's cabin, hoping Clytie would spin a yarn.

The adults sat around the maple table that Cornelius had recently finished. It was smooth and solid, the legs thick and leveled off smartly. It sat heavily on the puncheon floor Cornelius had also laid, the finest on the mountain. Four cherry, ladder-back chairs were arranged around it, all well-joined, the seats caned with white oak splints that Cornelius had stripped himself and dyed brown with the bark. Lydia sat on the floor with Cornelius' hawkbill blade. "What's this one for, Cornelius?" she asked him.

"That's for different things," he said. "But mostly I use it to shape wood and to cut the splints from trees to make the canes for my chairs. It's a kind of knife that gets pulled toward you, not like most knives where you push away. But you can push it, too, if you like."

"It's sharp."

"Yes indeed. Be careful."

Clytie said to Lydia, I heard you got you a hare and a squirrel today, little lady."

"Yes, ma'am."

"She's a good shot, Clytie," Preston said. Getting good with a bow, too. She took a turkey just the other day. Fletched her own arrows with the feathers, too."

Clytie winked at the girl and smiled.

Inez said, "I had to tell her to get that bow and those bloody arrows out of my pantry. 'Put those things the barn,' I said, where they belong. Men's things."

"Clytie used to be a pretty good shot," Cornelius said.

"How do you know I ain't *still* good," she said.

"Oh, lord," Cornelius said. I better watch my words. I could end up with a belly full of lead." He grinned at Lydia now.

Lydia said, "Clytie, did you used to hunt some?"

Clytie unplugged the bottle and passed it to Inez, who said "Oh, I reckon I'll have a tiny sup."

"That's the spirit, woman!" Clytie said. She took the bottle and plugged it.

Preston and Cornelius laughed, and Clytie started her story. "After my momma died," she said, "I used to go with my daddy hunting and trapping. There were many years there where we roamed them hills and took lots of game. He taught me all of it. How to bait traps, dress a kill, stalk a deer, everything. You see, when momma died, I took over all the womanly duties. I already knowed how to cook from her."

Cornelius interrupted, "And you are good, by God. Don't ever go back to hunting if you expect to give up cooking."

"Hush now, Corny," Clytie said. "Anyway, daddy was just so lonely without momma that he took me along with him on them long hunts. I had me a .22 single shot, an old one. I didn't have any interest in those repeaters. That little .22 killed plenty. Kept food on the table, it did. I still get a feeling from time to time that I'd like to get out there again. Come up on a deer or a bear, and POW!"

Cornelius smiled and said, "A bear, huh? Now that would be something to see."

"It's true I never took a bear," Clytie said, "but I would like to get out there again. Yes, I would."

Cornelius sensed that she was serious and said, "Well, there's nothing keeping you from doing so. We can go out together if you want."

Lydia nearly said, "I'll take you with me, Clytie," but she didn't.

Clytie smiled at her husband and pulled the plug to the bottle. "Maybe we will, Corny. Maybe."

Inez said, "If you go out there with that bottle like you do, Corny better lookout for where those bullets are flyin." Clytie opened her mouth wide to laugh at that one, and Lydia noticed her mother smile at her own success.

"Yes ma'am," Cornelius said. You can't go drinking and shooting at the same time."

"Like hell," Inez said. "Half the time all you men come back with is an empty bottle. Only thing you can kill."

"You tell it, woman!" Clytie said. She took a sip from the bottle and passed it over to Inez.

Lydia was glad to see her mother enjoy herself, pleased that she and Clytie had made everyone laugh once again. She watched the coals glow in the fire and listened to the logs pop. Cornelius had mortared a fine chimney that drew well, but it left enough wood smoke for Lydia to enjoy, like when she and her father made a fire in the woods to keep the chill off.

"Oh lord, I do have a good time over here," Preston said. "Tell you what, though, no joking, there ain't much up here these days. Am I telling the truth, Lyddie?"

"Yessir, you are," Lydia said. "It's like the animals have disappeared."

"It's that Railroad," Cornelius said.

"Scares off the game. All them explosions, all that commotion," Preston said.

"It ain't just that, either," Clytie said. "That Rail hires boys from the valley to come up here and hunt so as to help keep them workers fed. Anything to keep costs down. The food comes in from the Company, to feed them convicts, but if they can save money on that, they do it."

"I've seen them boys up here hunting," Preston said. "Many times."

"They're killing too much. Over-hunting is what it is," Cornelius said.

"What do you mean 'convicts,' Clytie?" Lydia said.

Clytie looked over at Inez, who gave her a little nod. "They use prisoners, dear," Clytie said. "That's another way the Rail saves money. Don't have to pay them. Just feed them and work them like slaves. They come from the penitentiary over in Hellerville, Lyddie."

"It's corporations and their greed, is what it is," Cornelius said.

He took a sip of whiskey and said, "In fact I heard something about some of them prisoners just today, when I was down there in town."

"What was it, Corny?" Clytie said.

Cornelius realized then that he should have kept quiet with Lydia in the room. He would have, too, had he not been sipping on the bottle like everyone else. He shot his eyes toward the girl and said, "Tell you later."

The talking and sipping went on for a while, but eventually the desire to know Corny's news was too great, and Preston sent Lydia back to the cabin. The girl grumbled openly. She disliked to be shuffled off when adults thought it best to keep her out of something. Wasn't it she who had provided the hare and turkey meat for their dinners, she thought? If she were too young to hear what they discussed, then they could find their own food, she reckoned. She was thirteen. A boy of that age wouldn't be shuffled off. Yet she could outshoot any of the boys on Black Boar, with either bow or gun. Hellfire, she thought. She would say something about it next time. Maybe Clytie at least would defend her.

But this time she stalked off to the cabin.

The instant she was out the door, Corny told what he heard, "What I know is that three of them convicts went on the run yesterday."

"Corny, what?" Clytie asked.

"Just what I said. They escaped. And there's more than that. Though this part I ain't so sure about. You know how folks can tell stretchers and outright lies. So, I don't know for sure. Anyways, I think it's true. Now--"

But Clytie interrupted him, "Out with it, Corny! This ain't the time for one of your preambles."

"Alright," Cornelius said. "The three of them boys were laying line up near the gap on Rusty Mountain. One of them took a

33

nine-pound hammer and laid it acrost the prison guard's head. Bludgeoned him to death and took his gun."

"Lord," Inez whispered.

"Well, Corny, what else?" Clytie asked. "Did they catch them? Are they still running?"

Cornelius said, "I heard the Sheriff and some deputies are out hunting them, up the mountain, but that's all I know."

"What mountain, Corny?" Inez asked. "Where, exactly?"

But Preston interrupted, "The Sheriff? Hell, he won't know the first thing about looking for anyone up there. He won't know how to go about it, or them deputies. They're valley people."

"How come the Company didn't tell us none of this? It's a danger," Clytie said. "Or that Sheriff. No one told us there's men on the loose. Hell, why didn't *you* tell us this, Corny?"

Preston took a pull off the bottle and said, "The Sheriff and the Company are one and the same. That Sheriff is practically an employee of the Company, the way he bends to them and does their business."

Inez said again, "*What* mountain, Corny? *Where?* Do you know?"

"Not for certain," he said. But most everyone thinks they're headed up Rusty Mountain. That's what people are saying."

Preston shook his head. "Those men will be desperate. Likely they don't know how to get food or even water up here. And they're convicts. God knows what they could do."

Inez was practically out the cabin door by now. She called back to the others, "I'm going to see about Lydia. We should tell the others, Press."

Preston rose quickly. "I'm coming with you," he said. They left without proper a goodbye.

Clytie was angry now. "Hell, Corny. Why didn't you tell us this earlier? We're settin' here sipping whiskey and there's desperate killers out there somewhere."

"They're on the run. Not looking to kill anyone. Besides, they headed toward Rusty Mountain, not Black Boar. I told you that. What would they want with us? They gonna come in and sip whiskey with us?"

"Oh, hell, Cornelius. Will you hush and get some boards on that window."

"What are you gonna do?"

"Going to tell people what you should've told them earlier, that we need to be on guard." She grabbed Cornelius' Winchester with the lever action.

Cornelius was humbled now, and a little angry at being henpecked. Under his breath he grumbled to himself, "You're not taking your beloved .22 single-shot?"

But Clytie had heard him.

She cocked the lever. "Not if I gotta kill three of 'em," she said.

Burr carried the rifle, but he made young Henry haul the irons and key taken from the guard. "Things like that can come in handy," Burr said. It was rough going through the rhododendron, and on rises over the limestone boulders, but Burr said such routes were the best way to slow down trackers, to make it hard to follow the trail. The difficult passage didn't seem to slow Burr much, but for the other two it was unfamiliar ground, and it wore on them.

As it turned out, the careful precautions were unnecessary. Burr's ruse about Rusty Mountain had paid off. How he did it was easy, too. On the morning of the escape, he told an inmate about his plan: Lay out the guard with the hammer, get the man's rifle, and head up Rusty Mountain. The convict he told was weak, given to gossip, and the tale spread like wildfire, just as Burr had expected. He only worried that the story would get out *before* the men made their move. At first, most of the prisoners told the Sheriff and the other guards they knew nothing about where Burr and the other prisoners were headed. But it wasn't long before the rumor was tracked to its source. The guards beat hell out of the man and the rumor was exposed. Once that happened, there was no need to keep quiet about things and the story was corroborated: Burr, Simms, and Henry were headed up Rusty Mountain, the prisoners said, the quickest way to get to cover, and the best way to put distance between themselves and any trackers. That's what Burr had said to the man.

And at first the prisoners headed that direction, too, right up the road the timber company had just graded. They were seen there, running hard in their prison whites. But what Burr didn't tell Simms and Henry--besides the fact that he planned to bludgeon the guard to death with the hammer, and not just lay him out like he said--was that they weren't heading up Rusty Mountain at all. And the men were surprised when he darted off the road just a half-mile from the base of the mountain. He led them through laurel slicks and briar patches, over boulders and through gullies clotted with vines and creeper. And then through a bottomland thick with high river cane. They followed the creek upstream, walking in the water itself, against the current, in case the dogs were called out, Burr said. Eventually they came to the base of Black Boar Mountain. Simms and Henry were exhausted before they even began the ascent, but Burr never slowed for them, and the threat of what he might do was greater than that of being captured by the Sheriff or the prison guards.

Burr was not right.

Of course, none of them were *right*, but Burr was a different sort, unlike any convict Simms or Henry had ever come across, either inside or out. Burr was in for murder. "The only one they caught me for," he would say. And he had killed men in prison, too, and not only one. There was no way he would ever see the light of day outside of an escape. But inside, Burr was the Bossman, a title earned on deeds, not talk. Both Simms and Henry had witnessed it, though they wished they hadn't.

One time, they watched Burr knife another prisoner over an alleged insult. Burr stood above the man, in the tunnel where they had been laying line. The man was bleeding out, but no one would move to his aid or call the guard to signal the doctor. Burr himself would have to do that, everyone knew, either by walking away or by calling the guard himself. For Simms and Henry, it was gruesome to stand and watch the man writhe on the ground, his hands a shiny red mess from the wound.

And Burr knew it.

He also knew that the longer he waited, the more his reputation would rise. He waited and watched, looked around at the others who either hung their heads, or nodded tight-lipped at Burr. It was an agonizing moment, and it seemed to Simms and Henry to go on forever. Burr asked for a smoke and a light, even though he didn't smoke. Someone produced a hand-rolled cigarette and Burr drew on it. He held in the smoke and eventually let it out the side of his mouth. The knifed man groaned and thrashed, his heels making little ruts in the dirt now, but from above Burr just shook his head at the man, as if to say, *Oh, no you don't. Not here.* He drew on the cigarette again and blew the smoke high this time. Then he turned to the man who gave him the smoke and said, "Thank you, kindly. I'm done with this."

With a shaky hand, the man accepted the cigarette and pinched out the coal. Burr stood with his arms across his chest, the bloodied knife still in hand, his knuckles red with gore. Eventually he slicked back his greasy black locks, tossed the knife on the ground, and walked away.

Simms called the guard then, when he judged Burr had moved far enough down the tunnel, and men snapped into action to stop the bleeding. As it turned out, the man survived, but he wouldn't say who had knifed him, nor would anyone else. He was sent back to the prison in Hellerville, and in the coming days, Burr told jokes about the incident. "That old boy was smart," he said, "Got hisself a ticket back to Hellerville. Only cost him a lung and a liver, too." Then he'd smile wide and reveal the silver cuspid he'd polish nightly with engine oil. It was a remark he repeated dozens of times in the following days, forcing tight smiles from the men on his work detail.

Simms was a world-class rogue, a man who lived violently wherever life took him. He had been jailed for fighting, stealing, maiming, and finally for rape. Had he not had a sixth sense about when to flee a place, he'd have been killed by vigilantes and aggrieved husbands ten times over. He was handy, though, and few men wanted to tangle with him.

Henry was a thief and a con man, but the violent men of the prison didn't make for good marks, and the idea of serving out his sentence was too much to be borne. Simms wasn't keen on him joining the crew, but Burr told Simms they needed a decoy for the attack on the guard, someone who wouldn't be seen as a physical threat. Guards drew down on men like Burr and Simms if they were approached. "Stay back or I'll drop you where you stand," they would say. But when Henry dropped his mattock and fell to the ground, the guard took the bait. He moved in to see what was happening, and when he did Burr came from behind and buried the nine-pound hammer in the man's skull. It would have been easy to leave Henry there, but he had done what was asked of him, and the convict code was strong in Burr. They let him come along.

The King cabin sat about a half mile from Clytie and Cornelius' place. Preston had to take long strides to keep up with Inez, who raced on, leading recklessly with her head and hands through the branches and briars of an overgrown shortcut, unconcerned whether or not Preston kept pace with her.

"She'll be alright, woman, Preston called out. "She only left just before we did."

Inez didn't answer him. She found her way by little shafts of moonlight that shone through holes in the tree canopy. The naked branches that twisted every which way under the silver light unnerved her more than they normally would have. Something was wrong. She sensed it. And why hadn't they heard Hez' dog, she wondered? It always made noise when it caught the scent of anyone on the night air. It should be howling with all the movement.

Tearing through the brush, she pushed on toward the homestead.

When Preston saw light in the cabin window he slowed his pace, but Inez still raced ahead. He watched her, well ahead of him now. She threw open the door and charged in. As Preston neared the cabin he heard a scream come from inside. He bolted and nearly knocked over Inez at the threshold. She screamed again, a primal wail of fear. Preston had never heard anything like it from her. Her hair was a tangled nest of twigs and leaves, and her eyes were wide like a startled animal's. This creature was not his wife.

"She ain't here!" she said. "Press, she ain't here!" Preston heard it again in the strange pitch of her voice, the fear. She was an animal in the woods now, a mother bear whose cubs were threatened, a queen bobcat protecting her kits. It took him some time to settle her, to find out if she had looked in the loft and around the back, outside of the pantry.

"Go on inside," he said. And again, he asked, "Are you sure she ain't in there?"

She wheeled on him. "Hell yes, I'm sure, goddamnit. Preston, we got to find her!"

Preston grabbed his gun from the cabin and directed Inez to wait inside. He would check down by the oak tree and in the barn. "Just wait here. Bolt the door. She's likely in the barn or down by that tree," he said.

"Oh lord, Press," she said. "Why didn't Hez' dog bark? Holy God, what's happened? Why in hell would she be in the barn?" Her breath came short.

Preston did his best to assert himself, despite his own mounting fear. "It's the only place she can be. Maybe she went to get her bow. Stay in here. I'll find her."

He worked the lever on the gun and trotted toward the barn by memory and the faint moonlight. The door was closed but Preston forced it with his free hand and entered low, his head on a swivel and the gun following it.

Nothing. In the far stall, a mare whinnied once and then stomped her feet.

Still, nothing.

The moonlight coming through the barn boards was the only light, and Preston squinted to see further back into the barn. He found the lantern on the ledge and lit it. When the flame had lifted, he crept forward toward the second stall, the empty one.

What he saw nearly did him in.

Lydia was tied with the hemp ropes he used to pull tree stumps and gagged with a dirty rag. Her face was wet with tears. A red mark spread out across the side of her face, like she had been hit hard, he thought. He set down the rifle and lantern and moved to free his daughter. The girl's eyes opened wide, and she squealed behind the gag, a feral sound.

It was a warning.

But there wasn't enough time to heed it.

Preston felt something hot and hard on the back of his head before he went down. When he opened his eyes, Simms stood above him, hammer in hand. Seconds later, Burr appeared and lifted the lantern. It lit up his face and oily hair from below, all shadow and light now.

Lydia cried out through the rag in her mouth. It was then, when Burr smiled wide, that she first noticed the silver cuspid that flashed in the lamp light.

Burr was a natural predator, and it hadn't taken him long to hatch a plan. Such thoughts came to him instinctively, it seemed. Once the crew got sight of the cabin, they simply laid in wait. When Lydia came home alone, the men followed Burr's lead. Taking her quietly was easy. A punch to her face told Burr that her parents were not too far away, and that they'd be home sometime shortly, she guessed. She begged for the men to take what they wanted and leave. Burr didn't answer her. "Where would your folks look for you if you was missing?" he asked her. That's how he learned of the barn down the hill. From there it was simple. Separate the parents. They would find the girl gone and the father would look in the barn for the girl. There was a gun. Burr saw it there above the hearth. The father would take it with him to the barn, and that's why he needed Simms with him there. (If Burr had taken the gun, he wouldn't have bene able to separate the parents.) Then let Henry take the mother, who would be left behind while the father went looking for their girl. The little ruse in the barn was all Burr, too. Tie up the girl. The father's instinct will be to free her, and to do that he'd need to set down his gun. Then they move on him, at that moment. The hammer Burr found in the barn came in handy, but there were other options, too. It's just that he didn't need any of them.

The whole thing seemed to come to Burr without effort, as if he had done it all before.

Henry was sipping on a bottle he had found in the cabin when Simms walked in. Simms had Preston's gun in one hand and Lydia in the other, held tightly by the upper arm, the gag still in her mouth. He whispered something to her and laughed. Inez yanked furiously on the hand irons, one end of which Henry had secured to a wall post. Through her own gag, she shrieked at the sight of Lydia, and Henry slapped her hard on the side of the head. But she thrashed on, wailing and pulling at the irons so that it seemed her shoulder would come out of joint. Henry hit her again and by now Lydia, too, was howling through the gag. The small space filled with a desperate, muffled wailing.

Henry was at a loss. He threatened to hit Inez again, but Simms broke in. "No!" he yelled. And to Inez he said, "Woman, you shut up or I will kill this young one. You hear now?"

Inez quieted, but her chest still heaved. "Take off those irons, Henry," Simms said. "If it goes nice and smooth with this one, we'll be on our way." It was a lie, but Inez hoped it wasn't.

Henry removed the irons and asked Simms, pointing at Lydia, "What about her?"

Simms shoved the girl toward Henry and said, "Take her somewhere out of the way. She'll likely raise a ruckus when she sees this," he said. "Use the irons."

"There's a room off the back there, a little pantry," Henry said. "I can take her there."

Simms was already directing Inez to the bed tick in the corner.

"Wherever, son. Just get her out of here, and stay there until I'm done in here. Then you can have a turn."

Then Simms said to Inez, "Now you lift up that dress for me, you hear?"

Chained to a timber post in the tiny pantry, Lydia realized that she was in the presence of something animal now. It was in the air, a wildness the prisoners had brought with them, and she sensed it viscerally. An memory came to her, something she had seen far out in the woods, a deer carcass. Chunks of flesh had been ripped from the haunches and flank. Something had preyed on it, a large cat maybe. At the time, she felt the primal nature of it all, a heavy sickness in the air around the mutilated animal, something the predator had left behind. She could feel it in her lungs back then.

And now, she felt it again. It was there, with her, in the cabin. The feeling of predators doing the only thing they know. To survive, she would need to become one of them, even though what separated her from them was the fact that they were savages, and she was not.

Deeply, she drew in the foul air through her nose.

Back in the barn, Burr waited for Preston to come to. He had some questions about routes to get off the mountain, possible trails that hunters and mountaineers followed, places where they could get water and such, and where it would be tough to track the convicts by horse. He had found a skinning knife in the barn and now he examined the grip, turning over the blade in his hand.

When Preston finally got his bearings, he moved to get up. "Lydia," he said groggily.

"Your wood nymph ain't here," Burr said above him.

"Leave her out of it," Preston said. He pressed his hand to his head. Blood still flowed from the wound and his hand came back a slick mess. He tried to lift himself up.

"Down, boy!" Burr delivered a vicious kick to the ribs that ripped through Preston. He collapsed with a grunt. Burr said, "First I need to know some things from you, gentle farmer. And you're gonna answer me about each and every one of them." He asked about routes, potential shelters, cabins, guns, knives, and everything else he wanted to know in order to hasten the escape. Preston did his best to answer him, begging all the while that Burr release Lydia and Inez. He told Burr he would even help him in the escape, so long as the women were let go. He knew every route in and out of the mountain, he said, even places where one could bushwhack into hiding places no one could ever find.

But Burr now had what he needed from Preston. As far as he was concerned, all that remained was to kill the man. There was no need to tell him that they were all planning on taking turns with his wife and with "that wood nymph daughter of his," before they killed them.

But Burr told him this anyway.

Then he plunged the knife deep into Preston's throat.

That was Burr.

Lydia was bound to an oak post that supported the shelves for Inez' bowls, some kitchen tools, and the remaining jars of canned food from last summer. Henry had closed the gate of the irons to the last notch so that Lydia's thin wrist was fully locked down. She couldn't see her mother, but she could hear her, straining in pain, her groans like death throes. She could hear Simms too, his grunting.

She also heard Burr's throaty laughter now. He had returned from the barn.

Eventually Simms groaned and it all stopped but for her mother's breathing, a furious wheezing, like she was struggling just to breathe. Simms called Henry into the room and Lydia hoped now Simms would release her mother, let her lay there unmolested. But she also knew that Burr would not allow that. She had seen Burr. She knew what he was. And so she thought now of her father, down at the barn, alone. She wondered what Burr had done to him, though part of her already knew. And she realized that she must do something, no matter the risk. Desperately she scanned the little room.

Then she saw it.

On one of the shelves was a knife her mother used for cutting meat. A good, sharp blade fixed to a cherry grip Cornelius had made when the old grip splintered from so much use. It was exquisitely tooled and fit the hand perfectly. If she stretched out, she could reach it. Once she had it in hand, she closed her eyes and took a deep breath. But she knew she couldn't think on it for too long. This would have to be done now, she knew.

In the other room, Henry took a long time with Inez, and Burr and Simms needled him all the while, drinking from the whiskey and hooting insults. When it was over, Burr ordered Simms to go get the wood nymph. But when Simms entered the little room off the main cabin, Lydia was nowhere to be found. The irons sat on the floor, one end still fixed to the post. There, too, was something else. The girl's bloodied thumb, the joint at the end still white and clean.

"She's gone!" Simms hollered.

Burr's eyes went wide. He said, "Now what exactly do you mean, Simms?"

"The irons are there, but she's gone," Simms said. "There's blood all over the place. She cut off her fuckin' thumb, Burr."

Inez moaned loud and long. Burr lifted his heel and kicked her brutally in the side. She let out a howl and then groaned. "Son of a bitch," Burr said. "She's likely gone down to the barn to see about the father." He wheeled on Henry. "Jesus, Henry," he said, "you made a mess of things. Go down there and bring her back. Take one of the guns. You think you can manage that much?" When Henry left, Burr said to Simms, "This could get out of hand if that girl gets away. Let's be done with this one and get moving."

"Agreed," Simms said.

Inside the barn, the lantern sat on a shelf near the doorway, still lit. Henry entered and made his way into the back. The mare stomped and whinnied. Inside the far stall, Preston's body lay on the ground. But there was no girl. Henry looked around again and then made to head out and search outside, around the barn.

But he never got there.

He felt a sharp pain and then a quick tightness in his chest, just above the heart, where the fletching of an arrow begins to moisten with his blood. Lydia stood directly in front of him, in the barn doorway, lit now by the lantern she had set there and the silver moon light from behind. The sleeve of her dress was soaked red where she had tried to stanch the flow of her own blood. Henry had just time enough to recognize the three-fingered grip she used before another arrow hit him in the neck. He clawed at it and fell. As he writhed on the ground, she appeared above him.

Somehow, this wasn't the same girl he had imprisoned in the little room off the cabin. The gag was gone from her mouth, and her hair was a tangled nest of bloodied, stray tresses. Her dress was reddened in large patches, and she was missing a thumb, but in no sense did she seem injured to him. This was no wood nymph. This was something feral, an animal bent on survival. The irons were gone and in her good hand she held her mother's knife, the cherry grip wet with her own blood. Henry still held the rifle in his hand but he would never be able to use it. This, too, Lydia knew.

She opened her eyes wide and dropped her knee to his chest. He watched as she raised the blade high.

Simms had found some of Preston's clothes in the cabin. A pair of woolen pants and a linsey shirt fit him perfectly. A second set of clothes were big on Burr but he pulled them on anyway.

At the bed tick, Burr roused Inez enough to tell her that her time on this earth was up. She groaned and swooned again, but Burr didn't bother to rouse her any further. He was about to move in on her, to strangle her in the crook of his arm, one hand over her mouth, when he heard voices from outside. But it didn't sound like Henry or the girl. "What in hell?" he said.

Simms cracked the door enough to poke his head out. A bullet splintered the door frame and sent wood flying over his head. He slammed the door and fixed the latch. Another shot hit almost instantly, right where his head had been.

Burr was already halfway to the back door when Simms caught on and followed. "What about Henry?" Simms yelled.

Burr saw the blood on the floor and the small, bloodied thumb. "Henry may be dead. And we'll be, too, if we don't get moving. We underestimated the wood nymph."

Burr and Simms headed fast for the trees beyond the King's plot when Clytie's scream rang out across the hillside. Another shot sounded, and Simms spun and fell to the ground.

"Burr!" he hollered.

Burr kept moving, the sole rifle in his hand now.

After a brief moment of terror, Simms realized he was hit in the shoulder. The bullet had passed through. It burned like hell, but he was up and moving after a few seconds. A bullet slammed into a beech tree nearby and he ducked his head. He looked back, and in the moonlight that fell through the trees he saw Clytie work the lever and level the gun. He dropped to the ground, and he heard the shot whiz by just above him. Then he was up and moving, trying to catch up with Burr.

Clytie took off in pursuit, but Cornelius called her from the back door of the cabin. "Clytie! Leave them. We're needed here, woman!" he yelled.

She cursed and ran back to the cabin door. When she saw Lydia's thumb and the slick of blood in the pantry, she nearly got sick. In the other room, Cornelius had removed the gag from Inez' mouth. Every bone and muscle inside her ached horribly, but she got to her feet and tried to work her way toward the door. She gritted her teeth and said, "The barn. They're in the barn." Cornelius slowed her but she tossed his arms aside. "Come on," she hissed. Clytie jumped in and forced Inez to tell them what had happened. "We need to know what we're up against, Inez! We can't go at them blind," she said.

Inez did her best to lay it out, quick as she could.

"How many are there?" Clytie said "I seen two running off, not three. Is there another one?"

Inez said, "Yes, I think he's down to the barn. I don't know. Come on. Let's go!"

Cornelius led the way out the front and down toward the barn, but when they got there Clytie told him and Inez to wait outside. Cornelius didn't like it but he knew, deep down, Clytie was faster, and a much better shot than him.

She entered the barn, crouched low with her rifle at the ready. The mare stomped furiously in her stall. Clytie jumped at the sight of Henry there on the ground, and drew down on the prone body, but at the same time she heard whimpering near the far stall. There was Lydia on her knees and with the lantern set beside her.

"Lyddie," Clytie said. "Girl, are you ok?" But she didn't answer, or couldn't. Preston's body was covered with a horse blanket. Lydia knelt with both hands atop it. Clytie winced when she saw the girl's mangled hand. She pulled the blanket from Preston's body, though instantly she wished that she hadn't, and she set it back over him. She knelt down and took Lydia into her arms. "Corny," she called. "Lydia's with me, but you and Inez wait out there for me, ok?"

Before she had finished speaking Inez had charged through the barn door. She gasped at the sight of Henry's body, two arrows sunk to the fletching in his chest and neck, but when she realized it wasn't Preston she moved to the stall where she heard Lydia and Clytie. Clytie tried to shield her from the sight, but Inez wouldn't be moved. A high-pitched wail rose up and filled the small space of the barn. It became a prolonged keening, a mixture of screaming and crying, relief and horror in the same sound. Cornelius had followed in behind. He swooned when he saw what faced him, but he managed to stay on his feet. The women knelt by Preston's body with their arms around one another now, howling wildly. In the end, it was Lydia who rose up off the ground first.

"Lyddie, girl," her mother said.

But Lydia was gone to her now, gone to all of them for the moment. She walked toward the barn door and stood above Henry's dead body. One of the arrows was broken, the shaft snapped with the impact of the falling body. But the other one, the one that had entered just above the heart, was intact. With her foot Lydia rolled the body onto its side. It was then that the others first saw Inez' work knife. The bloodied cherry grip was visible at the man's rib cage, but the blade was sunk deep. It dawned on Inez then that Preston must have been killed before Henry, that Lydia was the one to have killed this man. She had no time to study on it, no time to consider that Lydia may have saved them all. But she felt instinctively as a mother will, that her daughter was not her daughter anymore, or that she was something else now.

Lydia grabbed the bloody shaft of the arrow that had run fully through the body and yanked it free in one violent motion. She stood there, the wet arrow in hand, silhouetted by the weak light of the moon that made its way through the trees and the spaces between the boards on the barn walls.

At first light Hez Coombs mounted his mare and headed down into the valley with Abe Williams riding beside him. Abe carried his rifle in a special holster hitched to his saddle, and a six gun on his hip. But Hez carried his Colt in hand, though he had a holster on his belt. It made for a tricky ride in places and unnerved Abe terribly. Hez wheeled the gun at everything he heard in the tree line along the rough path, and also at everything he *thought* he heard. He had even fired once or twice, which angered Abe, though he kept quiet about it. Hez' thoughts were on Preston, first, and then Inez and Lydia. But to say he hadn't thought about his dog would be a lie. The animal had been beaten to death with a heavy rock, bludgeoned again and again on the head. Hez knew why it had been killed, and why the convicts didn't use a gun—stealth—but he didn't know why the dog had been stomped, something that had to have happened *after* she was already dead. When he found her, he saw muddy boot prints on the animal's flank. All four of her legs were broken.

The dog had been mauled.

The Sheriff's office in Queen's Tooth was adjoined to the Railroad's, a smartly painted building built by the company, with gilt-lettered windows and a porch with neatly joined, level boards. For those in town, the two entities had long ago become one. Town folk never thought of the Rail or the timber company as distinct from the law, but for those on Black Boar, this still seemed odd. The Sheriff sat behind his oak desk while Hez and Abe together narrated the events of the evening, best they knew. When they finished, the Sheriff rose heavily from his chair and took his hat from a peg on the wall. He took the news hard. It was clear he hoped the escaped men would be taken by his trackers—a mix of his own deputies and others from neighboring counties, along with a few local volunteers, hunters and mountaineer types. But they had come back empty handed. Burr's ruse about Rusty Mountain had worked.

Grimly, the Sheriff wondered what it would all mean. The death of a prison guard in an escape was one thing. With prison labor, you can expect some violence, the Sheriff knew well. But a citizen? And the violation of a woman on top of it all? It was bad for everyone, he thought. "Sonuvabitch," he said. "You sure the girl killed that convict?"

"Yes," Hez and Abe said together.

"Goddamn," the Sheriff said. "This is a nightmare, a goddamn nightmare." He steadied himself with a hand on the door frame.

Hez said, "Who did you send to track these men, Sheriff? Now you got two dead on your hands. And one convict dead, too."

The sheriff sighed and said, "Don't you think I know this much, Hez Coombs?"

"Well, where are your trackers, then? Your deputies?" Abe chimed in. "And how come we weren't warned there were dangerous men on the loose? And shouldn't you be up there looking, too? Hell, why don't you take some action *now*?"

"You don't need to tell me my business." The Sheriff said. "There are men up there tracking them right now. Good men. Mountain men." He didn't mention that his trackers had hours ago returned from Rusty Mountain without a clue of the convicts' escape route.

"Beg your pardon, Sheriff," Abe added, "but mountain men live in the mountains, not down here. There might have been even more damage if Clytie and Cornelius hadn't set out to warn folks when they did. And there's no one up on Black Boar now, no law men."

"We'll get those men, the Sheriff said. "They'll hang. Don't you worry on it … Hold on, what do you mean about Clytie and Corny?"

Abe said, "Cornelius Noe was in town and heard a rumor the convicts run off. Clytie and them got worried. Good thing, too. Lydia and Inez might have been killed if Cornelius and Clytie hadn't run them off."

The Sheriff fixed Abe with a stare, "You mean people *did* know about the escape? They *were* warned, you mean."

"No," Hez answered. Corny told what he heard from the town folk. A rumor was all it was. There was no *official* warning, like there should've been."

"Well, now," the Sheriff said, fixing his hat.

"And there's more," Hez added. "Lydia lost her thumb." It was a fact the men had left out of the telling. They explained it all then.

"By God," the Sheriff said. "She cut it off to free herself. Lord, that takes grit … Well, the Rail will compensate her."

"You speak for the Rail?" Abe asked.

"I do." The Sheriff held the door for them. "You two have had a long, worrisome ride, I imagine. I don't want to keep you down here longer than you need to be. I know you must want to be with your people. Why don't you head on back up to the settlement, men. I'll send some people up to get onto the trail. We'll find those men."

Hez shot back, "You sure they can find *us*?"

The Sheriff narrowed his eyes and said, "Now, I know you've been done wrong. I know you must be upset by all this. But the Rail plans to make it right. No need for ill will, Hez." The Sheriff opened the door wider and added, "Now, I've got to go set this in motion. Tell your people the Rail is behind them. The Rail is a friend in times of trouble."

"The goddamn Rail *caused* the trouble," Hez said.

"That is a reckless claim," the Sheriff said. "I'll leave you two gentlemen now."

"You ain't coming back with us? To investigate?"

"What's to investigate? We know who did this. Now I need to get my men back on the trail. Let me do my job."

Capturing the convicts *did* worry the Sheriff. But now he began to worry about something else, too—how he and the Rail could control the dark news about what had just happened.

Preston King was buried two days later, his body wrapped in a cotton shroud an old woman on Black Boar had spun and weaved herself. It had not been dyed in the modern fashion because the woman believed the natural fibers looked truer and kept their strength longer. It was beautiful, and at first Inez refused to accept it. But when she saw the tears brim in the old woman's eyes, she decided to take it. The woman was as thankful as Inez. She wanted to see the cloth put to good use before she left this earth, she said.

Lydia stayed close to her mother, and to Clytie and Cornelius. She fretted over Inez continually, keeping a close eye on her all the while. But at times, part of her thought it might be best to leave her to the care of Clytie and some of the other women there, at least for a little while. Her bandaged hand seemed a constant reminder to her mother of the violent event, and of what the woman had lost. Lydia sensed the pain it caused, and now and again she made off briefly on some excuse or other. With those who hugged her and cried when they spoke to her, Lydia accepted the pity and condolences. She cried, too, especially when she first saw her father in the natural shroud. Young as she was, she knew that she would never get over it, would never be the same person she was. But she felt something else, something bound up with those Railroad men, the ones who now stood aloof, who whispered amongst one another on the outside of the group. They looked different than the people of Black Boar, Lydia thought. They were dressed more formally, clean shaven with waxed mustaches. She didn't fault them for this, but their physical difference marked them. They were not of the settlement. Something about them unsettled her, though she wasn't exactly sure what.

The pain in her hand was excruciating, but she bore up as best she could. During the burial she stood nearby her mother and Clytie, with Cornelius beside them, rifle in hand. She heard Clytie whisper, "I want it at the ready, Corny. Don't stray from me." Others, too, carried guns, not so much because they feared the prisoner would return, but more as a statement, an expression of unity in the face of being wronged. There was a growing sense of the unjustness of things, and not only the violations and the killing. The Company was fast becoming more of a pariah than it already was, despite the oak coffin and the flour, sugar, tobacco, and liquor they brought with them. Men eyed the Railroad representatives sourly, spitting in their direction and shaking their heads. They blamed the Rail for what happened, especially since no one was told formally that the convicts, the *killers*, were on the loose. Why wasn't someone sent up to Black Boar with this information? How come some of the Sheriff's armed guards weren't sent right away to help protect the little community of homesteaders? For years, the Rail and the Sheriff had been telling them that life would be much easier for everyone once the line had been laid. Well? Look what happened. And where *was* the Sheriff anyway? Lydia remembered what her father had said about the Rail. That there was as much chance the Rail could damage Black Boar as it could help.

So far, she thought, it had done only damage.

The preacher, Isaac Nichols, spoke some words at the grave. Right away, Inez fell to her knees and wailed a noise that rented the air. Lydia tried to console her. Part of her thought her mother was ready to jump in the grave herself. With Clytie and Cornelius, she lifted her mother and restored her to standing, supported now on each arm. Lydia felt her mother could take no more of it. She would die of sadness on the spot, she thought, if she had to witness the earth laid atop the casket. Clytie, too, sensed as much. She and Cornelius ushered Inez away, but when Clytie touched Lydia on the shoulder and told her to follow along, Lydia shook her head. She would watch the burial. Another woman stepped in beside Lydia and nodded to Clytie to go on. She did.

Lydia stood stiffly as men shoveled dirt onto the casket. She listened to the sound of her mother's high-pitched wailing behind her, and the soft thud of the earth as it fell on the her father's coffin.

As she made her way from the site with Clytie and Cornelius supporting her, Inez managed to form a single, complete sentence. Lydia heard it clearly. "It was that body," Inez said, "up on the bog. That's what caused this."

Clytie and Cornelius hushed her the best they could.

After the preacher spoke, and after they lay Preston in the ground, the mourners gathered for a reading of the article in the *Mountain Sentinel*, something Clytie had organized. There was a chill in the air and some men dug a fire pit near Inez' cabin, but far enough from Preston's grave to maintain decorum. People huddled around the flames. A few of them wondered about the propriety of taking a snort or two while Connor McNeely read from the newspaper, and some of them took sips furtively. Clytie saw this, and so did Cornelius and some others. What Clytie said surprised a few folks.

"I see you men out there," she said. You want to be right and proper for Inez and her Press. That's thoughty of you. But let me tell you, it's ok to sup on whiskey. We need something to comfort us now, after this, after what these heathens done up here. These men are convicts, let's not forget. But who brung them here? Who brung them up to these hills? Well, the Railroad did. Now the Rail tells us they will make our lives easier when that line is done. But as I see it, they've already made things worse." She looked directly at the men around the fire pit and said, "You go ahead and have a sup, you men. Take your bottles out. It's ok. Not disrespectful."

The preacher didn't like it, but he kept quiet about Clytie's speech. Part of him felt as if he were being usurped. But to make a scene now would have been worse, he figured.

Clytie held her hand out to Corny who took a bottle from his suitcoat pocket and handed it to her. She took a sip. "We need to take away some of the pain for a moment. Take stock of what we have as a settlement and see what we can do, together." She handed the bottle to Cornelius who took a sip, too. Clytie then took up her rifle, holding it across her body so that all could see her. "Let's listen to Connor read this article from the newspaper," she said.

As defeated as she felt, as worried as she was about her mother, Lydia felt that there was something vital in Clytie's words, and an energy began to stir inside her.

Connor McNeely cleared his throat and read the article from the *Valley Messenger*:

"On Friday near 3:15 in the afternoon, three men escaped from a work detail near the Rusty Mountain gap where workers were busy laying line for the Railroad. They are Henry Byrd, Simms Jackson, and Burr Hollis, men from the State Prison at Hellerville. In the escape, a company guard was killed, Ephraim Knox. The escaped men also made

trouble in the small community on Black Boar Mountain where a man was killed. The details of this killing are not wholly clear at the time of this writing, but one of the convicts, Mr. Henry Byrd, was killed in the event as well.

An official from the Company suspects that some residents of the Black Boar community might not have heeded the news of the escape, though again, all the details are not yet known.

The men have not been captured. Reports should be communicated to officials at the company or the Sheriff's Office. The men are dangerous and should be avoided at all costs."

The reading was first met with a stunned silence. People looked at one another, and at Connor McNeely. They waited for him to turn the page, to carry on. But he simply folded the newspaper and said, "That's it, you all. That's all there is."

Eventually someone yelled out, "What about the violation of a woman? Are you telling me they don't know that much? Hez and Abe *told* the Sheriff what all happened!"

"A girl mutilated herself," someone else chimed up. "How come they don't tell that?"

Hez Coombs boomed from the rear of the circle, "And how about Preston? He was butchered, by God!" His wife hushed him then, telling him not to say such things in front of Lydia and Inez. But Hez wheeled on her, "They know what happened, Emma! Let me say my piece!"

From somewhere in the crowd a woman hollered, "Clytie Noe, what more can you tell us? How come this story makes it sound like we knew those convicts were coming? Like it was our fault?"

Clytie shook her head in disbelief and said, "I reckon I know no more than anyone here. I thought that this article would tell more on things. All I know is that the Rail says they're gonna help Inez, and Lydia, too." And here Clytie lifted her rifle to her chest again. "But I don't trust them. I don't trust they care about us. And I think it's possible they'll do as little as possible to pay the debt they owe to Inez and Lydia. You can tell as much from the story. The Railroad, and the Sheriff who works for them, I think they'll try to hush it all up. They don't want anything that's bad for business. And this, what happened here, is bad for business. And one more thing I got to tell. This could happen again. Them convicts have gotten away, or far enough away, to make other ones think about escape. And now everyone'll know where to take their chances: Black Boar. We need to defend ourselves!" She reached into a dress pocket, brought out her bottle, and drank from it. The men in the crowd, and a good many of the women, too, followed her lead.

But there was one fact Clytie didn't tell. She lied when she said she hadn't read the article beforehand. Lydia had watched Clytie read the article earlier, after Mr. McNeely had met her by the King cabin. Lydia pulled Clytie close and whispered in her ear, "Clytie--" But she didn't know how to say what she wanted to say. When Clytie took her good hand and squeezed it, though, she knew Clytie understood.

The representatives from the Railroad had already secured Henry Byrd's decaying, mutilated body to a buckboard and sent it back to town. They were long gone by the time the reading was done.

Lucky for them, they were.

There was something important that Clytie had kept from Lydia.

Earlier, when trackers from the Railroad had finally arrived on Black Boar, before the burial, but after Hez and Abe had already headed down into the valley, they learned that Clytie had winged one of the convicts, and that men from Black Boar had followed the trail but lost it somewhere near the bog. Clytie could only tell them that the men traveled up the mountain for some distance.

One of the Railroad men looked at the traces of blood on the fallen leaves where the convicts entered the woods behind the King's cabin. He shook his head mournfully and said, "This blood is old. Likely this trail is cold."

Clytie said, "It's cold now. But it wasn't when we set on to it. You're two days behind. Hell, if we had waited for you, half of us would be dead by now. You need to stick to layin' Rail, I reckon. Leave off mountaineering to those who know better."

The tracker bristled and was about to answer her, but one of his partners told him to hush. Clytie stormed off, further convinced of something she had decided on the night of the horrible event, a snap decision that had weighed on her ever since. On the night of the killings, she had found a tintype in the pocket of the prison whites Simms had left behind. It pictured a man with a woman, his arm around her waist. Behind them stood a small clapboard house, like a company home built for workers, Clytie thought. The man beamed broadly in the photo, and the woman, too, looked happy. Clytie hadn't seen the convicts' faces that night, and so she didn't know who was pictured in the tintype. She stared at the photograph in the newspaper, comparing it to the tintype, but she didn't know if it was the man she winged or the other one. Maybe the woman in the image was his wife. She and Corny had a tintype like that, taken outside his mother's house just after their marriage, and just before they became homesteaders. Such images were common. But maybe it was someone else, a cousin or a sister. She thought at first to give it over to the Railroad men, to the Sheriff. But after her exchange with the trackers from the Rail, she decided to keep the tintype. She told herself that she'd ask Cornelius about it first. If he thought it best to hand it over to the Sheriff, or to the Railroad, she would.

It wasn't until days later when they finally had a moment alone, and when Clytie judged Cornelius ready to listen to her. When Inez and Lydia had fallen asleep, she showed the tintype to Cornelius. He held the metal image close to the oil lamp and examined it.

"What do you think, Corny?" she asked him.

"Well, I don't even know who it is. I suppose it's one of them raiders. We should maybe give this over to the Sheriff's men."

"Do you think they'll make good use of it, the Sheriff?"

Corny sighed deeply. "I don't know, really. I reckon so," he said. "It's evidence in a crime, Clytie. They might need it to find the men." It was all Corny could do to look at the image again. Clytie could tell how it pained him. He shook his head in disgust, mostly at himself, and handed it back to her.

But as Clytie thought more about it, she began to question

the logic of turning it over. Corny was forlorn beyond words since the incident, blaming himself for not speaking up earlier about the rumored escape. His judgment was compromised, Clytie thought. And she worried about giving over the one piece of evidence to the Sheriff and his no 'count Company trackers. She needed the tintype, she decided. Later she could give it to the Sheriff. She could say she just now found it somehow, out behind the King cabin one day, if nothing came of keeping it in the meanwhile. Anyway, if it was an image of the convict and his wife, prison officials would already have that kind of information.

But maybe something else could be gleaned from the tintype, something useful. First, though, Clytie had to find out who was the man in the image. There was only one way to find out, short of showing it to Inez, and that she refused to do.

She would have to show it to Lydia.

It was the last thing Clytie wanted to do, to make the girl look at the image of one of her tormentors. Clytie shrank at the thought of it. But there was also something that heartened her about the idea. It was the image in her own mind, the one of Lydia standing over the corpse of the convict and drawing out the arrow. Clytie had seen men draw arrows from killed animals. Arrows were hand-made by people up on Black Boar. They were a resource much valued. But Lydia had turned the body over with her foot, grabbed the arrow, and ripped it straight out. There was something there, Clytie realized, something different--a hardness uncommon amongst girls that age, even among homesteaders.

If Lydia could so such a thing, at such a time, she could look at a photo of a man, even one of the man who had imprisoned her, threatened to violate her no doubt. This Clytie believed. Still, she also thought of the girl's gentleness, how she stroked her mother's hair in a way that made Clytie pine for that sense of maternal love—both of her own long-dead mother and of the children she never bore. How could she show this girl the tintype?

In the end she didn't know how she would go about it, only that she would.

But first she would have to get Cornelius to come around. As capable as she was on her own, she needed him. Unlike so many men on Black Boar, Cornelius never felt the need to bridle Clytie. Clytie knew the men sometimes teased him for his ease with her, and now and again someone might say he was hen-pecked, though not to his face. What people gossiped about on Black Boar always got around. She didn't want this for him, such talk, but she couldn't be someone she wasn't. In the past, when she fretted over these things, Cornelius would give her a squeeze of the hand or a kiss on the neck. It was all she needed. And she needed it now, his touch. She worried about what was happening to him, the daily decline she saw, and she knew she would have to talk to him, though she dreaded it and put it off for weeks.

The couple sat outside their cabin where Cornelius had set out a single chair he had caned years ago, something he believed was uncomfortable for the faulty measurement in the height of the seat. He had planned to use the hard hickory and smooth, treated cane in another project sometime later, but he decided the ill-fitting chair now suited his mood. He set it out back of the cabin, out of view of anyone traveling the path out front. Though now that Lydia and Inez had moved in with him and Clytie, he could never escape the thought of that night. Still, the view suited him, he thought. He sat mournfully, whittling just to keep his hands in motion, his galluses dropped and his boots loosely tied.

Clytie took a seat on the ground, cross-legged. She drew a small whiskey bottle from her dress, took a sip, and offered it to Corny. When he refused, she continued to hold the bottle toward him. "Corny, please."

He took the bottle and tipped it. "I'd let you have this chair but it's uncomfortable. Sits all wrong. Designed poorly, this first one was," Cornelius said.

"I'm fine here." She drew on the bottle and set it down. "Corny,

I ain't gonna try to tell you not to feel poorly about all this. That just ain't gonna make a difference, I know. You feel this is all your fault. It ain't, not one bit of it, but it won't do good to tell you such."

"Goddamn right," Cornelius answered. "It won't do any good."

"But listen, dear," she said softly, "you need to come out of it, even if you ain't out of it. For Lydia and Inez. And for everyone else. We need you, Corny. Black Boar needs you. *I* need you, husband."

Cornelius sighed. Tears brimmed in his eyes, but they never spilled over. He said only one thing. "Leave me now, Clytie," he said. "Please."

Burr knew that the creek that followed out of the bog would complicate matters for trackers. He also knew that if they walked in the stream for as long as they could suffer the cold and the wet, the trail would be tough to follow. They tied their laces and slung their boots over their shoulders. He insisted they walk for long stretches, as far as they could stand it, barefoot in the stream.

He was pitiless toward Simms, though the man had lost a good deal of blood and was in enormous pain. "You need to keep up, boy," he said time and again, using the diminutive he had reserved for Henry earlier. "This ain't no stroll around town."

"My shoulder," Simms said, "It's killing me."

"You're gonna kill *us both*, if you don't pick up the pace."

"Can we rest for a minute, Burr? Please. My shoulder. It hurts like the devil."

Burr never slowed. The cold of the stream seemed not to affect him, and he navigated the rocks with ease where Simms fell more than a few times. Once Simms cried out in pain when he braced a fall with his injured arm. Burr wheeled on him and drug him over to the side of the creek, though he made sure neither of them stepped on the bank. He said, "We're gonna take a lit breather, Simms, a real little one."

At first Simms thought the man had come around, but when Burr's tale began, he knew it wasn't so. "When I was little," Burr began, "my daddy raised chickens. We was just a small operation, but we sold eggs and meat both. Well, you see, with chickens you got to think about the larger herd, the healthy ones first and foremost. If you got sickly birds, you got to cull 'em. They can spread that sickness to the others, see. And if them hens ain't producing, they need to go, too. You got to look up at the vent, is what they call it, the place on the hen where the egg come out ... and the shit, too. Burr laughed, but Simms could tell where the story was going.

"So, if that vent ain't wet, or if a hen is sick, or even a little pullet, you gotta cull 'em. Well, my brothers didn't like it one bit, and they was *older* than me. But Hell, I took to it, boy! It was nothin' for me to wring a hen's neck." He fixed Simms with a stare and added, "If something's holding me back, well, culling is what's maybe got to be done. You know what I'm saying?"

Burr headed back into the stream, not looking to see if Simms was following, but he knew he would be, at least for now.

C lytie had taken to hunting with Lydia a few weeks after "that night," the way folks on Black Boar began to refer to the violation and the killings. As Clytie saw it, this served two purposes: she could get food for the four of them and take stock of how the girl was doing at the same time. The woods were Lydia's element, and to remove the girl from them was unhealthy, Clytie figured. Lydia didn't need "rest," as Clytie's neighbors advised. She needed to move, to walk under the sugar maples and elms, to listen to the bird songs and woodpeckers, to smell the rich earth and feel the cold air in her lungs and on her face. She needed to hunt, too. Lydia would heal in helping to provide for others, Clytie felt. The woods would restore her.

Inez was another story.

At times, the woman rallied enough to comfort her daughter, and to make it appear as if she were on the mend. She helped Clytie with cooking, and she even helped with planting and with the chickens and geese, tasks which had fallen entirely to Cornelius now. But Inez was not what she used to be. Unpredictably, she would just break down, collapsing right there on the cabin floor. These instances unnerved Clytie and terrified young Lydia.

But at least the hunting gave the girl a respite from it. And Clytie began to realize something about herself. The hunting and hiking was good for *her*, too. It was the first time Clytie had really got out into the wild since her marriage, years ago. It was true that Lydia saw things that Clytie couldn't—little animal markers, trails, traces of things. Not much escaped her. But Clytie's wood sense was reawakening, and she taught Lydia a few things, too. Together, they took to the woods.

One time, as they neared a giant, rotted out oak, Clytie said, "Let's circle around that."

"Why, Clytie?" Lydia asked.

"I'm being over-worried, probably, but bears like places like that, hollowed out logs and such."

"For their winter, you mean."

"Yes."

"Do they ever wake up?" Lydia said. Though she knew the answer, Lydia liked to listen to Clytie talk about the woods, about her time there when she was Lydia's age.

"They do. If there's a rain that floods their nest, or something stirs them up. But I just steer clear if I think maybe there's one in there. Even though we likely wouldn't wake one just by walking." They followed a wide arc around the fallen tree, but Clytie kept her eyes fixed on it.

Lydia noticed and asked, "Did you ever come onto a bear?"

Clytie didn't answer right away, and Lydia let it drop, but eventually she sighed and said, "Yes, Lyddie. Me and my daddy did, one time. We was on a winter hunt, just the two of us—." Clytie stopped to wipe her eyes.

"What's wrong?" Lydia asked.

Clytie sighed and said, "Well, we was on a hunt and we seen one. It looked at us and then moved on. That's all, really. Not much of a tale. Scared me thinking back on it. That's all."

But Lydia knew it wasn't all. She stopped and set her bow on the ground. She took Clytie's hand in her own. "Go on and tell me, Clytie. It's ok," she said. "Tell me about you and your daddy. I want to hear it. C'mon now, tell me."

Clytie looked at the girl's thumb-less hand on top of her own and she felt a tightness in her throat. She knew then she would tell the story, the whole story and the role her father played in it. She also realized then that there weren't many girls like Lydia, or like her when she was Lydia's age, or even like her now. In that moment she felt a tenderness beyond what she had ever felt for anyone, even for Corny.

"Let's walk," Clytie said. "I'll tell you now."

As the two made their way over a small rise and into a small clearing, Clytie took a deep breath and said, "We was on a hunt, must've been February, I think. We didn't for a minute think about bears. They were asleep, we reckoned. Their mast was dried up. But we come over a little rise and there he is, right there lookin' straight at us. A biggun', too. Three-, maybe four-hundred pounds I bet. My heart dropped. He was rooting around with that big brown snout in the ground, and when he sensed us, he lifted that giant head of his, a big old block it looked like. We stopped cold. Couldn't move, neither me nor daddy. Then that bear let out a growl. But he held his ground. Didn't move toward us any. I started to cry, quiet like, and Daddy said, 'Quiet now, girl. Don't you make a sound.' Well, we started backing out of there slowly, and sure enough that biggun' starts comin' toward us. I was never so scared in my life, Lydia."

The story unsettled Clytie even in the telling, Lydia could see, but Clytie gathered herself and went on. "Anyway, that bear all of a sudden moved on us, slow-like, but meaning to do something, you could tell. Daddy said, 'Run, Clytie.' And he moved toward that bear at the same time. Well, I just froze, and he said again, 'Run, girl!' He yelled loud. But I couldn't move. Next thing you know that bear is right up on him in a half-second, and he takes a swipe at Daddy. Knocked the shotgun from his hand. Daddy was cut bad but he had enough time to scamper off behind a log just like that fallen oak back there. The bear, he just stood there, swinging his head back and forth and rooting in the earth again with that big snout. I heard Daddy behind that trunk. Heard him gasping out. He was in pain. Seemed like it went on forever, listening to Daddy, rustling around behind that fallen tree. He was practically screaming. That bear swiped him good. You seen them claws, Lydia. You know."

"Yes," Lydia whispered, her eyes wide now with Clytie's telling.

"Well, that bear walked around some, back and forth, like it didn't care what was going on. Almost like nothing had happened at all. Then it come back all of a sudden and reared up on its hind legs. I heard a shotgun blast, loud as Hades, and I was knocked on my backside!"

"What?"

"I took half its head off. It dropped heavy right there ten feet in front of me. First time I ever fired such a gun. By God I don't know to this day how it all happened. I can't remember picking up the shotgun, but I must have. Daddy came crawling from behind that tree and I fell apart, Lydia. I cried to see him looking like that, with blood all down his arm, his shirt soaked with it."

"I can't imagine," Lydia said.

Clytie looked her square in the eye. "Yes, you can, girl. And I'm sorry to tell you this. But this story has a good ending. And we need good things now, even if some of them good things make us think on bad things."

Lydia nodded.

"So, we fell into each other there in the woods, Daddy and me. It was like me killing that bear had somehow energized him. He took command, and it was like I was a little girl again all of a sudden, like I hadn't myself killed that giant bear and saved my Daddy. I cried and cried. But we got home alive. Left that bear for the catamounts and buzzards." Clytie took a deep breath and

Lydia could see her eyes were glistening. She looked up into the trees and said, "I love you, Daddy." Then she checked the safety on her .22 single shot and said, "I hope it was good I told you that story, Lyddie, but I don't know for sure." Clytie took Lydia's hand and said, "C'mon now, girl, let's go."

After some time, when she judged Clytie was ready Lydia said, "That's a good story, a scary one. But I want to ask you something."

"What's that, honey?" Clytie said.

"How come you told Cornelius you never killed a bear. That's not true."

Clytie laughed and said, "You got a quick mind, Lyddie. You notice things, and don't soon forget them. I see you out here looking at tracks and traces. You don't miss a thing. You'd be a good detective, I reckon. Maybe go work for that Sheriff someday!"

Lydia laughed, but asked again, "Why, Clytie?"

"Well," Clytie said, "sometimes men don't want to be shown up, especially by a woman, even though most of the time it's not the woman who's trying to show them up. Sometimes it's best to just hush, let the men *think* they're the only ones can do certain things, like hunting and trapping and such."

"But Cornelius doesn't seem like that. He seems like he'd be proud of you to tell that story."

Clytie stopped again, and looked up into the trees, but whether to search for doves or to keep from crying Lydia didn't know. But she knew her words had touched the woman.

Lydia said, "I just mean that Cornelius seems to love you so, is all, and that he'd not care if you did men's things."

Clytie stroked the girl's long tresses. "That's thoughty of you to say such things, Lydia. And you're right, Corny don't seem to care about it. But sometimes in the presence of other men, even Corny can get touchy, though it doesn't happen much."

"My Daddy must've been some like yours," Lydia said. "Him and me, we would get onto these trails--" But she couldn't go on, and for a moment, Clytie again regretted opening her mouth in the first place, regretted telling the story. She was about to apologize for not thinking it out, for not thinking that the story would sadden the girl, but Lydia said, "That's a good story, Clytie. You should tell Cornelius, I think."

Clytie squatted down to examine something she thought she saw on the ground. She cleared some dried leaves and tossed twigs out of her way. Lydia could tell she was thinking about telling Cornelius the story. "Well," Clytie said, "maybe I will. Maybe I just will."

On the trek back to the cabins, Lydia saw a large hare sneak into a laurel patch. She could still see its flank though, through the leaves. She stopped Clytie and the two looked on. "What is it?" Clytie asked.

Lydia whispered, "A rabbit. Do you want it?"

Clytie smiled and said, "Naw, you take it, woman."

Lydia was still grinning when she released the arrow.

Clytie wondered if Lydia ever thought about the time she first set an arrow on the rest above the grip without a thumb to aid her. How she could have overcome the pain. It must've been tricky, she thought, but she had no choice then. Clytie never asked her about it, but each time she watched her take an arrow from her quiver between two fingers and set it on the rest atop the bow grip, she thought about the fear the girl must have felt when it happened. And the nerve it must have taken to let it fly. Twice.

And to kill a man.

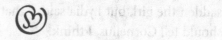

For all of Clytie's encouragement, Cornelius seemed to sink even deeper into despair. He did little around the cabin beyond some work tending crops and looking after the jersey cow. He would set to weeding but leave the job off halfway, or muck out a stall and then forget to set down hay. He sat out back of the cabin in the poorly made chair he now favored. At times just the sight of Inez, or worse, of Lydia, sent him into the blackest of moods, something Clytie had never seen before. And he would not be heartened by her words, no matter what she tried.

He took to drinking more steadily.

Clytie knew she had to take a new tack and she met him out back of the cabin one day. The sight of him made her second guess herself, though. His form had become even more gaunt, the round cheeks now hollows and the eyes deeply set, with dark shadows beneath them. But she knew something had to be done. "Corny, I mean to tell you a story."

Cornelius shook his head, "Please, Clytie. I ask you … please. I need no schooling about life or sadness or such. I told you this already, woman." He pulled on the bottle he kept between his legs.

"No, Corny. It's a story about me, one I never told you." She watched and waited for a response.

When she didn't leave after some time, Cornelius finally met her stare. He gave her the slightest of nods.

"Gimme a sup off that before I tell it," Clytie said. She pulled deeply on it, wiped her mouth with the sleeve of her dress, and without stopping she then told the story of the time she killed the bear, of her father and of her fear. By turns Cornelius gave over to the tale, his interest building. He was surprised never to have heard it before. Clytie was not one to keep secrets from him. But this time, Clytie managed the telling a little differently, spending more time on her fear, on her desperation both before and after the event. Clytie paused dramatically in places to take a sip of whiskey, or she ramped up the tension in the way she described the bear, how it bore its teeth and howled, how it swiped the ground in front of itself with its huge, sharp claws, and drooled from its long mouth. In places, Cornelius wondered if Clytie was stretching the truth, like she did when she told tales to others to make them laugh, or to scare people, to give them a thrill. But he saw the emotions pass over her face as she narrated the different parts of the tale--the fear returned to her in the telling, and the tenderness for the father.

This was no stretcher, he decided. The tale had worked him up.

When Clytie had judged that she had told it all, when she judged that Corny had sensed the desperation and the horror, and the love she felt then for her father, she said to him, "Corny, husband, I feel this same fear now." She looked into his eyes. "Only it's worse. You seem a different person, Cornelius. I know why, but that doesn't change matters. I ask you to return to me. I'm scared again, Corny."

Cornelius wiped his eyes and said, "How come your daddy never told this story?"

"Because, Corny, I told him never to tell it, my momma, too. I wanted you more than anything in the world, and you know how some men can be about women and men's things. I just didn't want you to think I was someone who was gonna hector you about anything like that. I wanted you to want me, the woman in me, what's feminine, not what ain't. Not some bear-killin' mountain witch."

Cornelius' voice caught in his throat, "But I wouldn't have---"

"Hush, Corny, I know that now, but the story ... it's hard for me to tell it. I told Lydia because I thought she might understand and it might help to heal her. But I don't like to re-live it, Corny. And like I said, I'm scared now, like I was then but worse. I'm asking you to help me. Come back to me."

Cornelius stood and wiped his eyes again. He took a deep breath and let it out slowly. He pulled his galluses up and said to Clytie, "Send Lydia down to the barn in a little while. There's something I've been wanting to do, but I couldn't then. Now I can."

Clytie saw something pass over his face, a change. He walked off toward the barn, the poorly-made chair in hand, and she thought she saw a spring in his step, though his clothes still hung off of his thin frame and he looked alien to her. He had left the bottle, and Clytie knew that at least this was a good sign.

Still, her hand shook when she tipped it to her lips.

Just After the Killings

In the days just after the killings on Black Boar, Burr and
Simms took turns catching some sleep, usually in a grotto
if they could find one, or alongside a rhododendron thicket or a
cluster of brambles they'd bushwhacked into. Anything that provided a little cover. More than once Simms considered hightail-
ing it when he heard Burr deep in sleep. But he knew the man
would be on top of him the next day, or the day after that, and
what else would that mean but certain death?

Maybe worse.

And more than once Simms thought about taking a rock to
Burr's head and ending their union right then and there. But
there was something keeping him from it, and it wasn't a con-
sideration of moral principles. When he stared at the situation
directly, in the cold evenings with only scant moonlight coming
through the canopy above, he knew what it was that kept him
from the deed--fear. But *what* was there to fear, exactly? This part
he couldn't figure. If Burr were dead, he could move at his own
pace. The pair were well beyond the Sheriff's reach now. If Simms
could keep his wits, and if he stayed in the hills for just a few

more days to put further distance between himself and the valley, he would have a good chance at freedom. He would change his name and move go to that town in western Tennessee, that place from his youth, where things were once good.

Or he could go West. Go North. Go South. Go anywhere outside of these hills and he'd have pulled it off.

Add to this the fact that it would be easy to kill Burr, physically at least. Simms was large and strong. A good piece of limestone and he could crush Burr's skull with a single thrust, even with his bum shoulder. A second pass would finish things for sure. Hell, Burr likely wouldn't even awaken. There would be no rifle report either.

But he couldn't do it.

After much thought, he realized that this fear was a complex matter. First there was the fear of Burr, of the man himself. If Burr woke while Simms approached him, he would kill Simms instantly. And so Simms was paralyzed to approach the sleeping man. This he was certain of because he had, in fact, already tried to carry out the killing. One night he had found a heavy rock and had made his way toward Burr's prone body when he began to shake and sweat. With each step closer his resolve weakened, and then a blind terror beset him--that Burr would awaken and see Simms holding the rock. At once the fear transformed itself. Now the goal became setting the rock back to the ground *before* Burr awoke, and in the depression where the rock first sat so that Burr would not see anything amiss. He stood there with the rock in his hands, too scared to turn his back to Burr and retreat, too scared to move an inch. It took him a full twenty minutes to set the rock back in place. His hands and arms shook uncontrollably.

Simms realized that one fear had simply replaced the other.

But there was still another side to this fear, one less rational than the first. It was a terror borne of the *idea* of Burr, of what was beyond the man's mortal self. He had seen this in prison, too, and during work on the road. The convicts were forever in fear of

Burr, always, but in an unformed way. His very name unnerved men who had no dealings with him. This Simms could see in the quiet that followed mention of his name, and sometimes in the anger men showed at someone *careless* enough to mention Burr's name without good reason. It was not uncommon for men to slip away from a group quietly upon a reference to Burr, and Simms himself had left groups of men if he sensed even that a conversation *might* move toward mention of Burr. The man was ever-present.

And it was such a fear now that Simms felt, as if Burr would reach him from beyond this world. For Simms, the whole night-time regimen was a study in terror.

In the barn Cornelius had set out bevellers, knives, punches and mallets—all his leatherwork tools—along with a slate and chalk he used to draw up plans. The ill-made chair, reduced to a heap of hickory and cane, sat on the floor with a maul beside it. He used twine to measure the thumb on Lydia's left hand and drew a three-dimensional image of the entire hand with the chalk. Lydia was stunned by this skill she knew nothing of, but she kept quiet, sensing that Cornelius was in his element. He used the twine again to gauge the circumference of the digit at several places and then made indentations with an awl on a piece of buckskin he had nailed taut to a work bench. Lydia watched his hands move, both on her own hands and then on the leather and slate, and then once more over her own hands. He had her demonstrate to him what motion she had left in the area where the thumb had been, placing his fingers on the nub of her hand. She was embarrassed, but Cornelius wasn't. He examined the place where the girl had removed her own digit, continually going over the area and asking her to repeat the movement, closing his eyes as she worked the remaining muscle and tendon.

Finally, he again used the twine to take measurements of her thumb, and with these he drew the image on the slate. But it was her right hand that he drew now, the hand without a thumb.

When he had finished the drawing, he showed it to Lydia. And something shifted inside of her. Images began to appear to her. She thought of shooting her gun, and of setting traps with her father. She thought of stringing beans and of writing the letters her mother had taught her on a slate much like the one on which Cornelius had made the rendering. She recalled the image of the hickory axe from the bog site grave, how neatly it fit in her grip, how perfectly weighted and balanced it felt.

Somehow, at least for now, Cornelius had returned to her the appendage.

Not in fact, but in feeling. Through some kind of alchemy, some mixture of science and art, Cornelius had wrought something from nothing. And did she not just then feel a tingle where her thumb should be, a feeling of its presence returned? She watched Cornelius slam the maul on a piece of the hickory from the old chair, and then again, and again still. He took up a saw and reduced a small piece of the wood even further. Then he looked deeply into it, turning it over in his hand and running his finger along the grain.

He slicked back his hair, matted with sweat, and fixed Lydia with a stare. There was an energy in his eyes, a determination, something alive that had been dead, or nearly so. "Lydia," he reached out and touched her shoulder softly, "I'm gonna make you a thumb."

"Well, that's fine, then ..."

"But it won't be real, girl. It won't be like the thumb you lost. I reckon it to be my fault that this all happened. But I can at least do this much."

"Corny, it's not your fault that this happened. I'm grateful for you doing this much for me and momma."

"Lydia, if you wear this prosthetic—that's what they call it—
you'd be doing something for *me*."

Cornelius began to trim the leather, carefully with his beloved
hawkbill. He didn't remember saying goodbye to Lydia when she
left the barn, but he must have done so, he thought afterward.

I saac Nichols walked up and down the wood floor of the tiny church up on Black Boar Mountain, his linsey shirt wet at the armpits and his fiery red hair matted with sweat to his forehead. He spoke to the little congregation about forgiveness, and about the dangers of harboring ill will toward neighbors. The pronouncements were vague. Occasionally he referenced the kinds of disputes familiar to mountain people: debts owed, damages caused to animal stock, accusations of indolence and failure to help out neighbors. Such disputes cause hardness, he said, and can poison the settlement in the long run. The residents on Black Boar must do better, he said. They must learn to forgive and forget, to move forward. Finally, he mentioned the Railroad, to the surprise of more than a few congregants. "There was a time the Rail seemed like an enemy," he said. He slicked back his red locks and moved down the aisle between the rough pine benches. "Truth be told I was no supporter of the Rail, nor of that Sheriff who does their bidding. In fact, I felt as most everyone did back then. We can do without the Rail, I thought. We don't need 'em, and by God why won't they leave us be?"

In a pew near the rear of the chapel, Clytie reached down and took Lydia's hand in her own. She ran her thumb along the soft buckskin that cinched the prosthetic to the girl's hand. Lydia thought about how Clytie knitted her brow nowadays when the preacher spoke.

"In those times, the company and the people of Black Boar didn't understand one another," the preacher said. "We were poor neighbors. But things have changed, brothers and sisters. Yes they have, and they are *still* changing. I want to tell you about something. Now this might surprise you, my friends. But I've visited with some of these Railroad men. Yes, I have." The preacher took a rag from his pocket and mopped his forehead. He walked up to the simple lectern Cornelius had made years ago and removed his black coat, adjusted his galluses and forged ahead. "The Rail, and the timbermen they support, are good for the town of Queen's Tooth. And this means they're good for us, too. We must be good neighbors, my friends, for the Railroad will be our boon, our windfall. It will be a good friend to us, a dear and loyal friend, I tell you. Right now, we are a-strugglin'. It's hard to find game out there, I know. But in my talks with these company men, I'm learning about ways that our lives can be made easier, much easier."

Clytie's grip tightened on Lydia's hand, and Lydia reached across herself to smooth the top of Clytie's hand with her own. Clytie released the pressure, but she whispered to Lydia and Cornelius beside her. "What's he mean, *back then*, like our differences with them are in the past?"

"Hush now," Cornelius whispered.

"And what in hell does he mean about making our lives easier?" Clytie added. "It's the goddamn Railroad that's scared off the game to start with."

"Hush, Clytie. We'll talk on it later."

"*You* hush," Clytie hissed at him. And again Lydia felt the pressure on her hand.

The preacher continued, "In towns all up and down these mountains where the Rail has come, mountain folk have improved their lot. But here, up on Black Boar, we continue to toil, my friends, and for what? For so little. And we're at the mercy of the weather, of the seasons and of the untelling ways of the game we hunt. But the Rail, now it can help us. It's insurance against such troublesome things. The Rail is a benefactor, I say. Look at other hill folk. The Rail makes it easy for drovers, for growers, for traders—that's all of us right here. Just you ask." Here the preacher reached down into the cavity of the lectern and pulled out a large clay jug. He held it aloft for a moment and then sat it on the floor with a heavy thud. "Now you know I don't hold with drinking overmuch. Many-a-man I've seen taken by the creature." He swept his wet locks back again and smiled broadly. "But this bottle come from the Rail. I could have rejected it. But I saw this as an expression of goodwill, of neighborliness. It would have been unkind to turn it away." He flashed a Cheshire smile here, as if on cue.

The men in the congregation stole looks at one another. The women, in turn, looked at their men. But when the preacher unplugged the jug and took a pull, both men and women held their breath. "Oh!" the preacher said, wiping his mouth on his sleeve. "Now, this is fine corn. Better than fine. And I invite all those here today to share this with me, this gift from the Rail." He slipped his galluses off and walked down the narrow aisle again. "But let us try to put our disagreements with our neighbors to rest. Settle your disputes about stock, about favors and debts, and about any injustices you feel. Be charitable with one another, and with the Railroad. Let us put any nastiness behind us, and any sorrows and mistreatments—real or imagined."

He never mentioned the King family by name, nor the convicts, nor that night. But it was there, beneath the slick words, woven in alongside the Christian sentiment. To name it openly would be like opening the very wounds he sought to close. Lydia sensed this instinctively. It wasn't as if she disbelieved the words the preacher spoke. Even her father had told her long ago that the Railroad could be good or bad. It just depended on how it all worked out. But the preacher reminded her of a huckster she had seen in town once, a man selling cures to townsfolk, remedies made from herbs and animals he said came from Asia, cures that simply couldn't be found around the hills of Kentucky. Her mother had scoffed and pulled Lydia by the hand, bent on completing the few errands for which she had to go to town. But Lydia noticed then that the townspeople were gathered in a circle around the man, in rapt attention, his voice booming out and his glance taking in the crowd. Like the preacher, the huckster's voice rose and fell according to the points he wanted to emphasize. He was working the crowd, bending them to his will. Those were townspeople back then, Lydia thought, and if they wanted to throw away their money, what was that to her? But now the preacher was speaking to the people of Black Boar, to her neighbors, the ones who comforted her, the ones she spoke to every day. Righteous people. This was different.

Even so, there were some who were inclined to believe the preacher, to trust him. The Rail planned to help the people of Black Boar, he said. He hadn't been known to fabricate. Wasn't he a righteous man, a man of God? Why would he deceive the people, his very own flock? Now that would be downright nasty, dangerous even, for both body and soul.

And then, too, there was the jug.

"Lyddie, honey, there's something I need to talk to you about," Clytie said.

She and Lydia hung the last wet clothes on a hemp line stretched taut between two trees. Inez was out walking somewhere, without purpose, as she often did now, and Corny was at work in the barn. Clytie pulled the tintype from the pocket of her dress.

"Now, I don't know why I kept this. But I did," Clytie said. "Something told me to, and now I'm glad of it. Let's go set down." They sat on an oak log Corny had hewed flat and set onto four thick posts to make a rough bench. She pulled the girl close, with an arm around her shoulder. Clytie said, "That night, the night your daddy was killed and your momma violated." She fought through a sudden tightness in her throat, as she expected she might have to. "That night you killed that prisoner, Lydia, I found this. It's a picture. I thinks it's of one of them raiders, the one who attacked your momma. I got it from his britches he left there, the cretin devil. Damn him to hell. I wanted to destroy this little keepsake of his, but then I thought how this could be a clue, and I don't trust to give it over to the Sheriff, unless you say so, of course. And I don't think your momma has been in a state to judge what we should do. I showed Cornelius, but he left it up to me what to do. So now I come to you."

She set the tintype in the girl's palm, but she kept her own hand on top of it. "Lydia, there's a reason I want you to see it, even though I know it might pain you some, and that pains me, too. Well, I reckon maybe we can find out where that devil has run to. You see, Lydia, you have a gift. You can see things that others don't sometimes. You got a keen eye. And like I said, I don't trust that Sheriff and that company, that prison or anyone from that Railroad. I think they want to forget about what happened. Give you a little money and such and hush it all up. All of it makes me wonder, how come they ain't caught them two? So, sweetheart, can you look at this picture? If you can't, I will understand, and we'll give it over to the Sheriff. I'll say I just found it out in the woods behind your cabin. Do you think you can look at it?"

Clytie took her hand away and Lydia looked at the tintype. Her breath caught in her throat, and for a moment Clytie thought she had made a terrible mistake in showing it to the girl. But then Lydia pulled the image closer to her eyes. She ran her finger over the face of Simms and the woman, turning the image this way and that.

With her arm around Lydia's shoulder, Clytie squeezed the girl close to her and asked, "Is that him? Is that the devil that attacked Inez?"

Lydia nodded. "Simms Jackson is his name, the newspaper said. I remember."

"Now that woman there," Clytie said, "That could be a wife or a sister, I think. He's got his arm around her, and that likely wouldn't be a friend. Maybe a relative, though. What do you think?"

"Maybe," Lydia said. She examined the tintype, holding it at arm's length, and then pulling it up close to her face, alternately squinting and opening her eyes wide. Finally, she said, "I don't know if it's a sister or a wife, or maybe a cousin. That I don't know. But I know this much. He loves her. And she loves him."

Inez spoke little these days. But Lydia could gauge her mood from how she moved about, how she boiled a shirt or worked a row in the corn plot, and whether or not she finished tasks or gave up mid-way through. Sometimes a garden row would end up half-hoed, the tool cast to the ground, blade up, and Inez nowhere in sight. To retrieve the tool in those moments, and to finish the job, was much more trying for Lydia or Clytie, or even Cornelius, than it should have been. The cast-off tools and kitchen things became for Lydia forlorn objects that startled her when she came upon them, and she felt pangs of sadness and loss at those moments: an oak bucket full of wash water, the stiff brush on the floor beside it; half a basket of beans left unstrung; a dress patched, but the needle and thread yet attached. Usually, Lydia or Clytie knew where they could find Inez at such moments--in the little cabin addition Cornelius and the other men had built for her and Lydia, asleep on her tick, or lying there eyes wide open. She was not able to do many of the things she used to do, like harness the plow to the mule, or skin a rabbit or squirrel. Either there were too many steps involved, or the knife and the guts repulsed her. No one ever asked specifically. They all simply went on. This was Inez now, they reckoned. She was not the Inez of the past, nor would she ever be.

For months after that night, the women on Black Boar tried all they knew to bring Inez around, to restore her to her old self, or as much of it that could be restored. Some made remedies like those Inez herself used to make, curatives sure to restore her vigor and such. Others visited with her, tried to make conversation. Some even dared to broach the topic of her trauma, reasoning that this was only path toward recovery. Others came over and made pies or simply helped Inez with domestic duties. Still others took her for walks along the wooded paths or further out even. But little seemed to do any good, and often Inez would simply stop dead in her tracks, or wheel around suddenly and head back to the cabin.

One time Lydia and Clytie walked her to far ridge, high up where a person could see all of Queen's Tooth down below in the valley. Here she seemed to regain something of her former self, some kind of ease that issued from the beauty of the vista there, though it made Clytie and Lydia anxious to stand directly on the precipice as Inez did. Just looking along the sheer drop all along the ridge made them swoon. Still, if it made Inez happy, they would stand on the giant rock formations there, well back from the edge, but with a commanding view of the town below even so, while Inez stood so that the toes of her shoes hungover the ledge.

"Set down here with us," Clytie would say to her as Inez looked out at the rows of intersecting hills, one after the other, receding far in the distance. The sight mesmerized her.

"What? Oh, yes, yes," Inez said, as if she had been in a trance or a reverie.

And so it went.

At moments Inez showed flashes of her former self, but generally speaking, she was wrecked. Even her moments with her daughter, quiet times when the two were alone, made Lydia feel uneasy. She was buoyed when her mother took her hand, or stroked her hair, talking softly to her about finding a young man someday, or about what a fine wife and mother Lydia would make. But just as quickly Inez' mood could change. If she took hold of the girl's right hand, she would fixate on her wooden thumb, staring at it and caressing it as if it were real, as if the girl could feel the comfort she intended. Lydia did her best to sit on her mother's right-hand side and give her the good hand. But Inez seemed determined to touch the wooden thumb, and she would reach across Lydia to take it in her hand and caress it. It was a gesture even Lydia couldn't interpret, and she never asked about it, though it unnerved her.

More and more Clytie served the role as Lydia's mother, though Lydia needed less direction and instruction than other girls her age on the mountain. Clytie could tell that the girl missed maternal love, the sweetness that had come so naturally before that night, the feminine succor that flowed both ways, equally in measure and in its power to hearten. For her part, Clytie felt guilty about it. She wondered if she were assuming a role unfairly, and even if she were taking advantage in some way, stealing from Inez something she herself didn't, and wouldn't, ever have. Before it all happened, Clytie had never felt a sadness for that which she did not possess, a child. But she knew now that she could not go back. She had felt it now with Lydia, a closeness unlike anything else. And whether or not Inez would eventually recover was in some ways of no moment to her now. Yes, she hoped and prayed that her dear friend would mend, but she had no choice but to serve the role that had been foisted upon her. It was Cornelius who one day assuaged her feelings of guilt over it. When she explained it all to him, tearfully and with a desperation that scared him some, he simply said, "Sweetheart, that girl needs a mother. If not for you, she ain't got one."

When it overwhelmed her, when it seemed Inez would never be herself again, Lydia took to the woods, sometimes roaming entire afternoons, exploring areas farther and farther out, rarely announcing her departure. Clytie knew to let her be on these occasions, and she never hectored the girl about work around the cabin or out in the field. More often than not, Lydia would return with some food, or some herbs, or both, and Clytie figured this made up for her absence. She worried about the girl out alone in the woods, but adults in the community often headed out to hunt alone, or to gather, and Lydia was more attuned to her surroundings than most of them. She was armed with her bow and arrows, though Clytie and Cornelius worried about animals that could surprise, like a bear, or a catamount. But there was no way to dissuade the girl, and in any event, Clytie knew that the walks were good for Lydia, good for her soul and her spirit. The risks were weighed against the benefits and Lydia's need to roam won out. On her return from these excursions, she usually recalled what she saw or heard for Clytie, or for Clytie and Cornelius both, often with Inez in earshot, though deaf to it.

Early one morning, when the faint rays of the rising sun struck through the hardwood canopy, Lydia set off for the overlook, a ledge that sat high above the banks of the Empyrean River. It was close to eight miles each way, with some rough terrain in places, though she felt confident about navigating it. It was losing her way that gave her pause. In the weeks before she had asked Hez about routes and precautions. He told her everything he knew, having made the trek many times himself, but he asked that Lydia not go alone, and he offered to make the hike with her. But Hez knew the girl would up and go on her own, and Clytie and Cornelius knew the day was coming, especially now that Hez had told them that Lydia had been asking about a route to the overlook.

When Clytie rose early that morning to find Lydia gone, she knew. She worried, of course, but she would keep it from Inez for now. No use in two worrying when one would do, she reasoned. She would tell Inez that Lydia was helping a neighbor for the day, if Inez were aware enough even to ask.

Cornelius had made a hemp and buckskin halter for Lydia, something to hold both her quiver and bow. This allowed her the movement she needed to navigate the rough mountain terrain. The route crossed sandstone boulders and laurel hells that tore holes in her dress. A deep gulley and a steep rise gave her some problems, but she managed, though she worried after the fact if she had marked her way as well as she should have.

Earlier, Hez had told her that she would start to see large stands of hickories and walnut trees just ahead of the ridge that overlooked the river and Rusty Mountain. Men from over that way, he said, would sometimes hunt for bear there.

"There's plenty mast that the bears feed on near that overlook. Maybe you'll see one," he winked when he told her.

"Lord, Hez, I hope not."

"Just listen close and if you see one, move away. They mostly don't want to do with us, mostly anyway."

"Well, I hope I don't see one."

Hez laughed and winked again. "Law, girl, it's not the bears you should worry on, not right now anyway, but the black boar hisself. He's been seen out there."

She laughed. "Aw, Hez, that's just a tall tale and you know it."

"Well, how do you think we got the name of this hill, then? There's a black boar out there, somewhere. Got huge, sharp tusks and big cloven feet on him. People who seen him say he's huge. Bears are scared of him, they say." He grinned as he said it.

"Hush, you."

Hez laughed. "Anyway, I never saw him, but they say he's coal black, all over. Some says he's mean, and he'll charge you. Killed many a-man with them tusks, they say. But others say he just roams and eats. They say he protects the mountain."

"Law, Hez! Protects it from what?"

"I don't know. Maybe outsiders. Maybe men who come to do harm. One thing I heard some old folks say, though, is he don't go after females, just menfolk."

"Hez! That's crazy talk."

"Maybe so, but let's hope it ain't, because you're going out there. Just listen careful, you hear, and watch like you always do. You're as good as anyone out there. Just watch and listen, dear."

"OK, Hez. Thank you."

Closer now to the overlook, hickory husks, half-decayed and rotted black, crunched under Lydia's boots with every step. Along with the shriveled and darkened walnuts that lay everywhere, the mast released a sharp, moldy scent that cut the thin air. At one point, she thought she saw something dark moving up ahead of her, but her view was obstructed by the trees. She stilled herself, slowed her breathing, and waited. She looked around, in every direction. Nothing.

She thought she could hear the river now, faintly up ahead, and she picked up her pace. But here and there she got reckless, and she cut herself in some briars and on a thick laurel branch she should have seen. She stanched the flow of blood with the hem of her dress and moved on before she should have. Soon the dress had reddened at the shoulder and down the side. She stopped again to make a mud paste with water from her gourd. This she smeared onto the cut before she hurried on. A kestrel sounded far off and a squirrel peeked its head from a drey. A killdeer trilled its false call on the ground nearby. She knew to slow herself before she got there, before the vista that promised so much. It would not be good to arrive harried, out of breath and unready for the sight. And so she stopped and steadied herself against a tall walnut tree. She took ten deep breaths, in slowly through the nose, and then out her mouth. In time her heart rate slowed and she was part of it all again.

She headed off toward the sound of the river.

Just After the Killings

Burr and Simms were still moving through the hardwoods, traveling the most difficult of routes, through dense brush and up hellish inclines. The pace exhausted Simms, but Burr said that tough routes were hardest to track. A few more days, Burr said, and they could go their separate ways, but until then they would stay together. Burr gathered small sassafras leaves and roots, wood sorrel, hickory nuts, and black walnuts. They nauseated Simms, but Burr ate them mechanically, chewing the raw meat of the nuts without comment.

"Ain't we supposed to boil these first? Or rinse them?" Simms asked. "They're bitter as hell."

"In what?" Burr said flatly. "How?"

"Well, we can at least wash them in the creek water, can't we?"

Burr shook his head in disgust and fished out the meat of an acorn using his teeth to crush the husk.

Simms knew better than to insist. He forced down the acorns and chased them with the sassafras leaves. He couldn't wait to be shut of Burr and he only hoped that the few remaining days would pass without incident.

But it wasn't to be.

The men had been moving steadily along a high eastern ledge for the better part of a day when Burr decided to follow a line that angled up the slope for what seemed like hours. Simms had ceased asking about such decisions long ago. He simply gave over to Burr, figuring that if Burr had wanted to kill him, he'd have already done so. Now and again Burr stopped to look at something on the forest floor or in the brush that surrounded them. For hours they moved on like this, with Burr leading the way.

And then Simms, too, finally saw what Burr had seen long ago—footprints.

"Hellfire," Simms said, "why are we following this, Burr? There might be a little hamlet up here, like where we already come from. We don't want that, do we?"

"There ain't no hamlet, as you call it. Just someone. One person, maybe two. I'm guessing some mountain man lives alone. A hermit. Maybe he got a pretty wife … or one not so pretty. Don't make a difference, do it?" Burr laughed softly.

Simms waited to find out what more Burr might add. But the man said nothing and finally Simms asked, "But why do we want to see *anyone* at all? Don't we want to get as far from people as we can?"

Burr chuckled. "Well, you said you was tired of eating raw nuts and such. So I just thought maybe we could take advantage of some mountain hospitality."

Simms watched Burr move up ahead of him, a sickness growing in his stomach. Again he thought of picking up a rock along the way and dashing apart Burr's head. God only knew what the man intended in following a route to some tiny cabin or hovel, maybe some crude lean-to or a cave where a hermit eked out a simple life. But again he couldn't summon the courage to follow through and kill Burr.

And now he was sick with fear, both for what he wanted to do, but couldn't, and for what he thought Burr *might* do once they arrived at their end, wherever that was. He envisioned another night like the one on Black Boar, more terror and death, much of which he himself had caused, though now regretted.

Burr slowed the pace when he smelled wood smoke. Eventually, Simms smelled it, too, and soon enough, a tiny cabin came into view as the men topped a small rise. Burr ordered Simms to move a ways back down the path they had just followed while he made a wide arc around the cabin. He was gone a full hour, and Simms didn't even hear his approach until Burr was practically on top of him.

"We'll move a ways back a bit until nightfall, I reckon," Burr said.

Simms followed him further down the path they had just come up. "And then what?" he asked.

"Then we enjoy some mountain hospitality, I figure," Burr said.

Simms hoped to God there was a legitimate, neighborly reason to wait for nightfall, though he didn't think there was. But he didn't have the courage to ask about the real reason, the reason he imagined was behind Burr's plan, and so he said nothing, hoping against all that the men would spend an uneventful visit at hermit's home. His stomach churned and he could taste the bile rising in his mouth. For his part, Burr crushed an acorn hull with his teeth and began to chew the bitter, dense meat with relish. He flashed a smile at Simms.

Long after the sun had gone down, the men still set in place on the dry leaves and earth well away from the cabin. Eventually, Burr gave the word, "Let's go." He rose and started moving up the path. Simms followed, his stomach sour.

At the top of the final rise, pale moonlight fell through on a little clearing where the cabin owner had girdled some trees but had not dug out the stumps. Simms could see a few plots for fall crops, tiny little spaces with enough food to sustain one or two. The moonlight made for a pretty picture where it fell on the cabin, Simms thought, but it only lasted a second or two. Burr set the rifle up against a tree stump and called out, "Hello, there! Hidy, neighbor!"

The sound of a chair on a wood floor came from within. And then the sound of something metallic. A levered rifle, Simms thought. His eardrums pounded with his own heartbeat. Burr took a few steps toward the cabin and called out again, "Hello, neighbor! We intend no harm. We're lost. Out hunting and lost our way." He took another acorn from his pocket, pulled out the meat with his teeth and spat the husk to the ground. It was dark, but Simms thought Burr had winked when he looked back at him.

Burr whispered, "What you scared of now, boy? We're just friendly mountain folk here." Moonlight glinted off the cuspid tooth.

The cabin door cracked and a shaft of soft orange firelight shone through the opening. Seconds later, the double barrel of a shotgun poked through. "What do you want?" a man said. "There's nothing here for you." Simms heard the fear in the high, thin voice of the old man. He knew that fear can make for recklessness, and he worried that he'd end up dead any second now. His heartbeat whooshed in his ears.

Burr only heard the fear.

"Friend, we've lost our way. We've been out looking for game. Ain't had any luck and kept on moving. We ain't had but some acorns for three days. And we just run out of water. You see my gun over here against the tree stump. I'll leave that where it sits. Friend, could you let us inside. We're cold and hungry. Thirsty more than anything. We're friends. Mountain people, like you. We don't want trouble."

The door opened a bit further and the barrel swept across the area around the cabin. "Turn around so's I can see you," the old man said.

Burr and Simms showed the man their backs.

"Where's all your gear? Cover and such."

"We left it below, maybe a few miles from here," Burr said. "Though we ain't got much left. Once we lost our way. We tried to find the stream, but we're lost mister. We're in bad straits, I'd say. Will you help us, kindly?"

"How come you only got one gun?"

"Ran out of buckshot. No use in carrying a gun hasn't got any shot. We've been trading off carrying that one. Don't either of us have much strength left," Burr said.

In the long pause that followed only the sounds of the chill fall night could be heard. Something thrashed in a tree above and a covey of bats darted low across the cleared land, their small wings working furiously across the space before they were lost to the woods beyond. In a moment they tore back across the space, and then again a moment later, flying low and terrifying Simms each time they came in sight and dived toward him. He gritted his teeth and waited for another approach of the bats, or the gunshot, or both.

"Turn around and come in," the old man finally said as he opened the door. Simms saw the man framed in the orange light of the cook fire from a stone hearth inside the cabin. He had set the gun aside and turned back into the cabin. The glow cast itself out onto the cleared space around the sturdy wood structure, lighting the chinked walls and heavy timbers of the cabin. It was warm and welcoming, Simms thought. Just then it seemed a great stroke of luck to have come upon it, at this very moment, nearly free and at the end of their mountain trek, he hoped. But when Burr turned and smiled at him, Simms wondered what would happen in the coming hours, time he would have no control over, events over which he would have no say. Burr led the way into the cabin, and the light from the hearth instantly became a hellish vision. Simms nearly fainted with the fear of it all, but he righted himself and followed Burr into the cabin.

For better or ill, he didn't know.

The ledge wasn't far now, and Lydia could better hear the river's flow with every few steps. But there was something else there, a sound she didn't recognize, underneath that of the river. And as she got nearer the ledge this other sound grew more distinct. She could still hear the water as it coursed over its rocky bed and surged around the boulders that created fierce rapids. But the sound, the other sound, rose against the sound of the river, something discordant. Soon she could see light ahead, where the ledge opened up onto the vista of the river and trees below. She was nearly there. She wondered about the sound, though, that which now threatened to overcome the sound of the river, an unnatural sound, something from outside the forest. What was it? How could anything drown out the sound of the Empyrean River, with its violent rapids that had awed even Hez, to hear him tell it, a man who had seen everything in nature? It puzzled her, and she moved fast toward the ledge in order to find out.

In her final approach to the overlook, she was beset with a feeling that something was wrong. Throughout the day, she had felt the pleasurable promise of beholding something new, the nervous anticipation of a reward that would come at the end of a long journey: the vista. But the feeling was gone now. In its place was something baleful, something foreboding. She raced the final steps to the ledge, bushwhacking her way through rhododendron and briars that tore sharp cuts all along her arms and legs. She ran with a sense that something was wrong, that some emergency presented itself.

And there it was, finally.

But it was not what she had hoped, not what she had been told the vista would be, and she felt as if a promise had been broken. For acres and acres on the far side of the river, the earth lay bare of trees. Huge stumps dotted the landscape far and wide, giant pock marks amongst the mass of fallen slash that covered everything. It was an unending blanket of limbs, leaves, and tree crowns. Closer to the river bank, spread out as far as she could see in either direction, sat massive piles of logs, huge trunks shorn of limb and thrown every which way into a small mountains that lined the river bank. Men moved about everywhere, tiny figures swarming the logs and the landing. They were dwarfed by the huge trunks, but like flies on a carcass they trucked about fearlessly, as if victories over foes much larger occurred every day. Then Lydia saw how this was so.

On two rails of iron fixed together by wood ties sat a boxy black machine that poured thick smoke from a metal chimney. The loader. Men scurried around this machine and around the logs it dropped between heavy iron stakes that ran along the sides of rail cars. Inside the machine, a man stood behind a steel crane that stretched out high in front of the box. As he turned wheels and levers, men on the ground attached long, thick cables that ran from the crane to the logs in the landing. When the men scampered away, the cables were drawn up by the man in the box and the massive log was lifted and dragged along the ground, leaving a wide trench in its wake. The box pivoted on the rail and the log was lifted high above the flatcar, miraculously hanging in the air for a few moments before the cables lowered its great mass onto the car where men guided the bulk into position to lay atop the others already loaded.

Once in place, the process would begin again with the machine pivoting and the men affixing the tongs at the ends of the cables to the logs. Lydia heard the wheels and chains grinding and pulling inside the black box, creating torque form the steam produced by the fire. The whole effort produced a ceaseless mechanical whine, a jarring, continual din. She watched for a long while as men hurried about, trying to keep pace with the activity of the loader.

The mystery of the sound had been solved.

The trees themselves had been leveled by crosscut saw, Lydia knew. She had seen the sawyers on Black Boar use them, in fact, after the trunks had been girdled, in order to make space for the homesteads. She'd seen Hez and her father fell substantial oaks and maples with the crosscut saw, and hew them with their sharp broadaxes for cabins and barns. It was an artful thing, using controlled strokes of the broad-axe to create the planed surfaces for rafters, joists, and walls. It was work that took days, weeks sometimes, depending on the amount of wood needed for a structure. And there was finer woodwork, too. Cornelius could shape a table from a log, or cane a chair using the very strips from just inside the bark. But such work was done by hand. When it was complete, there would follow a little gathering with corn whiskey and maybe music and dancing.

What Lydia saw below her, this was different.

She saw no joy in any of it, no sense of craft. She reckoned it was the loader that governed it all, the clamorous black box that sat at the center of things. Eventually, all of the work seemed to end up there, where the muscular machine hauled the logs on to the flat cars. She marveled at the its tireless industry as it pulled log upon log and loaded it on to the rail cars. These in turn were followed by more rail cars and then moved out, and so on. But unlike a man, the machine needed no rest. So long as there was fuel to feed the hungry boiler, more logs would be pulled and loaded.

It was a cycle that could never be sustained by crosscut saw alone, unless the crosscut saw became a hundred crosscut saws, or a thousand, with sawyers on either side of that saw working continually. And so she figured that must be the way of it: the work of hundreds of men and hundreds of crosscut saws. How else could an entire forest be felled?

She figured that the men themselves must also be a sort of fuel for the machine, sawing and felling, sawing and felling, and over yet again, and again after that. Men had built the loader to make the work *easier*, she guessed, but now they had to work continually to keep pace with it, becoming in the process like machines themselves. This is how she saw it. Man had given life to a hauling, swinging, grinding machine that breathed smoke. In the end, she decided not to climb down to the banks as she had planned, but to turn back and hike home. Walking right up to the rim of the ledge, she took a last look at it all, still trying to make sense of it, to account for the death of the hardwoods. It dizzied her and she stepped back from the ledge knowing that a slip on the sheer rock face would be deadly at this height.

Though she knew it was the men and their crosscut saws that reduced the forest to slash, it was the loader that seemed to matter most. The loader controlled it all. And though just a machine, it seemed alive somehow with its intelligent movement, its arm that lifted and swung, its cable that grasped and hauled, its waist that pivoted, and its dense black breath sent high into the air. It was alive, absolutely, she thought, in the same way that a monster was.

She turned and headed back.

Just After the Killings

Burr sat on the only chair in the cabin, a roughly made oak ladder back that the old man insisted one of them take. Simms and the old man sat on wood crates the man had emptied of the few potatoes and turnips they held. On a heavy clapboard table, he set out a bottle of whiskey and a jug of water.

"My name is Hiram Knoll. Now, this ain't the greatest corn in the world, but it'll do the job," he said and laughed. He passed the bottle to Burr who took a pull and handed it back to the man. But the man passed it on to Simms before he sipped on it. Simms realized that Burr had been right about the mountain hospitality, and again he tasted the bile that rose in his throat behind the liquor.

"Thank you kindly for taking us in. I'm Wells Napier and this is Jefferson Reed. We're from all the way over on Black Boar, above Queen's Tooth. Do you know that place?"

"I do," said the old man, "but it's been years since I heard of anyone from there. When I was younger, I knew some folks over that way. But I've been here alone near twenty years now, or thereabouts. How I like it." He offered the bottle again to the two men and took a sip after them.

"You been alone all them years, then? No woman?" Burr asked.

"I'm alone. Always have been since I've been up here. I built this cabin myself, though I'm no expert carpenter. More of a farmer, I guess you could say."

Burr nodded and asked a few questions about crops and yields, about the year's weather and such. Simms noticed that Burr's eyes would now and again catch something in the cabin, something to be stolen, used to advantage and then tossed aside likely. For his part, Burr was careful. If he thought the old man saw him eyeing something, he'd make a remark about it. "Them knives on that shelf over there. I seen them when I come in. Did you use deer antler for that grip? It's nice work."

"I made them, yes. Thank you. If I take a deer, I try to use all I can from it."

"Hell, that's impressive, that is," Burr said. "I'd like to be able to do that kind of thing. No one ever taught me, though."

The man rose with a groan and picked up the knives from a shelf near his bed tick. He set them on the table where Burr sat. "Now, this one I use to scrape hides and such," the man said. But this other one here, this is to gut and clean. I keep this one extra sharp."

Simms wondered if the man had just selected the instrument of his own death.

In time Burr wound the discussion back around to Black Boar, talking about life there, about the little church and the different people and the trades they plied. The man seemed to delight in talk of the community there, though he knew none of the people Burr mentioned. Of course, the people weren't real, but the *types* were, and the old man recognized them from the time before he became a hermit.

"We had some trouble on Black Boar sometime back," Burr said. "Was a killing amongst us. You hear about that?"

"By God, no. What happened?" the old man asked as he passed the bottle around again.

Simms heard a whooshing in his ears that kept pace with his racing heartbeat. He felt hot all over and declined the bottle when it made its way around to him. He could hardly believe it was happening. Burr was relating the tale of their own escape from the railroad work, and the violation and killing. He told it as if he were one of those men who traveled from town to town and charged people to hear him read the newspaper aloud, adding flair to a particular incident, or slowing his pace when he neared a climactic event. He told it all, every sickening detail. In places, he added dialogue that Simms didn't remember, and little details that made the tale more gripping.

The old man was riveted, his eyes glistening. "Lord above," he whispered. "Now that is terrible, more than terrible."

Me and Jefferson, we know that family well. Like kin to us, they are. Well, most everyone up on Black Boar is like that. Close, I mean." Burr tossed his head Simms' way and added, "Jefferson here almost married the woman who was violated, a ways back, I mean. But she favored the other one in the end, the one that got killed, I mean. Ain't that true, Jefferson?"

Simms' mouth was bone dry but he managed to say, "Yes."

"Well," Burr said, "I guess that might be hard to talk about, Jeff. Sorry about that. But I guess you gotta be glad you never married her. That might've got you killed, maybe." He sipped from the bottle and smiled.

"Lord above," the old man said again. "I guess you're right there." He wiped the moisture from his eyes.

Burr leaned back in the chair and thumbed the blade on the sharp knife, turning it over in his hands and admiring the work on the grip. "You're left-handed, ain't you?" he asked the man.

"Yes, I am. Now how did you know that? It's that grip, huh?"

Burr laughed, "Yes it is. You're good. This fits like a glove." Burr turned over the knife in his hand and ran the blade against the hairs on his forearm leaving a tiny shaved patch. He held it to his side, arm extended, as if he were going to make a pass with it. Simms waited tensely for the slash, for the gore that would follow, and tried to steel himself against it.

But it never came.

Burr set the knife on the table and said. "Lord, I am tired."

"You men need some rest," their host said.

"Well," Burr said, "we thank you dearly for your hospitality, Mr. Knoll. And you're right. The truth is, sir, I don't think I can keep my eyes open much longer. Do you mind if we find a place on the floor here?"

"I feel almost beholden to you for that story. It's a tragedy, and I hate it. But I have no means of news up here, and you told it fine. You two can take the tick over there. I'm gonna stay up awhile and put some things to rights for tomorrow. I'm fine on the floor. You two have had a real ordeal. Tomorrow after breakfast, I'll show you how to get back to where you're going."

Simms didn't want to accept the offer of the bed tick, but it seemed easier at this point. And it was obvious the old man suspected nothing about them. He hoped Burr would accept the offer and they could be on their way tomorrow without incident.

She was still lost in all of it when she first heard it--the sound of something rooting around in the earth and mast, something back there in the laurel that edged the path. She stopped and realized that she *had* in fact heard whatever it was a full mile behind her, and then again somewhere in between. She had heard it, in the back of her mind, but thoughts of the timbermen, of the rail cars and the loader at the center of it all had kept her mind occupied, kept her from fully *sensing* it. She had been taken out of her element, out of the forest. And now whatever it was in the brush was almost on top of her. Though she knew it to be a wives' tale, images of the black boar flashed in her mind's eye.

She moved on through the laurel that narrowed the path, finally becoming almost like a tunnel, the waxy leaves and gnarled branches closing in on her. It was a part of the hike she enjoyed on the trek out to the ledge, a natural enclosure that ran near a quarter mile. She had even considered doubling back to enjoy it again, but she worried about time and consoled herself that it would be something to look forward to on the hike home, this odd and lovely tunnel where peepers chirped and tiny brown hares crossed her path and eyed her before they darted back into the brush.

Soon she heard the movement again, back in the laurel on her flank. She ducked low and tried to get a fix on it, but when she stopped, the sound stopped. And then when she began to walk again, she heard the sound, the animal, whatever it was, forging its way through the thick brush. The snap of broken branches and crunch of the dried leaves and mast followed her, though she couldn't see what made the sound. Even the thick laurel was no match for this creature.

She picked up her pace, hoping to get to the head of the tunnel, a place where she felt she could gain some advantage, or at least get on equal footing, where she could get into some space and take stock of her surroundings, maybe get a fix on the animal and nock and arrow. But the sounds kept pace with her. And now her eye caught something black moving in there, low and quick-like, but it would disappear from sight just as soon as she saw it, or *thought* she saw it.

When she eventually heard a snort she knew, and her heart sank. It was a boar. A bear might run off when it saw her, but a boar was more likely to charge, and she had nowhere to move. The laurel had narrowed so that she had to duck under branches and slide sideways through places.

There came another snort and a high squealing. Lydia stopped dead. A final thrashing up ahead of her now, just twenty feet, and the boar entered onto the path in front of her. Lydia froze. It snorted and rooted in the earth there, its hind end facing Lydia, but it moved on ahead and was soon gone from sight around a little bend. Lydia heard its hoof falls on the leaves, moving farther and farther away. She waited a full five minutes there, her heart racing, long after she had heard anything but peepers. Finally, she moved on. It would be a story for Hez, she thought. Every now and again she stopped and listened, scanning what she could through the thick laurel. She figured she was nearly at the opening of the tunnel now and she moved on with real purpose, stepping high and fast, avoiding anything on the ground but moving with greater pace. Her dress caught on snags she didn't bother to avoid, and her wound had opened up again. When she rounded a bend in the path she saw where the tunnel exited onto a stand of red maples and where some light filtered through the canopy. She was nearly there.

Then the boar wheeled into the small space to close off the tunnel.

It snorted and threw its head wildly, not fifteen feet from Lydia. What struck her first was not the size of the animal, but its color. Black as coal. Even its snout was dark from the wet, dark loam it rooted in. Its head turned and she saw the glassy eye, shiny and black. It saw her, too. On either side of its lower jaw the curved tusks, yellowed with age, flared wide. The boar was old. It sniffed the air and snorted again. She noticed the huge, cloven hoofs when it made its way down the path toward her, slowly. Part of her thought to nock and arrow. If she kneeled in the earth she could get off a fine shot. She had killed many animals this way. It was a position she had practiced.

But she didn't.

Instead she froze, terrified, as the boar moved heavily toward her, snorting and swinging its head in vicious, wide arcs. As it neared her, it turned again and rooted in the ground for something. When she saw its full flank, she felt the true size of the animal. It must have weighed five hundred pounds, maybe more. She saw now how black mud covered its coarse hair up to the top of its haunches and along its rounded gut. The huge testicles were covered in it, too. It lifted its massive head high and moved toward Lydia, holding her in its gaze with its shiny eyes. For a moment Lydia thought it intended to pass her on the narrow path, but after it brushed by her, leaving a patch of mud and excrement on her skirt, it stopped and returned along the other side of the path. And again it rubbed its filth upon her. Now she smelled it, too, a feral scent mixed with the smell of wet earth and pig filth. The old, yellowed tusks, gnarled along the edges, caught on the hem of her day dress and tugged her forward before the fabric gave way and ripped. The animal took no notice. It moved back down the path and snorted yet again. Eventually, it turned and faced her. Lydia felt her heart pound and she nearly swooned.

And then the animal burst into a charge.

Lydia wasn't sure if she screamed or not, but she thought maybe she had. At the last second the boar darted to the side and ripped its way through the thick laurel branches at the edge of the path, leaving a swath of destruction in its squealing wake. It flew down the path behind her, and she felt its rumbling in her legs. When she looked at the path, she saw the boar's thick black hairs spread about the broken laurel branches. Waxy leaves from high in the bush fluttered to the ground. She saw traces of mud and excrement, and the wide, cloven prints that made an arc off the path and into the dense laurel.

It had avoided her, had spared her. She fell to the earth and cried.

As dusk came on, she arrived at the cabins. Hez was the first one she ran into. She dove into his arms and cried again, though she never told him about the black boar.

She didn't have to.

Just After the Killings

When they woke in the morning, the old man was at work at the hearth. He had made some biscuits and set out some jam he had canned from the wild blackberries that grew everywhere. "I got some serviceberry jam, too, if you'd rather," he said.

"Sure," Burr said. "That would be nice. Can't believe the good luck we happened on here, Mr. Knoll."

"Hiram, is what you can call me, friend." he said. He rooted around on a shelf and set the jar on the table.

"Thank you, Hiram," Burr said.

When they were full up and given a gourd of water for their trip, the old man told them how to descend the mountain with the least difficulty. Burr repeated the directions to the man twice to be certain of the route. The convicts thanked him.

Then Burr grabbed the left-handed knife from the table and plunged it into the old man's throat.

Long, Long Ago

BLACK BOAR MOUNTAIN

The woman followed the cloven prints across a little clearing and into a stand of yellow poplars. When she came across fresh pig droppings she felt a familiar, pleasant thrum in her ears. Her palms were moist with sweat and she wiped them across her buckskin breeches. She thought she heard some movement up ahead, but when she stopped to listen for it, the shrill trilling of a warbler got in the way. She took a deep breath and stilled herself. She listened. When she finally heard it again, she nocked an arrow and moved ahead. Now and again she would hear it moving, but when she stopped to get a fix on it, the animal, too, would stop, and then only the warbler could be heard. It went on this way for a long time.

And then it appeared, a huge black mass moving slowly between the trees. But she would need to get closer to get a shot that would kill. She inched forward. At one point, the boar swung its head suddenly and fixed her with its large dark eye. She readied her longbow and braced for a charge. But the animal only snorted and rooted around in the earth, intent only on the mast and earth. When she got close, she watched it working its large snout, grubbing and snorting. Its tusks curved out wide from the jaw and the sight of it made her shudder. Still, she crept up on it. Once she was in range she drew hard on the bow string, and the boar lifted its head at the creak of the bending wood and stretched sinew.

It stopped chewing for a second.

But before she let loose, she saw the eye again. The boar was aware of her. And he turned his flank just then, giving her the clearest shot she had ever had. It couldn't have been easier. In the space of just a few seconds she realized that there would be plenty of meat from the kill, enough for the clan to roast together at night, where the fire would cast a glow on the children and old women, their lips wet with fat from the meat. She could imagine the shadows thrown from the firelight, long shapes that moved as the people circled the fire and talked and ate and laughed. She would thank the boar once she had tracked it by its blood to wherever it finally fell, and had killed it there if she needed to. She would use her axe if need be. She would dress it and cover whatever portion she couldn't haul in green leaves and freshly cut branches. She would come back with others to retrieve what remained that very day. She would provide for the others like they, too, provided for her.

The boar worked its snout, its tusks making sharp slashes in the earth as it rooted in. Just as she was about to release the string, the boar fixed its eye on her yet again. She saw it blink this time, saw the bristles above the eye move.

And then something happened.

She didn't know what it was, though she would think about it at times over the course of her life. Sometimes she thought she had reasoned it out it nicely, had figured out what happened that day. At other times, though, she would admit to herself that she didn't understand why she did what she did. Or what she didn't do. In the years that followed, she would kill many animals-- boars, deer, turkey, even bear, without hesitation.

But she didn't kill the boar that day. She never told anyone that she had seen it. Instead, she watched the huge black mass move amongst the sugar maples up ahead of her. She watched it grub in the earth. She heard the hulls of acorns crunch in its jaws and she listened to its hooves and the crinkle of leaves as it eventually left her sight.

She released the tension on the bow and lowered it. Then she turned and walked back the way she had come.

1905

BLACK BOAR MOUNTAIN

(Lydia, age 17)

Cole was excellent in the woods, good with a rifle, and he knew things, too. He knew about trees, about what bloomed when, about what animals ate, and where they hid and how to flush them out. He knew about mating seasons, about gestation periods for different mammals, and about how the creatures of the woods and streams cared for their young. He had books he got down in Queens' Tooth, he said, that talked about these things, and he read them again and again. It was something that drew Lydia to him. That, and the fact that he was one of the few boys taller than her. She had grown in the last few years, sprouted straight up like a white birch, as Clytie put it. Her feet and hands were larger than that of other girls her age, and Cornelius had to refashion a leather cinch for a new thumb he had made. She was seventeen, and she prayed that she would stop growing now. She and Cole had courted for well over a year, and there were plans for a wedding.

They took to the woods often, hunting, trapping, and exploring together. Lydia's height made no difference to Cole, nor did her disfigurement. Before he and Lydia had become so serious, a boy had made a coarse joke about Lydia's features, about her height and her missing thumb. Cole had thrashed him.

No one ever made a joke about the tall girl with the wooden thumb after that.

They were headed all the way to the ledge, to the vista above the river where Lydia had seen the timberman working alongside the loader years ago. Word had spread about a huge fire that consumed the old tree crowns and decayed brush from when the area beneath the ledge was first cut, and Lydia and Cole wanted to see the damage for themselves. They planned to hike down to the river, too. They were nearly there.

They had just gone through a patch of thick briars when a large brown hare peeked out from under some brush and ducked back in when it saw the couple. Lydia looked at Cole, "Ain't you gonna take it?"

"Take what?"

"That hare."

"What hare?" but Cole was smiling now.

"Aw, give over that rifle, boy. You haven't got the skills to take him, I can tell."

Cole laughed with his mouth wide open. "You make me laugh, you do. Naw, I saw it, but I don't want to carry him all the way. We'll look for something later, after the ledge and closer to home."

Lydia was laughing, too. She teased, "Game's pretty scarce now. Maybe I'll take that gun on the way back. We can't risk losing anything."

"Yes, ma'am," Cole laughed.

"I can smell that burn, can you?" Cole said.

"Not yet … maybe a little, I'm not sure."

"Well, your nose ain't as good as mine, I guess. A true woodsman has a good nose."

"Aw, you hush, Cole Clemmons."

Up ahead Cole and Lydia could see where the light entered

into the forest. They picked their way over boulders and through some rhododendron. Finally, they came out onto the ledge.

"Holy Jesus," Cole said, his voice just a whisper.

Lydia took it all in. "Lord," she said, "looks like something from the Bible, some pestilence, some plague or something."

It looks like Hell on earth is what it looks like," Cole said.

As far as they could see, the earth was a mass of scorched tree crowns, ash, and blackened stumps. In places, little plumes of smoke still rose skyward. Lydia recalled the flurry of activity she had seen when she last visited, when the loader hauled logs and men buzzed around the landing everywhere. She could still see the scars in the earth where the machine had operated. That was the beginning of the end, though only now did it really dawn on her what it meant. For a time, neither Lydia nor Cole said a word. They simply gazed, spellbound at the destruction. Except for the river, which still flowed alongside the now abandoned track far below, there was no life, no movement.

Eventually, a little sound came from Cole, a stifled cry it seemed like, a moaning that came more from the throat than the mouth. Lydia couldn't tell, but she didn't respond, didn't look at Cole then. He shook his head, "This is bad, Lyddie girl. Really bad."

Lydia said, "Hez told about fires over on Rusty Mountain and everywhere else now, because of them woodhicks cutting everything in creation."

"He's right. The brush gets dry and any little spark will set it off. A lightning strike is just about guaranteed to set it off. A goddamn shame is what it is. Goddamn woodhicks."

A curse word from Cole was startling, no less taking the lord's name, Lydia thought. She stayed quiet. Cole sighed and said, "Let's climb down there and get into the river."

Once they finally navigated their way down, they picked their way through the charred slash, climbing over burnt logs and walking across patches of softened ash that blackened their boots. Here and there they stopped to listen to the roiling water. The hem of Lydia's dress was stained black all the way around by the time they reached the banks of the Empyrean. Recent heavy rains made for some fast rapids and Lydia watched the water race over the rocks. Translucent and green-hued, it rushed forth and made spumes of white water. The little breeze that blew close to the river's edge threw droplets onto her face and neck. She had to raise her voice to make herself heard. "This river's raging, Cole!"

"Yes, it is."

She threw her arm around Cole's shoulders and yelled, "It's loud, too, by God!"

Cole laughed. "Hell yes, girl."

The two watched the water race, a green and white maelstrom, a vein of life that raged on, unaware of the fire's destruction on both its banks. Lydia and Cole made their way down toward a place where the riverbed deepened, and the water moved slower. They took off their boots and stepped onto the uneven rocks of an eddy. Even there, Lydia could feel the pull of the current over her ankles. "It's colder than I thought it would be," she said.

"The cool air makes it so."

"I know that much, Cole. I just mean it's colder than even I thought it would be."

Cole laughed. "Well, yes, it is cold, by God."

"What do you think you could catch in these eddies?" she asked.

"Don't know. Trout, I guess. Muskellunge. I'm no fisherman, though. Bores me to tears."

Lydia watched the river move. Here, where the bed was deep, it made less noise, but she could still see and hear the violent rapids. Her ankles stung with the cold of the river but it was bracing and with Cole it felt good, too. The flow of the water on her legs thrilled her. She felt alive, part of the living river and a part of Cole, too, who also stood to his ankles in the cold water.

"I guess a fire can't kill off a river, can it?" Lydia said.

"No," Cole said. He took her hand and smiled at her. But then Lydia saw something serious pass over his face. He said, "But the animals that live here, the ones that used to live here, I mean ... they're gone. Lots of things depend on the river, but they need the trees, too, Lyddie, the shade of them. Even the fish need it. The woodhicks didn't leave anything here on the banks. Just took it all. And that's what caused this fire, all the dead wood they left, all the slash." Cole skipped a rock across the water. He smiled at her again, but it wasn't the same careless smile he had given her before.

Lydia said nothing in answer, just turned a foot around in the water and splashed it around. She looked at Cole, who stood with his hands on his hips looking out across the river at the scorched land. Finally, she said, "Well, you know what, Cole? Maybe it ain't so bad. My daddy once told me that the ash from a fire is good for the land. It's just that we don't see it in our own lives, in our own lifetime, I mean."

Cole didn't answer. Lydia heard only the great sound of the river and she wondered if she had lost Cole for the moment, or worse, if he had ignored her altogether. Finally, he said, "Is that right?"

"Yes," Lydia said, "the ash has got things in it that are good for the soil, and another forest will grow here because of that ash. It's just part of nature's cycle, he told me. But like I said, we only see some of those things, like this fire. To us, it's bad, and to the animals, too. But over time this will become a fine place again."

Cole turned to her and said, "Is that so?"

"It is so."

Cole knew all of this, but he acted as if he didn't. Still, it was Lydia who reminded him of it, who reminded him of their place in the larger order of things and of the resiliency of the earth. She sought to lessen the anguish he felt for the loss of the woods, he realized. He felt then a tightness in his chest, and a tenderness of feeling for her swept through him.

"Well," he said, "I guess that's so, too."

He smiled at her and splashed her lightly with water from the river. She squealed and he was on her in a second. He kissed her deeply and squeezed her until she felt breathless, almost scared but not exactly that either, as if maybe there were some danger here. Cole reached his hand into her dress and touched her breast. Her nipple hardened and she arched herself towards him in his embrace. He moved his arm across her back then and lifted the dress to touch her between her legs. She felt the heat rising in her and heard her own heartbeat in her ears, a thrum deep and full. She stood on one foot and then the other as Cole removed her bloomers and stroked her. She surprised herself with the sound of her own moaning. The water continued to swirl about her ankles in the eddy, but she no longer felt the cold chill or the numbness. She felt the heat radiate from her skin and she could smell Cole's musky scent now, coming from his neck and arms, from his chest even. He moved his fingers inside of her and all around between her legs. When she felt like she could take no more, as if she were in some kind of physical danger even, with her heart about to explode, she shuddered and fell limply into Cole's arms.

Cole kissed her softly on the neck and held her to him, supporting her entire weight in his lithe arms and legs. She was no longer sure if her feet were in or out of the eddy water now. As she recovered her breath, she saw over Cole's shoulder a grey and red cardinal on a charred stump. The female flapped its wings once or twice and the male shifted closer to her. They twisted their beaks every which way and then when the male rose in flight the female followed. She saw her bloomers on the black ash of the riverbank at her feet, and she knew things would never be the same for her. She wasn't sure what it was that had happened, but she knew it was right that it happened with Cole, and that it happened here, out of doors, with the river beneath her and the mountain behind her.

"We can lie down on the ground here, Cole, I mean, if you want," she said.

But Cole said, "No, Lyddie girl. We can wait 'til we're back home for that."

"Cole," she said, "It don't matter to me if we're married to lay together. It don't matter to me … marriage … before we lay together."

Cole kissed her on the cheek and neck and said, "Naw, it ain't that. It's just that a bed tick is nice for that. I can wait, Lydia."

For some time, the two stood on the river bank and watched the water move. In places Lydia could see the grey rocks beneath the glassy water, but in other spots the water moved darkly over the deeper part of the bed. She took a breath and removed her dress, tossing it behind her onto the earth. Cole was startled but something inside of him told him to keep still. He watched Lydia wade out knee deep. Her bare back and buttocks made him feel cold, and his impulse was to race ahead and pull Lydia from the water, to shelter her somewhere in his own warmth. But again, something inside of him stilled this impulse even as it arose.

He watched as Lydia disappeared beneath the water, and then shot up in the center of the river where the current started to take her. Cole was on the verge of rushing in, of screaming to her to make for the bank. But it was Lydia who began to swim toward the far bank in hard, muscular strokes. She kicked powerfully, and turned her head to take in air as she glided across the surface. When she reached the far bank, the panic in Cole subsided. Cole could see the water fly from her long hair in droplets as she slung her head to the side. She was far away now, but she walked back upstream along the riverbank, well past the point where Cole stood on the opposite bank. Her skin had reddened from the air, but she didn't appear cold. She looked down to watch her footing in the rocks at the far bank as she waded back in. When she was knee deep, she looked at Cole once more and smiled. She went under again and came up floating on her back in the eddy, her breasts and face above the surface. She turned again and stroked hard across the river. Cole watched her until the current had taken her beyond him again, downstream a little ways but on the same side of the river now.

Cole wanted to strip down, to join her in the water, but he wasn't sure if that's what Lydia wanted, and he was overcome with a feeling of not wanting to disappoint her, not wanting to counter her will. It was something he hadn't felt before. And the truth of it, too, was that he feared the cold water and air, unlike Lydia. He was unsure of what to do, and it was as if Lydia could read this in him. She laughed and reached her arms across a rock that created a little riffle in the water, letting herself hold on to the rock as the water sent a little wave across her face. She was stretched out fully, anchored by the rock and her feet downstream behind her. The water flowed over her long locks and down her back and buttocks. Cole was struck with the image of her, not sure if he should do anything, or even speak. He noticed then that the leather cinch that held her false thumb had darkened from the water and Lydia's fingers had whitened with her grip on the rock. Again, he felt that he should act, should enter the water to aid her, or to comfort her. But as soon as he had decided to strip and enter the water, something told him not to, told him that Lydia was fine without him and that maybe he was meant now only to watch her, to remain silent.

Lydia pulled herself up to her full height and pulled back her wet tresses with both hands, her body fully open to Cole. Rivulets fell from her hair and breasts and shiny droplets clung to the hair between her legs. Far in the distance, beyond the scorched earth, were the hills in their browns, yellows, and reds. It was as if she had come from them, Cole thought, like a figure from some story, some Greek myth. He saw it all at once, this one complete image of her, a beautiful creature born of the hills.

She set her feet on the uneven rocks and walked right by him. She pulled herself into her bloomers and dress and looked back at Cole, who still stood on the bank watching her. Once she had tied her hair back with a little piece of inner bark she had pulled from a branch earlier, she held out her hand to him and said, "C'mon, Cole Clemmons. Let's leave this place."

Long, Long Ago

BLACK BOAR MOUNTAIN

The woman removed her breeches and tunic, slipped off her buckskin shoes and waded into the river. She knew it would be bracing at this time of year, but she also knew that she would catch her breath in time, that she would warm up if she could keep her shoulders beneath the surface, the hardest thing to do at first. She lay down in the eddy and watched the water race white over a set of riffles in the center of the river. It was low and a few of the rocks remained dry at their tops. The woman enjoyed the river this way, once she regained her breathing, low and quieter than normal. Though she also enjoyed it when it raged. She thought about this for a while. She would ask her husband later which way he liked the river water best, and if he felt like she did, that she liked it no matter what.

BLACK BOAR MOUNTAIN

(Lydia, age 19)

I t troubled her to think about it. But she couldn't help herself much of the time. Lydia considered her wedding day the last time she had lived as herself, as her *true* self, she thought. Of course, she knew beforehand that her life would change with marriage. This she wanted. She looked forward to it more than anything in life, to be Mrs. Cole Clemmons. But the union brought complications that she hadn't foreseen.

And it wasn't just the marriage. It wasn't just her relationship with Cole that complicated things. It was that, yes, but that and everything else that happened on account of the Railroad and the timber Company, which, for everyone on Black Boar, amounted to one and the same thing. When she thought back on it, long after the wedding itself, she realized that the signs had been there, even on the wedding day. And that she should have seen it.

Isaac Nichols, the preacher, had performed the wedding. Clytie had asked Lydia about this beforehand, asked if she were sure about Nichols. Clytie felt the preacher was a scourge to Black Boar, "an agent of the Company," she said. She and Corny had stopped going to services because the man seemed always to turn a sermon into an opportunity to stump for the Rail or the timber Company, to encourage the people of Black Boar to "get out of the hills," to modernize. The Company would pay good money for their land, and jobs in Queen's Tooth were plenty, he said. There was the sawmill, or work felling trees and hauling. The little farms and drover operations on the hillside would not generate income for much longer, he said. Farming methods had changed, and the operations down in the valley were expanding and would soon make obsolete the small farmers and drovers on the mountain. "We need to get with the times," the preacher was fond of saying from the pulpit. "Lest we want to be seen as ignorant bumpkins." And yes, many families had already made the move, selling their acres to the timber Company and moving to Queen's Tooth. Even Cole's parents had accepted an offer from Cole's Uncle to live and work on the farm he owned in North Carolina. The uncle's wife got along with Cole's mother, and it seemed an easy way out. Cole told them he understood, but that he would remain and make a life on Black Boar.

Reverend Nichols said that, come the end of the year, the church up on Black Boar would be no longer. He planned to take up at the lovely church and meeting house in town. All were invited.

"Good riddance to him!" Clytie said. And she asked Lydia, "Are you certain you want that Railroad man to issue your vows? He don't care about us. He's just doing the Railroad's business." It may have been true, but Lydia thought her friend could have been more thoughtful in the weeks before her wedding, and the whole affair caused a small rift. A woman only got married once, Lydia reckoned, and that's if she's lucky. It seemed as if Clytie was spoiling things for her, as if she were jealous. Lydia resented her interference.

For her part, Clytie felt the girl's coolness, and in the final days before the wedding, she tried her best to support the arrangement. "I'm sorry for telling it the way I did, Lyddie dear," she said.

And the two made peace. At the wedding, though, it was Lydia who began to wonder if she had made the right decision. The preacher blessed the union, but before the crowd had begun to dance and sing, he decided to make a little speech.

"All of us here are happy for Cole and young Lydia, two children born and raised on Black Boar," he said. "And we hope their union brings more children, more such good people to the region. There are those who couldn't be here today to see this righteous union, people like Preston King, whom we all remember today. Now there was a good man, friends. We know that Preston looks down on us now, the last residents of Black Boar. And we ask you, God, to bless this marriage as we have done here today, with him looking on."

He came out from behind the lectern to walk down the aisle: "This marriage represents the future, I think, a future where people like us take our mountain skills into modern times, to the town, where we can show folks who we are. It's happening fast. There's several families have moved from here to town. You know them. The Neelys and the Wrights, the Holbrooks and the Wilsons. Others, too. People down in town are beginning to realize who we are up here. Clever people with skills, not ignorant dirt farmers. And we offer our spirituality, too, our sense of God. Amen." He took a handkerchief from his pants pocket and mopped his brow, the way he did in church, Lydia thought. "In fact, it's us mountaineers who're teaching the townsfolk in so many ways. But we need to get off these hills if we want to continue to thrive as a community. Town's where we can make the best of ourselves. And in young Cole here, I see a strong man about town, a respected worker. Maybe a mill hand, or a timberman. You know, that Cole's got a head for numbers, too. Maybe he might even work in the Rail office. I don't know for certain. The main thing is that there are *opportunities* for mountain folks like us down in town. That's where the future is. But I've talked on long enough." And just like that day a few months after Preston was killed, when he talked about the Railroad during the church service, he pulled a jug from beneath the lectern.

"This ain't no church service, and it ain't no lecture," he said, slipping back into the speech of the mountain man. "This here is a celebration of the union between Cole and Lydia!" He took a pull from the bottle and wiped his mouth with his sleeve. "Ahh," he said. "Tastes good to a man." He lifted the bottle high to let everyone see the amber liquid in the clear glass jug. The bottle had a printed label affixed to it this time. "Go ahead and sample some of this fine whiskey," he said. "It's a gift from the people at the timber Company, in honor of Lydia and Cole."

Clytie bit her tongue. She never looked at Lydia during the speech, nor did she mention it later. But as the men and women began to sing and dance, and to feel the fine whiskey warming them, Lydia felt her stomach tighten. It wasn't that the feeling put a damper on the celebration. Lydia thrilled in Cole's strong arms as he threw her about, dancing on the hard packed earth. She sipped on the whiskey with Clytie, Corny, Cole and everyone else. And the musicians amazed everyone with reels and jigs. The women of Back Boar had brought all manner of food. There was cured ham, rabbit stew, cornbread, biscuits, cream corn and grits. And there were sweet things, too, like apple stack cake, blackberry cobbler, and black walnut cake. But back of it all, in her stomach now and again, Lydia felt a tension, especially when she looked at the preacher, though for his part, he seemed every bit the reveler, dancing and singing.

Still, there was something else there, something bound up with the preacher's words that made Lydia uneasy. Everyone knew that Reverend Nichols favored a move to Queen's Tooth. The Railroad had built a fine church for him down in town, where he sermonized to larger crowds than he did on Black Boar. Nowadays he came to Black Boar once a week, though the services took place late in the afternoons, and not always on Sundays. But the reverend had singled out Cole and Lydia, had said that they were the future, they and their children. It seemed like he fully expected Cole and Lydia to move to town, though he had never said such a thing to her. The next day Lydia asked Cole if he had said anything to the reverend about moving to town.

"No," Cole answered.

"Well don't you think that's quare? Him saying all that?" Lydia said.

"I do. I do think it's odd, Lyddie dear."

Lydia sensed that the preacher's words didn't affect Cole like they did her. Like maybe it wasn't so terribly odd that the reverend took the liberty of laying out their futures for them. "I think it's downright quare, Cole. Him saying that stuff about us," Lydia said again.

"Ah, maybe so," Cole said, "but why let it worry you, Lyddie? The reverend ain't got any say over us." He reached out and pulled her down to the bed tick.

Cole and Lydia were living with Inez in the old King cabin now. With the help of neighbors, they had a "working," and built a room on to their cabin for Lydia's mother. But the event was carried off without the sense of celebration that normally came with a working. Lydia was disappointed that no one brought a fiddle nor did anyone want to stay around in the evenings after the work was completed to sip on whiskey, or to talk and eat. On the last day of the work, Lydia had fixed a stew with rabbit and venison and made an apple stack cake. Some other women brought vegetables and cornbread. Hez's wife made a blackberry pie. But much of the food was left uneaten, and after some small talk, most of the neighbors made their way back to their own cabins. They were plagued by the same worries as Lydia and Cole. It only occurred to Lydia after the fact that maybe the gifts had stressed their neighbors' food stores. It was nice to have the added space for Inez, but the business-like mood of the whole affair sat wrong with Lydia. It was saddening on the one hand, but she had to admit that it angered her, too, that everyone just up and left when the work was over. Still, she and Cole had no plans to move.

But all that would change.

Long, Long Ago

BLACK BOAR MOUNTAIN

The woman and her husband topped a rise and made their way to the ledge where they had sat, talked, laughed, and even lain together. The mists lifted and the gray-blue peaks came into view, extending as far as they could see. They were quiet, but this was not unusual. Sometimes it was best not to talk, but to look instead, to listen to the bird songs and to watch the mists move. But it was not that kind of quiet today. It was a quiet borne of frustration, of failure. Normally they would have arrived with a hare or a squirrel, or even a fat dove if an arrow stayed true.

But not today.

Inwardly they both felt it, knew that the return trip would yield nothing, though part of them hoped they would be wrong. After a time, the man moved off and the woman followed.

1908

BLACK BOAR MOUNTAIN

(Lydia, age 20)

Lydia felt Cole's sweat in the spaces between her fingers. It fairly poured off of him. But this was different than in the first months after the wedding, different than their heated love-making of those days, when they would fall together in an exhausted heap after coupling. Back then she would lay atop Cole afterward, her entire weight on him, his sturdy form supporting her. They would lie entwined, sated, but fully alive. Lydia recalled a vitality that seemed to hang in the air after those sessions, an energy that poured from their bodies as much as from their common love. Nowadays, though, it seemed that Cole had to work hard to release himself. He grinded on her roughly, laboring in order to finish. She had come to think that sex was a chore for Cole, an inversion of the mountain code about a "wife's duty," she thought. It seemed like sex had become *Cole's* duty, and she hated that.

For her part, there was less physical excitement in love-making, but to have Cole inside her was just as important as ever, maybe even more so. She wanted the closeness, wanted Cole's body like at first, but even more so, she was desperately trying to become pregnant, and she encouraged Cole to the bed often. But she felt that it was also this frequency that wore Cole out, that removed the sense of passion. The irony was that the more she wanted Cole inside of her, the more she was pushing him away. At least that was the way she thought about it. She could feel the tension in the muscles of Cole's back and buttocks as he stroked and stroked. She held her breath at times, for fear she would somehow interrupt his concentration and he wouldn't deliver the seed. Eventually, though, he would groan and release himself. Then he would roll off of her and reach for the bottle of corn on the floor beside the bed.

He always seemed relieved to have it over, she thought.

Once, after one of these sessions, when she felt that enough time had passed and Cole had gotten his wind back, she said, "I talked to a woman in Queen's Tooth, Cole, private-like. She doesn't know anyone up here. She told me about how to use black cohosh and milkweed. She said it will help … you know? To get a baby."

She thought that Cole might laugh outright at the folksy remedy the woman recommended, and she was prepared to answer him. She knew of bona fide testimonies, and even medical doctors who advised the elixirs. She was hopeful, and she would explain why. But Cole never gave her the chance. He only said, "That's great, Lyddie. Anything you can try." He took a pull from the bottle. It was a patronizing remark, Lydia thought, but to say so would have provoked Cole to more surliness than was usual these days. It was as if he had given up on the idea of having a child. The burden was hers entirely.

And it wasn't the only one.

There was also the problem of meat now that the timber Company and the Railroad had chased away even more game. Like most families still up on black Boar, Cole and Lydia raised some corn, beans, and other vegetables. They kept a few chickens for eggs, too. They could sustain themselves, but a family needed meat. By now, wide swaths of Black Boar had been clear cut, and the noise of the engines rattled the nerves of animals and humans alike. It maddened Cole, a man known always to return with something in his gunny sack. Nowadays he often returned with little, sometimes nothing.

"Maybe we can try together, Cole," Lydia said to him one time. "We used to hunt all the time, me and you, before we were married. Why can't we? You used to like having me along, didn't you?"

But she already knew the answer Cole would give: "I'm not gonna have my woman provide for the two of us. By God, Lyddie, what kind of man can't provide for his woman? What man needs help to bring home some food?"

And then there was that one time Cole was drunk and feeling sorry for himself. "Oh, hell, Lyddie," he had said. "Maybe it's best you can't get with child. I can't manage to take care of the two of us and Inez. How am I gonna manage with yet another." Lydia stormed out of the cabin then and both Cole and Inez heard her scream in anger. Inez worried Cole about it, asking all sorts of questions then. But Cole only reached for the jug. It was his answer to all of their ills now. And he had let go his personal appearance, too. He'd reddened and bloated in the face from drink. Less and less did he bathe, and though Lydia boiled all the clothes regularly, he preferred the same muslin shirt and pants, wearing them for weeks on end.

The neighbors who had stayed on Black Boar were good about sharing, but Cole wasn't beholden to anyone. He forbid Lydia to accept any "charity," as he called it. In the third year of the marriage, Lydia gave up and began to head out to find food on her own. She was better than Cole in the woods, and she came back with meat more often than he did. But it left a bitter taste in his mouth. Once when Lydia had taken a few hares and cooked them in a fine stew, Cole said, "Well, at least there's one man in the house. Maybe I ought to learn to do the women's work around here."

"Cole, what difference does it make who goes out there?" Lydia said. "We could do better if we went together, like we used to."

"Naw, Lyddie, I'd be a burden to you. You're more man than me." It wasn't the only time he had said it, either.

At such moments Lydia felt like there was a heavy rock inside, a large weight she felt in her chest. And she wondered, too, if there were more to Cole's remark. On the face of it, the slight was yet another bit of self-pity, Cole saying that she was more man than him. But Lydia thought maybe this was also a slight on her femininity, on her inability to conceive. She knew he said such things when he was angry at himself, but she also felt he blamed her for the lack of a child. It was maddening. Then the self-pity turned her way. She would go about forlornly, speaking only when she had to. It made it worse that neither Cole nor Inez seemed to notice.

These days she swung between sadness and anger, self-pity and rage. She didn't know what course to take next. A pregnancy could change things, set her and Cole back on course, but it might not ever happen, she knew.

What then?

On top of that, people were leaving Black Boar and food was tough to find. Cole's instinct was to isolate himself now in the face of such worry, not to partner up and figure out a solution.

"Do you plan on going fishing, Cole?" she asked one day. "We need to get something in here besides the vegetables and all what's down in the root cellar, all that I raised and canned."

Cole's sorry smile told her that he was not too drunk to feel the slight she intended, but that he didn't care enough anymore to allow it to affect him. It was his answer that threw her, though. "Naw," he said, "I can't manage to do much in the way of men's work, Lyddie dear. Maybe you can teach me canning and such things, and then *you* can go out to get us something worth eating. You're the provider in the family now."

And he delivered a cruel close to the sad remarks. "If only I could get with child," he said, "we would be ok."

It stuck with her, and she decided she couldn't go on this way. She just couldn't.

And so she set out to do something she had resisted for a few years now, since she had visited a young wife named Bertie Hysle on the edge of Black Boar to ask about how the woman finally managed to get pregnant. The day following Cole's harsh words, Lydia dressed and quietly removed a soft leather pouch from a tin. She stuffed it in an inside pocket of her father's mackinaw that she had thrown on, the one he used to wear so often when they explored the hills together, back when she was just a little girl. She left with her bow and the quiver she had rolled into a gunny sack and slung on her shoulder. On a belt cinched around her waist she wore a buckskin sheath that held her field knife. She had told Cole the night before that she was going hunting in the morning, without him, whether he liked it or not.

Part of her felt absolutely free, and the promise of a day in the woods excited her in spite of everything with Cole. Still another part of her felt unfaithful. She knew Cole didn't want it this way, with his wife headed out to provide for them. Outside the cabin, she paused before she headed off. The bare branches of a sycamore bent at crazy angles against the grey-blue light of the moon that poked through the tree canopy. Its patchy bark looked like the strange skin of monster, Lydia thought, a witch with dozens of arms and long thin fingers that spread out from her scaly body.

What was she doing out here, in the cold with her husband back inside? What *in hell* was she doing, she wondered?

She thought about turning back into the cabin then, about going in to roust Cole and to talk about things, maybe to force him to get up and go out with her, on a hunt. She would demand that he go with her. She would threaten something if he didn't, though she didn't know what that would be. Her eyes burned, and her cheeks flamed despite the raw chill about her. She was at a crossroads, she thought. But she didn't know which way to turn. Her breath hung on the air and she dug her hands into the mackinaw where she felt the leather pouch. She crushed it to her cheek with both hands. The scent of the soft leather was faint, but still there. Lydia remembered how she had helped her father clean that deerskin, how he had guided her little hand that held the blade across the hide. She gripped the pouch in her palm, remembering his firm touch. "You got to *hold on* tight now, Lyddie. This is a sharp blade and can hurt you if you ain't careful," he had said. She stuffed the pouch back into the pocket, wiped her eyes, and started walking.

It was dark but she knew her way to the stream. The moonlight was enough for her, and the sun would rise soon enough. She hadn't been out in the woods in this way in a long time, and she recalled it all in what seemed like a single emotion that included her father, Clytie, and Cole. The chill air stung her nose and cheeks in a way that made her feel more alive than she had since she had married, and the sound of her boots in the snow made a rhythm that thrummed inside of her.

She hoped she would find something to kill, but she also knew that wasn't her main intention. And if she came back empty handed, it wouldn't seem unusual. In time a little cabin came into view and Lydia's heartbeat picked up with the recollection of her visit with Bertie Hysle, several months after her own wedding, and the woman's tale of Black Mary.

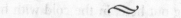

Back then, when she still hadn't conceived, Lydia told her woes to Bertie, a woman who hadn't become pregnant until long after she herself was wed. It tortured Lydia to have to ask Berite what she knew, but she reasoned it wouldn't have done any good to consult

140

Clytie, who never got pregnant in the first place, and Inez was too tormented now to talk to about such things. Lydia could recall the visit in detail. She had walked to Bertie's cabin one Saturday, at the edge of the settlement on Black Boar, a few years ago.

"I wondered if you would ever come to visit me some day, Lydia Clemmons," Berite said back then. The two women talked about their husbands and their lives. But Bertie said nothing when Lydia asked her how it was that Bertie eventually became pregnant. Bertie turned from Lydia and lay a swaddled infant onto a pallet alongside her other child, a two-year old girl who wriggled inside a feed sack nightie. A soft light came from the hearth fire behind. The scene stung Lydia's heart. Still, the woman didn't say anything at first, though she looked up to the loft and to the ladder that led there. Lydia thought maybe she had offended her and was about to apologize and explain her desperation. But Bertie put her finger to her mouth and gestured for Lydia to head outside.

It was cold outside the cabin, and the two women drew their arms around themselves.

Bertie said, "My husband don't know about this, Lydia." She turned her head to look back at the cabin. "He's asleep up there in the loft. Hell, that sawmill wears him out. He has to rest up all Saturday."

"He stays in town?" Lydia asked.

"Yes," Bertie said, "The Company has bunkhouses there, for the workers, you know."

"I heard that's how they do it," Lydia said. "But it's mostly men without wives there, isn't that so?"

"Mostly, but there are men from other places, places like Black Boar and other little settlements. Men who work at the mill and save up to get a place with their wives and children. Right now it's just men who live there, but the Company is talking of building real homes for the workers' families. When that happens, or when Luther puts away enough to get us a little place in Queen's Tooth, I'll take the girls and leave this place behind."

"Well, now," Lydia said, "will you really?"

"There's nothing left up here, Lydia. I used to love Black Boar, but I've got to think of my family. Now that Luther's at the sawmill, there's no reason to say up here."

"Well, yes, I see now." It was all Lydia could think to say. She drew her arms about herself.

Bertie said, "Lydia, it's cold out here and I don't want to talk on this inside, not where Luther can hear. So you got to listen to me close now. And I tell you this only because I know the sorrow you feel. It's not something I've told others. But if you should ever tell what I'm about to say to you, I'll deny it, and I'll curse you in my thoughts. Forever."

Lydia's saw her own breath on the cold air when she said, "I won't tell a word."

"It ain't that it's a bad thing, really," Bertie said. "It's just that I don't want people knowing I needed the help. And it's strange nowadays to believe in such things as I'm about to tell you." Bertie craned her neck in the direction of the stream that ran not far from her cabin." She inhaled deeply and let out a long plume of breath onto the cold air. She shook her head as if to say she knew she might be doing something wrong. "Hell, Lydia, I'll tell you but you need to keep quiet. This is a women's thing, amongst us. Do you understand me?"

Lydia looked Bertie in the eye and said, "I do, Bertie. I do."

"I figured you to come talk to me sometime, seeing how long it's been for you, and how long it took me. How long have you been trying?"

Lydia looked away. "It's been long," she said.

The woman shook her head again, but Lydia couldn't tell whether in pity or sympathy. Maybe both. She said, "Took me a long time. Almost ended my marriage. Lydia listen, it ain't no doctor I'm gonna send you to, nor no granny woman. Nor do I have any such herbs as to make you fertile. You understand this much, I hope." Lydia nodded and Bertie continued, "You need to follow the water upstream. It's a long hike. All the way up to the spring where it starts. There's no springhouse up there, either, just a pool. You'll see it. The climb ain't terrible hard, but it's long. But it if I made it, you surely can. Up there on the near side of that notch is a cabin where a lady lives, a spinster woman. Just beyond the spring on a little flat spot. Her name is Black Mary, because of she only wears black, if you believe what you hear anyway. She was wearin' it when I went to see her. That's the truth. My mother-in-law said Mary's husband died when she was just married, and she's worn black dresses ever since. She's the one who told me about Mary, my mother-in-law I mean, when I come to her same as you come to me now. But she ain't never told Luther, I know. I was desperate and afraid, like you are, I guess. Anyway, Black Mary comes from up by that notch, near where my mother-in-law was raised, but nobody lives there no more except Mary, and my mother-in-law told me of what she can do for a woman who wants a baby. It's a long ways, though. Take you half the day to get there and half to get back. Leave early if you go, before the sun come up. There's no guarantee either. Just so you know that much."

The talk had made Lydia's heart race. She was afraid to ask, but she could tell Bertie was scared to say any more. But Lydia needed the answer. "What did she tell you?" Lydia finally asked.

The woman rubbed her upper arms with her hands and looked back at the cabin wall behind which her husband rested. "Have you heard that name, Black Mary?"

"No, I have not."

Bertie shook her head slowly again, and Lydia thought she might not go on. But finally, she said, "It's old mountain ideas, Lydia. Not many people hold with it anymore, but I was desperate. Like you are, I think." Lydia could see the woman's breath on the air. It was coming harder now, in thick white plumes.

"Well, what did she do, Bertie? Tell me."

"You got to make a tribute. Something valuable, not just some trinket. I gave my mother's rosary. It was everything to her, you know. She was a Catholic. Gave it to me on her deathbed, Lydia. Wanted me to have it. It was the most valuable thing I ever owned, and I don't own it anymore. It about killed me to give it up. You got to give something of *value*, Lydia, but not money. It must be something that *means* something to you."

"She doesn't know of any medicine to help?" Lydia asked.

The woman rubbed her arms furiously now, visibly uncomfortable in the cold. She closed her eyes tight and shook her head firmly. "I can't tell you no more, Lydia," she said. "It's bad luck to talk on it too much. You need to go see Black Mary. That's all I can tell you."

Lydia nodded, and her voice caught when she said, "Yes, I will. Thank you." She was about to ask Bertie how she knew that the tribute had worked, but she heard crying from inside the cabin, and the woman hustled back inside to nurse her baby. Bertie offered Lydia some coffee, whispering again so as not to wake the husband, or the other child asleep on the pallet. But Lydia felt out of place now. And the little domestic scene she saw in front of her gave her a hollow feeling in her chest. Things seemed even more out of reach now that she learned of Black Mary. Lydia has expected to hear about some regimen of medicines, or some information about what to do after sex, or when to couple. Black Mary and her tributes was just a bunch of mountain lore, she felt. She knew better than that. Like she expected, Cole laughed at the whole story when she got up the nerve to tell him. She laughed along with him then, but it pained her not to have some answer for him. She blamed herself, and Cole had begun to sink into his depression around then.

But now, as she passed the woman's cabin on her way to the notch, she thought of how her life had changed since that day, a few years ago. She cursed herself for not having done at the time what she was doing now. Smoke poured from the chimney of the cabin, and Lydia thought she heard a toddler crying, but she wasn't sure. She didn't stop, because she couldn't. She didn't have time. She would have to keep moving to get to Black Mary's and get back home without Cole sending out a search party. Maybe she would stop in on her return. Bertie was still living there, she knew. Lydia had seen her a few times since her first visit, once just a week past. Bertie had told her that the Company was still at work on the family homes. She would soon move there with her little girls, she said, soon. It had been over two years since that first visit, and Bertie confessed it was tough going, seeing her husband only on Saturdays and Sundays, and even then, only if he wasn't too tired to make the hike. She had another child on the way now, and she was determined she would move to town to have the baby. She only hoped the homes would be ready by that time. The few times Lydia had seen Bertie, neither one spoke about Black Mary, but Lydia figured Bertie must have thought she never visited the woman.

Still, Bertie never asked about it.

Lydia pressed on, following the stream for hours. She saw nothing to kill, though she was more bent on her destination than on food. Maybe she would see something on the way back home, she thought. The hike was more long than difficult, and Lydia began to wonder how long she might have to visit with Black Mary, or if the woman would even welcome her in, and then if the weather would hold out for her return. At length she came to the spring. She had never been up this way before and she wondered if even Hez knew of this place. Off a little ways she saw smoke rising and she soon came onto the little clearing where the cabin stood. As she approached, the cabin door opened and a tall woman dressed in a black day dress emerged. It was if she were

145

waiting for her, Lydia thought. She wondered what kind of reception she'd receive, dressed as she was in the bulky men's clothes. She wasn't sure why, but it occurred to her then that she didn't want to be mistaken for a man. She was wearing one of Cole's slouch hats, with her hair tucked up underneath. She pulled the hat from her head and yanked the bark tie out of her hair. It fell out unevenly all around her shoulders as she shook it free of the bind. She called out, "Hidy, ma'am. Hidy. I mean no harm. I'm in no trouble."

The woman stood still.

"Hidy," Lydia said again as she neared.

The woman turned and entered the cabin. She left the door open, though, and Lydia crossed the threshold, leaving her bow and quiver outside, along with the knife and sheath. The woman crouched on her haunches with the poker, her back to Lydia. As she pulled on the logs in the hearth a shower of orange sparks flew about her head and shoulders, and the fire blazed up brightly behind her. When she turned to face her guest, Lydia realized how striking the woman was. She stood almost six feet, taller than even Lydia by several inches. True to the tale, she was dressed in black, with a little muslin cap that covered every lock of hair she had, if she had any at all. Suddenly Lydia wasn't sure of this. She looked middle-aged, with some crow's feet at her eyes and lines above her thin lips, but not the seventy or eighty she must be if Bertie's mother-in-law had known her. She extended her hand and asked for Lydia's coat and hat. Lydia noticed her long, thin fingers and her clean nails. She smelled faintly of rose. The cabin, too, surprised Lydia. The puncheon floor had been leveled and sanded, and the tables and two chairs sat clean and smartly on it. Everything seemed in its place, and Lydia wondered how a woman living alone way up at the notch could manage to keep both her home and person in such fine order. She reminded Lydia of the royals she had seen in photographs from newspapers and books. A regal mountain woman, she thought.

"You keep your cabin in fine form, ma'am. I'm Lydia Clemmons, from Black Boar, just above Queen's Tooth."

"Thank you. My name is Mary. It is a pleasure to have you here."

She even *sounded* regal, Lydia thought, formal and without as much mountain accent as she had expected. Though she wasn't sure whether or not it was really the pleasure she said it was. A greeting on Black Boar would have been warmer, even for a stranger. And where did she come from, Lydia wondered. She thought to ask the woman, but something stayed her, and she kept quiet.

"Why do you come this way, Lydia Clemmons from Black Boar?" Black Mary stared at Lydia, stiff and upright, a rigid black figure with near ivory white hands and face.

Lydia thought it best to let it all out at once and hear what the woman had to say. If she didn't want to help, Lydia could be on her way, out looking for food on the return trip. "A friend of mine," Lydia said, "a mother down on Black Boar. She told me you helped her to get with child. I've been trying a long time. It's not working." She halted, not sure what to say next. "I want a baby, Mary," she finally said. "Can you help me? I brought a tribute for you." Lydia went to the mackinaw Mary had set on a thick wooden peg in a timber on the wall and pulled the buckskin pouch from the pocket. "It's my father's pocket knife," Lydia said. "He taught me how to use it when I was just a little girl. How to dress an animal, and just how to do everyday things with it."

Black Mary took the knife and turned it over in her hands. She opened the blade and felt its edge. "Sharp," she said. She looked at the grip. And then she looked into Lydia's eyes, staring again. With a little flourish she spun the blade around in her palm. Lydia didn't catch all the movement, but the grip was presented to Lydia. Mary held only the very tip of the blade between her thumb and index finger. Lydia took the blade, not sure if her offer had been rejected and if she were about to be sent home.

"It's not a knife that would cost much money," Lydia said. "But it was my father's. It means the world to me. My friend told me you want a tribute that's *means* something." Lydia began to worry now. This could be the end of things between her and Cole if Black Mary refused to help. She closed the knife and held it out to Black Mary. "Please," she said.

Mary saw the water in Lydia's eyes. She cleared her throat and said, "I can tell it's dear to you, but I don't want it."

Lydia only said, "Please" once more. The tears came down her red cheeks in straight rivulets that fell onto her shoulders. Mary turned from her and took a heavy poker to the logs in the hearth. "I can see that it's a real tribute," she said. But it's not for me. Did your friend tell you anything else?"

Lydia wiped her face and said, "She acted like it wasn't right to say anything about it. She said she *couldn't* tell any more than what she had already told."

"She's right to say so," Black Mary said. "But the tribute isn't for me."

"It isn't? What do you mean?"

Black Mary said, "How come you think it's your fault you can't get a baby?"

The question surprised Lydia. "I don't know. We've been trying regular. And nothing's happened for nearly two years."

Mary reached out and took Lydia's hand in her own and ran her thumb along the prosthetic, like Inez had done so often in the days after the incident. "But how come you don't figure it's him, your man?"

Lydia's face flushed and her heart pounded in her ears. She had never considered that it could be Cole's fault. "I don't know," she answered. "I never studied on it."

"Too many times," the woman said, "I've seen women blame themselves for something that could be the man's problem." She shook her head. "What about the seed?" she said. "Isn't that an equal part of things?" There was an edge to her voice now. "Maybe it's his seed that's the trouble. Don't you women ever think about that?"

Lydia could barely hear her own voice. "I suppose so. I never thought about it the way you tell it."

Black Mary squeezed Lydia's hand, "You need to listen carefully to what I'm going to say."

Lydia nodded.

"There's a giant oak that grows over a ledge about an hour's walk from here," Black Mary said. "It's easy to get to, but it takes time to get there. Bury that knife at the trunk of that oak." Mary took a blade from a shelf and cut a strip of black fabric from what looked to Lydia like an old dress. Tie this around a rock and set it over where you bury that knife. That oak stands high above the other trees there. And its branches grow out over the ledge. You'll see it if you follow the signs I tell you." She looked Lydia hard in the eyes now. "And listen. This next part is the most important. "Leave right away. Do not look around and do not wait. Just leave."

"Yes ma'am," Lydia said. She swallowed hard and asked, "Who's the tribute for?"

But Black Mary was done talking about it. She only said, "Ask your friend. It's alright for her to tell about it now that it's done." Mary kneeled to rattle the logs in the hearth again. When she stood, she became the center of it all, at her full height, totally erect and with the orange glow of the hearth behind her—like a vision from a dream, or from some mountain tall tale, the widow witch. Maybe good, maybe bad, maybe both … or neither. Lydia couldn't be sure.

But she sensed that it was time to go. She thought it was right to ask, "Is there anything I can give to you, Mary? I'm grateful to you."

Mary reached for Lydia's hand. She took it in her own again and examined the prosthetic, turning over Lydia's hand to see it. "You're that girl who killed that prisoner, aren't you? The ones who defiled your mother ... and killed your father. I heard about that."

"Yes, ma'am."

She set her hands then on Lydia's shoulder, like Lydia's father had sometimes done when he had something important to tell her. Lydia felt the strength in her long, thin fingers. "I just want you to carry on. Lydia." Lydia noticed then that the woman had green eyes, deeply green like the color of a laurel leaf, or something just come up from the ground. "Remember what I told you," she said.

Lydia had been gone from Black Mary's cabin for over an hour. The snow whipped up around her face and she wished now that she had thought to bring a scarf. She bent forward and led with Cole's slouch hat and her shoulders, trying to stay the course and keep the snow off her face at the same time. Naked trees creaked and groaned with the growing gale, and up ahead a heavy maple limb snapped and fell to the ground, shearing off smaller branches on its way down and making a terrifying sound as it thudded to the earth. The massive limb had fallen directly in Lydia's path, and as she stepped over it she felt a violence that still hung in the air. Naked, jagged barbs shot out from the place where the branch had met the limb. A fresh wound, Lydia thought. All she cared about now was to get to the giant oak and leave her tribute.

In time, she finally saw up ahead where the forest ended, where the furthermost trees sat out against the grey sky above the valley. The oak was there, wide and towering. The wind and snow ripped through its upper branches and Lydia watched them sway. It looked absolutely alive to her. She heaved a heavy rock from the ground, tied the black fabric around it, and dug a small hole with her field knife. She set the leather pouch down in there and covered up the spot with earth. Then she rolled the rock over the hole and set both hands atop of it while she rested. Her fingers were black from the cold earth, and she rubbed her hands together fiercely. She worked to clear the dirt and snow from the leather cinch that held her prosthetic and then stuffed her hands into the pockets of the mackinaw. She turned her back to the wind, hunching herself over behind the oak's huge trunk. Now she must be on her way, she knew, but first she would walk out to the ledge and look over the valley. The wind and snow would be fierce, and she would only linger a minute, she told herself.

But she hadn't taken three steps toward the ledge when a clowder of bobcats began their yowling. Lydia felt it deep in her stomach then, like a queasiness come on her suddenly. She abandoned the view and headed back the way she came. Not far gone from the oak yet, she heard something moving behind her, and she picked up her pace. She wanted only to get back to Black Boar now. Whatever followed her, whether a deer or family of bobcats, it made no difference. She was bent on return.

But soon the snow began to come heavy in gusts that tortured Lydia's face, and she struggled to navigate the course, so hard was it to see the way forward. Again, she heard something moving, like footfalls on the icy crust, but up ahead of her this time, she thought, not behind her. She could see nothing, though, and she pressed on with her head down and her shoulders forward against the wind. When she heard the sound yet again, the heavy footfalls, like an animal on the move, the memory of the black boar, years ago, flashed in her mind and she felt a roiling in her stomach.

She was practically running when she saw something move between the trees up ahead. A darting form with limbs and a shock of long white hair. The image was so brief, but it looked to her like some animal, something that moved on four feet, bounding between the large trunks. She slung her bow off her shoulder and nocked an arrow, holding it in place as she trudged ahead.

Then she lost sight of it altogether, but she moved on faster than was wise, she knew.

For a while, she had made good progress, and eventually she slowed her pace. Whatever it was, she thought, was gone. But no sooner than she had stowed her bow and arrow did the form appear again, noiselessly this time. Lydia thought it moved on two feet now, but the snow half-blinded her and she couldn't be sure. She stopped and squinted, nocking an arrow again and sighting where she thought, maybe, the creature had moved. She drew the bowstring to her cheek and scanned a wide arc out in front of her. If anything, *anywhere*, would have moved, she would have let loose. Above her, limbs creaked in the fierce wind and smaller branches snapped and fell to the earth.

That's when she saw it, saw it truly, for the first and only time in her life.

In a dark hollow of an old chestnut tree, in a hole shaped like an inverted V, something moved. Lydia stopped dead. She sheltered her eyes against the snow and squinted hard to see. From inside the dark hollow a long tress of white hair flew up with the wind. Against the deep, brown bark it rose straight up, undulating like some kind of white flame before falling back into the hollow, and suddenly rising again, the tresses alive on the air. And then, a human hand, mottled with dirt and patches of red at the tips, reached out and took hold of the hollow's rim. Whoever, or whatever it was, just as quickly pulled the hand back inside the hollow. Lydia heard a violent rustle of leaves come from the place, and then the keening of bobcats, though she couldn't see them. She hurried on, turning her head every few steps to see if she were being followed. When she had fully put some distance between herself and the tree she stopped and looked one last time. She could see the cats now, outside the face of the hollow. They crawled about one another, a living clump of animals in a tight formation that moved in a serpentine way. They keened loudly, a high feminine wailing that pierced the air and raised the hair on Lydia's neck.

It was a nest.

Lydia ran until she couldn't. When she slowed to look back she realized she still had her bow in hand, though the arrow was long gone. There was a metallic taste in her mouth, and she worked to get air into her burning lungs. She moved on before she was really ready, pushing hard toward Black Mary's and slowing only when she finally saw the cabin come into view. Smoke poured from the little chimney and the promise of a few minutes of warmth tempted Lydia. But something inward told her that she needed to push ahead, that stopping now might undo the work of the tribute. She contented herself with a few minutes rest in view of the cabin. At least there was another human in her midst. She felt safer, for the moment. But once she got her wind she moved on, following the water downstream toward Black Boar and leaving the warm cabin behind her. The snow had slowed but the air was bitterly cold. Lydia worked her fingers in the pockets of the mackinaw. Now and then she would stop to blow her breath on them. In time the snow picked up again but she bent forward against it. She would keep up the pace, she told herself, until she arrived at Bertie's cabin. She had made good time given the conditions, but the winter sun was on its way down.

When Bertie's cabin finally hove into view Lydia nearly collapsed. The cabin was on the outermost edge of Black Boar, but Lydia knew where she was now. She could make her way home by the scant moonlight that fell through the canopy if she had to. At last, she was home, she thought. Praise God. She would stop in to warm up.

"Berite!" Lydia called from outside the cabin. "Bertie. Woman, are you there?"

Bertie opened the cabin door, looked out, and then closed it again."

"Bertie!" Lydia called.

Bertie came outside now. This time she held a rifle. She cocked the lever, levelled the gun and hollered, "Don't come any closer, you. I know how to use this."

"No, by God, Bertie! It's me, Lydia."

Bertie lowered the rifle. "Lydia? Lydia Clemmons, is that you?"

"Yes," Lydia said as she made her way toward the door.

"Hellfire, Lydia. You look like a man in them clothes. Come in. I'm sorry. I'm here alone, just my babies and me."

Lydia was pleased to get out of the cold and to be with someone from Black Boar. The cabin was just as she remembered it, warm and welcoming. Bertie's little girls crawled about on a bed tick in the corner. The smaller one banged a wooden spoon on the floor until Bertie took it from her. "You hush now," Bertie said. "We have company." But the girl just smiled and laughed.

"What are you doing here, Lydia?"

Lydia shrugged out of the bulky mackinaw and warmed her hands at the hearth. "I've been to see Black Mary," she said.

After a long pause Bertie simply said, "Oh ... why ... I ..."

"I should have done it long ago, Bertie, when you first named it to me. But I didn't. I'm not sure why."

"Well," Bertie said, "it's an odd thing, and not everyone holds with such ideas. I was scared to go myself. But I'm glad I did. Did you ... leave something?"

Lydia was just now beginning to get warm, and it pleased her some to say, "I did. My daddy's penknife."

"Oh, well ... that's good, then ... that's good."

"Bertie," Lydia said, "Black Mary said that now you could tell me more. Who's to receive the penknife? Who's up there, Bertie?"

Bertie turned away, pretending some issue with the baby at her breast.

"Bertie?"

Bertie took a deep breath and said, "Did she really say it was ok to talk on it?"

"Yes, Bertie. I swear."

"Well then," Bertie said, "I guess it's ok, if you swear it's so."

"It is, Bertie. It's so. She told me."

Bertie said, "Did you ever hear of the wild woman of the notch, Lydia?"

"No."

"Well," Bertie continued, "my mother-in-law told it to me. Seems there was a girl years and years ago, a young girl, when the first people come up here to settle. She had a baby, but she decided she didn't want it. Like I say she was young and didn't know any better. That's how my mother-in-law tells it, anyway. She didn't know what to do and so she brung the little baby girl up the mountain, way up by the notch. She left her there. Told people that someone stole that baby in the nighttime, right out of the cabin where she lived with her parents. Everyone poured sympathy on that girl. But there was a granny woman who sensed it was a lie. And she slapped the truth out of that young girl. Her people headed up there, to the notch, to see if the baby was still alive. But there was only the feed sack nightie on the ground. No blood, nothing like that. But here's the odd thing. The people all said there were bobcat prints all around where the baby had been left. And the nightie was covered in catamount hairs."

Lydia felt goose pimples rise up all over her.

"Well," Bertie said, "they followed the prints but they lost them at the stream. That's what some say anyway."

"Good lord," Lydia whispered. "I ... there was a nest up there, of bobcats."

Bertie nodded. "Yes, and here's what they say. Over the years that little baby became a woman, raised by them bobcats. She must be old now, but my mother-in-law says people have seen her over these many years. Some say she runs around up there in animal skins, and others say she's got a spear, you know, with a fire-hardened tip."

"Good lord," Lydia said again.

"Those who claim to have seen her say she's got long white hair down to her hips. And that she walks about with them cats, always screaming how they do. Loud and high, like an injured woman. She helps mothers who can't get with child. Don't ask me how Black Mary is involved. I only know that she is. I never asked her about it. My mother-in-law told it all to me. I don't ask questions. And you shouldn't either."

Lydia said, "But Bertie, how's anyone alive that long? She must be over 100 years old."

"Don't ask that kind of thing," Bertie said with an edge. "Just don't ask, Lydia."

"Alright, Bertie, alright."

Lydia's face was flush now with the heat from the hearth and with the story Bertie had told. It scared her, but it also gave her hope that the story was true. Once she settled her nerves, she asked Bertie, "Do you think it will work, the tribute? " But the instant she said it, she was sorry she did.

Bertie didn't answer, at least not in words. She looked Lydia in the eye as she adjusted the baby to her breast.

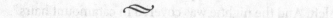

It was a long walk from Bertie's cabin to her own, but nothing compared to what she had put behind her that day. Lydia navigated by the light of the moon, though her feet followed the route mostly by memory, which allowed her to wonder on things. The wind was cold on her face but she knew she was safe now, and she straightened up and faced it with her head high, knowing she would soon be home, and hopeful that she had accomplished something. She thought about what she might have asked Black Mary, about whether or not she should lay with Cole more often, or what she should do, and how? She thought about what the regal-looking woman had said about how it could be the man's fault. She had never thought of that until then. What would Cole think if she proposed such a thing?

She pushed ahead hoping that Cole would be home, and not too gone into the bottle. She would lie with him tonight. She felt that she needed to do so right away. Tonight, despite the fatigue she felt, she would do this. Cold wind circled around her and she stopped to stuff the hair that blew across her eyes back under her cap. It made her think of the feral woman, her white tresses flying high and wild around the tree hollow, and her pale hands with the red spots at the tips of the fingers. And of the nest of cats. And of Black Mary. And even of Bertie with her baby at her breast and warm in the cabin. Somehow it was all connected. It all ran together in her mind, these women. They *knew* something she didn't, Lydia thought, they *had* something she wanted, but more than ever, now she felt connected to them. Something was operating inwardly, something that told her now was the time.

She must have Cole inside of her.

Years of listening quietly in the woods had sharpened Lydia's sense of hearing. Long before she could see the cabin, she heard people. The voices carried far on the thin air. There was Cole, she thought, and that was Clytie, though she sounded more shrill than normal. She thought, too, that she heard Hez's wife, Emma, out there, too. Lydia broke into a trot, a pace she thought she could manage until she got into sight and could call out without alarming the group. She tried to measure her pace, not to go too fast so that she couldn't call out when the time came, but it was Cole's voice that drew her. He above all she could hear. There are times in the woods when a frightened animal will sound an odd call. For a hunter this can be a boon, a marker of place or of the fact that one has wounded the prey. But when Lydia heard the shrill tones of Cole, she bolted toward the cabin, running full out, reckless of what might obstruct her in the light only of the moon. She began to cry out, "Cole! Cole! It's me. It's your Lyddie!"

Her heart raced and she worked to get air now. She decided to cut through a rhododendron patch that looked navigable, a shortcut, she thought. But the gnarled branches and thick vines that grew from below and clung to the bushes slowed her more than anything. She cursed and picked her way out of the patch back onto the course she had been following. Now she would be even longer.

"Cole!" she screamed.

This time he heard her. Lydia slowed when she heard the voices calling her name. They would know the path she was on, but she called to Cole again and again. When she saw the party come to meet her, she tore into a run. She fell into Cole's arms and kissed him on the lips and on the cheek. He smelled of wood smoke and she dug her face into his neck. She ran her fingers through his hair and when he pulled away finally to ask her where she had gone for so long, she dug her face back into his neck. She only said she had gotten lost in the storm, out hunting. Clytie and Cornelius, Hez and his wife--they all kissed her or touched her and went their own way. Lydia asked about Inez and they told her they had left her in the dark about things. Cole had made some excuse to get her over to Clytie's cabin, where she lie in bed for now. They would send her back to the cabin tomorrow, they said.

Clytie and the others never asked about how she got so lost on a hunt. They would find out later what had happened. It was enough to know Lydia was safe.

Lydia told Cole it was the storm that made her lose her way. With the blinding snow, she she had gotten lost out there, out hunting. No surprise she found nothing to kill either. She told him she spent most of her time finding her way back home. She also told him about seeing Bertie, but not what they talked about, nor did she tell him about Black Mary, or the wild woman and her brood of cats. It was a lie, one she knew ahead of time she would need to tell if things went the way they should have. But Cole took it all at face value. He fussed over her but never chastised her. Nor did he browbeat himself, as he was wont to do, about his failures as a provider and such. Lydia wondered why she didn't feel more uneasy about it. It was a bold-faced lie, and she had never lied to Cole before. But at the same time, she thought maybe it was all part of the way things were to be, all part of her plan from the outset. For now, she thought it best not to think of it at all. She told herself that any lie she told worked in the interest of her own marriage. A lie like that would benefit Cole as much as her, wouldn't it?

The fire Cole had stoked warmed her fingers and skin. She removed the bulky men's clothes and crouched by the hearth. Cole sat on his haunches behind her and wrapped his arms around her. She pulled off her cap and her hair fell about her. Cole buried his face in her neck, and she became warm again inwardly.

She knew what she had to do.

"Cole," she said, "I need you now." She led him to the bed tick. Cole felt the heat in her fingers and skin, and he undressed quickly. He kissed her deeply, like he used to do when they courted and in the early days of the marriage. His fear for her had awakened an old tenderness in him and instantly he was aroused. But it was Lydia who led him this time. It was she who would direct the course of things. She opened her legs and Cole entered her, burying his head in her neck.

Cole smelled of musk and the sweat that came with their exertions. It was something he had never sensed with Lydia before, something raw, he thought. And Lydia was different in other ways, too. With Cole's deep strokes she grunted more than moaned. Cole felt her fingers dig into his shoulder blades. She bucked him wildly in the end, grunting and squeezing. A brief fear entered Cole. Who was this woman, he wondered? It was not his Lyddie. And yet his arousal was greater than ever, greater even than on their wedding night, and in the days that followed, when Cole would take Lydia roughly in the woods they loved so dearly, when he would fairly throw her to the bed tick on returning from a hunt.

Now, though, it was Lydia who controlled things, and not the other way around.

As he neared climax, he felt Lydia's heels on his back, just above his buttocks, driving him into her with a force in step with the noises she made. It was a force he couldn't have resisted had he wanted to. Her legs and body shook. Cole felt an incredible tightness all along his length, and at first he couldn't pull himself free. He simply waited then until Lydia's convulsions had stopped.

When Cole finally pushed himself off and rolled to his side, Lydia reached out with her arm and drew him close. He felt the sweat from her breasts and stomach on his back. He was surprised at the heat that radiated from her.

"Don't get up," Lydia said.

"No, I won't, Lyddie."

"Not yet."

"I'm right here," Cole said. "I can barely breathe anyway. Got to catch my breath, woman."

He felt Lydia's warm breath coming in shallow, hard exhalations on the back of his neck, and again he felt a certain strangeness sweep over him. He didn't know the physical being who lay next to him, who held him fiercely with a new strength. Lydia wrapped a leg around him, and he felt the heat in her thigh on his side. She slipped her foot between his legs beneath the knees, and for an instant Cole felt that fear again, as if he were trapped, or as if her were about to become the prey of some animal. It was irrational, a moment of terror that subsided as quickly as it arose, but it was there. Cole had felt it deeply, in the most primal way.

Lydia had him.

Finally, they got their wind back, and Lydia released her hold. Still, Cole remained at her side. He felt he wanted to ask her about their coupling, about how it was different, but something in him told him not to. He wasn't displeased in any way, he thought, and so he said only, "Lyddie, dear, I'm pleased that you still love me."

"Yes, of course I love you, Cole Clemmons."

For a moment, Cole's voice caught in his throat. He said, "Law, woman, that was some kind of lovemaking."

Lydia said, "Yes," and she ran her fingers through Cole's curls. "And maybe something will come of it."

Cole wanted to avoid the issue of a baby for now. The last thing he wanted was for Lydia to feel shame, and he decided then he would never again make her feel like things were her fault. He had done enough damage with is words and his self-pity. For now, he wanted her only to know that she had pleased him, that he felt an irresistible need for her, a renewed desire that came with this coupling, and with the good news he would share with her soon. Maybe, he thought, the news was somehow a part of something larger, part of God's plan for the couple, maybe. The news might even be connected to the desire he suddenly felt again. He would think more about it later. Now he wanted only for Lydia to know that he was still drawn to her, that the fire of physical need was still so hot within him, like it had been before. "Lyddie," he said, "that was like an explosion. I think when you put your heels into me you might have left me some bruises." He laughed.

Lydia said, "My heels? Cole, what?"

"On my back, above my backside. How you drove me into you, Lyddie."

"Oh ... yes," Lydia said. But she hadn't dug her heels into Cole's lower back. She was sure of it.

Cole finally got up and threw a log onto the fire. From the bed, Lydia watched him moving about the little cabin. She saw then the two red marks on Cole's lower back. Her heart raced and a dizziness swept over her. As Cole adjusted the logs in the hearth she saw something else in the light of the fire, a thin filament, a fiber, maybe a thread from something she had sewn, clinging to the sweat on Cole's back. It hung nearly to the ground. She rose and removed the thing that clung there, looking at it carefully, drawing it up close to her face. She gathered it loosely around her finger, removed it, and then cast it off into the hearth.

"What was that?" Cole asked.

Lydia tried to keep her voice even. "Nothing," she said. "A loose thread. Maybe from that quilt I finished. Don't need it anymore."

But it wasn't a loose thread at all. It was a long white hair.

Inez still hadn't returned to the cabin by the time Cole and Lydia had risen for the day. Surely Clytie was keeping her there to give the couple some privacy after the scare. Lydia knew she'd have to thank Clytie and Cornelius later, and to thank them also for their worry last night, something she saw in Clytie's face when Lydia appeared to them at last, torn by briars and looking something like a wild animal. She hadn't seen Clytie in some time. She knew that her trouble with Cole was behind it, and that she had been ashamed to see her friend.

Cole and Lydia had slept in later than they ever did, exhausted from the passionate throes that carried on throughout the night. Cole joked that he was "powerful sore" in the muscles and that his manhood was wore out. He needed a few days to recover, he laughed. Once he stoked the fire at the hearth Lydia took down a bowl and began to make cornbread. There was a little bit of cured ham left that could be used, and some beans. She could make a credible meal to start them off, and to give her enough energy to do what she needed to. She didn't worry about telling Cole this time, either. Things had changed since her experience in the woods the day before, she could feel it.

162

"Cole," she said, "The reason I returned empty handed is because I got lost and fretted about getting back so. I didn't track or look hardly at all. I'm going back out today."

Cole's answer surprised her.

"I'll go with you," he said. "Maybe we can find something, together. But it ain't because you got lost that you didn't come across anything. Or at least that ain't the only reason. It's because they run off all the game with their timberin' everywhere. Black Boar won't be around too much longer, I don't think. Not if the Rail and the timber Company have their way. They'll get this land in time. Not much anyone can do about it neither." Cole squeezed Lydia's shoulders from behind. "Even the goddamn preacher is on their side," he laughed.

Lydia wasn't sure how to take this from Cole. She was pleased beyond measure that she would be out in the woods with him today, together, looking for food like they had done when they first courted. But what was this about the end of Black Boar? "That will be real fine, Cole, us going out there," she said. "It's late but we may see something still. We can stay out all day. Hares and squirrels, we can find maybe."

"We can, Lyddie. We can."

"But what do you mean about Black Boar? You really think the timber Company can get this land? It's ours, Cole, no matter what that preacher says."

Cole took a deep breath. "Lyddie, I've been thinking hard. All over these hills the Company has done its business, had its way with the land and the people living on it. It ain't lost a battle yet, dear. But it's just a matter of time."

Lydia said, "But Cole, we *own* this land. My daddy bought his parcel from old Mr. Covington. He owned the whole hillside one time."

"That's true, Lyddie, but it don't matter. The Company has control of most of the mountain, most of *all* these mountains, in fact. It can cut all the timber around us. And then what do we have? I'll tell you what we'll have, and we have it already. Fires, mud slicks, and dirty streams. On top of that the game has been run off. I used to think people who sold out up here were traitors. Now I think different. They were smart to sell then, and get out."

Lydia took her wet hands from the bowl and turned to stare directly at Cole. He took a deep breath. "I know this sounds strange, Lyddie. But there's more I got to say. Even if we hold out, we can't truly *live* here. We're not living now. We might be alive, yes, but we ain't *living*. Leastways, not how we want to, not from the woods anymore. It's going to be too tough even to raise food around here soon. That's if we don't get burned out by fire first or swallowed in a mud slick. The Company hasn't done anything yet with the land and cabins they bought up here, but that's only because they need *all* of them first. And they're gonna get them. Lyddie, it's depressed me, the whole thing. You know how much this place means to me. Even my momma and daddy sold. Now that tells you something. They're long gone. You know this. And they loved it here. They just couldn't make it. But I couldn't go with them, out there to my aunt's place, out to North Carolina, to that farm my uncle owns. That ain't for me, living under someone else's roof. It's fine for my folks, and I think my daddy will like it just as well helping my uncle to work that big farm. He and my momma are *needed* there. They're *useful*. But I got to take care of my own family, Lyddie. Even though I ain't done a good job of it. Not yet, at least. But I'm going to."

Lydia stood still. She was stunned to hear Cole talk this way.

"I went to Queen's Tooth yesterday, Lyddie. And that's what I need to talk to you about. And also my mournful ways and everything that's come from it. My drinking, my being a worthless husband."

Lydia saw the moisture in his eyes and heard the desperation in his voice. "But, Cole—"

"No, Lyddie! Let me finish. I went to town, yesterday, when I knew you'd likely be away all day. I went to ask about a job at that sawmill." He stopped and looked Lydia in the eye. She was surprised, he could see, but he had to finish. His voice wavered when he said, "I got a job, Lydia. I'm going to start work at that sawmill. I'm gonna live at that boardinghouse with the other men. When I save up enough, I'm going to get us a place to live, in town."

"Cole," Lydia said. "We don't ..." But she couldn't finish.

"I know, Lyddie dear. But listen to me. My life ... I can't go on like this. I can't be a man up here no longer. I took the job. I had to. Now I just got to save up enough to get you and your momma down there with me. To get up enough to rent a little place we can live in. I can do it, Lyddie. We can do it. We can live good lives in town, righteous lives where a man can make do. But we can't do it here. At least I can't. Black Boar, Lyddie ... it's not long for this world."

Lydia didn't know what to say. She was saddened, and scared, but she heard something in Cole then, a confidence in the way he spoke those final words, as if there would be no debate on the matter. It was the old Cole, the self-assured Cole who had so often promised to take care of his Lyddie in the days when they courted. And then Cole did something else. He grabbed the bottle of whiskey, threw open the cabin door and walked outside. Wind blew a sheet of downy snow into the cabin and Lydia said, "Cole!"

Framed by the door, Cole stood tall, shirtless but with his galluses pulled up. Lydia watched as the white dust blew around his form. He threw out his arm and tipped the bottle, pouring out the amber liquid. Lydia saw the muscles flex in his back, the gentle curve of his bicep, and the powerful, long fingers that gripped the bottle. She looked at the nape of his neck, just beneath his curls, where she had buried her face just last night. Instantly, desire surged through her yet again, and she was swept up in feeling for Cole. When the bottle was empty, Cole cast it out into the trees. He laughed and came back into the cabin. Lydia went to him and wrapped her arms around him. He was wet from the snow, and cold to the touch, but he didn't seem to feel it.

She led him to the bed tick.

Long, Long Ago

BLACK BOAR MOUNTAIN

When the gray light began to peek through the chinquapins, the couple rose and moved out together, without a word. The woman walked beside her husband, not behind him. He liked it this way as much as she did. There were hares and deer and squirrels to be taken. They only needed to take care to look out for the large cat said to be prowling high up. That would be a prize, they had said to one another, but not one that should be stalked. It was best if the cat and the people could both take what they needed and steer clear of one another. Only if the cat threatened them should it be hunted. Up ahead of them a fat hare poked its nose out of a thicket. It ducked back when it sensed them coming, and the couple waited silently. Eventually the hare peeked out, and the man nocked an arrow and released it into the side of the animal. The woman drew the arrow through it and dressed it on the ground.

In time they saw another one. The woman took this one and the man dressed it. There were signs of other game, too, deer and elk. But the woman thought she saw movement up above, a serpentine slither, something there, but then gone behind a patch of brush. The man wanted to know more, but she countered him. Better to be safe, she said.

They returned the way they had come.

1908
BLACK BOAR MOUNTAIN
(Lydia, age 20)

Cole led the way over the snow that crunched underneath him. He and Lydia had covered this ground dozens of times before, but it had been a long time since they had hunted together. The snow had stopped, and the wind had died down, but the air was still cold, and Lydia saw her breath even through the scarf she had drawn close across her face. Now and then, Cole stopped dead and listened for something he thought he had heard. Lydia scanned the trees and the ground with him, but they hadn't come across anything for hours. The trunks of the dark hickories and walnut trees stood out starkly against the snow on the earth, their naked branches twisting and reaching across the flat grey sky that peeked through the canopy.

From a little rise Lydia eventually spotted a cottontail partly burrowed in a rotted chestnut trunk. She signaled to Cole and the two stopped and watched. Lydia nocked an arrow and waited. After a while Cole whispered, "Take him, Lyddie." But Lydia just shook her head. In time another cottontail appeared from under the log. Lydia let fly the arrow and hit her mark. The other hare bolted but then stopped. It turned its head toward Lydia, but it was too late. The second arrow hit its flank and the animal shook and fell.

"By God, you are good," Cole said.

Lydia laughed and said, "Sometimes, yes, Cole Clemmons."

She tore the arrows from the hares. Cole then dressed them and dropped them into a feed sack. She didn't say it openly, but Lydia felt freer now that they had taken something. It was a sort of relief, proof that they could still live in the way they wanted, even though they had decided to live differently.

They walked on and finally Cole said, "Lyddie, it's not like we can't come back here. We can come up here on the weekends and look for something, or we can just walk."

"If there's anything left."

"Well, that's true. Maybe not Black Boar, but there's still much of these hills that haven't yet been timbered. We can find a place to get away from town when we want."

Lydia reached out and took Cole's hand. He ran his thumb over the leather cinch the way she liked. She said, "Maybe town will be nice."

"Oh, Lyddie it *is* nice. There's things to do there, and lots of people like us. We can have a good life in town."

Lydia nodded and said, "Bertie's man works at that mill. She's leaving soon enough to be with him. I'll talk to her again. She's a good woman. Could be a good friend."

"Yes, Lyddie."

They walked on, hand in hand, and then Cole stopped short. Lydia saw his eyes open wide and she knew he was listening, not so much looking. But Lydia didn't hear anything. "What is it?" she finally whispered.

Cole put his finger to his lips and signaled for her to stay put. He moved off ahead, crouched low, stopping and listening and then moving. Lydia watched him creep between the trees, circling back and popping up here and there where she didn't expect to see him. He was quick, but quiet. She could tell he had sighted something, or sensed it, heard it. Maybe it was a deer, or a bobcat, she thought. She hadn't heard anything but the birds and the wind that made the branches groan above her. Cole disappeared for a little while and an unformed fear began to rise in Lydia. She worried, though she knew Cole was on a trail. Still, something unnerved her.

And then she heard it. Something moving fast in the briars. She caught a glimpse of Cole then, running and then drawing up to raise the gun. But it was hard for her to get a good look at him because of the brush. She didn't see Cole lower the gun but a moment later she saw him moving again off to her right now. And then she heard a growl. She wheeled and saw it coming in her direction. A large bear. It roared again and then broke into a run, straight at her, a huge black mass gaining speed by the second. She broke off to one side, but the bear saw it and turned to chase. Lydia screamed, "Cole!" and the bear growled yet again. She ran blindly now, just trying to put distance between her and the animal. From behind a tree Cole stepped into her path. She raced toward him with everything she had in her. With a single movement he shouldered the gun and drew down on her. She saw the black barrel pointed at her and she screamed. This was it, she realized.

Cole aimed to kill her.

This was the end of everything. Before she hit the ground, she saw the muzzle flash. And then heard a sound like nothing she had ever heard before. A wild groan, deep and long. The bear fell not ten feet from her. She rose and backed away, toward Cole. When the animal let out a final groan and shifted its tremendous weight on the ground, she squealed out in fear.

Cole broke the gun breech and loaded another shell. He snapped it closed and took Lydia with one arm from the ground. She buried her head in his chest and shook there. "It's alright, Lyddie dear," he laughed. "Just a four-hundred-pound bear is all. Out and about when it should be sleepin'". Must've woken up.

Maybe them wood hicks cut down his den." Lydia let out a sound between a cry and a laugh. Cole moved up on the bear, the gun barrel pointed at its head. "Turn away, Lyddie if you don't want to see this," he said. But Lydia watched the bear's head buckle with the gun's loud report. Blood had begun to redden the snow around the animal and Cole said, "We need to get busy here, girl."

Lydia hesitated, but when she saw Cole draw his knife and get to work another feeling began to rise in her. She realized then what had just happened. Cole had saved her. And now he was at work on the food they would eat. It was the old Cole. She dropped her bow and quiver, drew her knife and went to help her husband. They worked fast, without a word between them, and soon their hands were red with the gore of the animal's steaming innards. Cole took as much of the meat as he thought they could carry. He looked over at Lydia, across the dead carcass, and smiled. He had touched his face in the process and his cheek was streaked red with blood. She felt something catch in her throat and her chest swelled. Tears brimmed in her eyes and she felt hot all over despite the cold.

Lydia took the pieces from Cole and removed the fat which she stowed in a corner of her sack. When she had taken what she wanted, she twisted up the corner of the sack and turned it inside out, keeping the fat from the meat they piled in on top. They headed off then, back to their cabin carrying all they possibly could. It had begun to snow, and the wind had picked up, too. But it was an inward warmth Lydia most felt. She had Cole back, she sensed, and then there was the bear meat on top of this.

As they marched the long trail, she wondered about things, about Cole's return, about Black Mary and about the feral woman. She wondered if she would ever become pregnant, and even if she were in fact pregnant even now. But it was no longer a worry like it had been, no longer something that bedeviled her. She watched Cole walk ahead, the sack of meat far heavier than the one she carried. He would heft it, though, hard as it would be, and again her heart swelled.

They walked on for a while without talking, but more connected than they had been when they talked daily in the cabin. After some time Lydia said, "I still have that bobcat foot you made for me when we were little." Cole didn't say anything but she heard him laugh softly from up ahead. He figured that she had heard him laugh, and she reckoned that he knew she had heard him, too. And Cole knew what she had intended by saying this, about the bobcat foot.

And so there was no more to say on it. They walked on toward the cabin.

There were other ways to do it, and Cornelius took pains to make this clear, but Clytie insisted he and the men haul the cauldron down to the King cabin to cook the burgoo. There were far fewer men around now, and the only way to get it over there was to carry it by hand, which amounted to a mixture of carrying and rolling it on its side. The men complained about it, but in a half-joking manner, taking frequent breaks to sip on the bottles Hez Coombs and Abe Williams brought along. It had been a long time since someone had killed a large animal up on Black Boar, with meat enough to feed others. The promise of a gathering, with food, liquor, and maybe even some music, eased the burden of life on Black Boar. At one point, Hez claimed his whiskey tasted better than Abe's, but Abe countered this opinion. Cornelius and the other couple of men made a case for another tasting so that the men could decide a proper winner. This was met with great laughter and a passing of both bottles at the same time. By the time they arrived at the King cabin, they were half hilarious with the liquor, but full of energy to help out. They split logs and hauled wood to the cauldron where Clytie and some of the men's wives had gathered. Inez and Lydia sliced up chunks of the meat and Cole and the men warmed their hands at a fire pit nearby, awaiting any orders.

Even Inez seemed lively. She recalled to Lydia the bear killing of years ago, mentioning Preston without crying or breaking down. There was a young bride working alongside them, one of the few young people still living on Black Boar. She was heavy with child, but she labored on at the cutting table and the cauldron like the others. Inez said to her, "My Press knew how to tan a hide. Knew how to kill and dress an animal like this here. Knew lots of things young people don't know nowadays. It's nice to see you and your man still know these things," she said.

The young bride lowered her eyes and said, "Thank you, ma'am."

At the cauldron, Clytie laughed and joked, sipping from a little bottle she kept in a pocket somewhere inside of the heavy, manly clothes she wore against the cold. "Eye-God," she hollered, "tastes good to a woman!" Cole and the men stoked the fire in the rocks beneath the cauldron. The winter sun had already begun to set, and the powerful glow from the flames cast itself on the faces of all who had gathered around on benches and logs stools. The burgoo was dished out in bowls and the hungry guests ate it with little talk. Lydia sat with Cole on a bench and savored the warmth from the bowl in her hands. She let the steam rise on her face before she dug into the stew, so hungry was she from the hunt and the hike.

In time, someone took up a fiddle and played some tunes. Even those who hadn't finished eating set down their bowls and sang along. Lydia felt a powerful energy rise in her with the music, food, and the presence of her Cole. She rose and took Cole's hand, and the two of them danced in the orange light of the fire. Cornelius, Clytie and some of the others danced, too. It was like old times, Lydia thought. After she had danced for a while, she stopped and sat with Clytie on the bench. Clytie passed Lydia a bottle, but Lydia shook her head no. Her dear friend talked on but Lydia's mind was elsewhere. She nodded at the right places and squeezed Clytie's hand, but Clytie saw that Lydia was looking at Cole across the fire where he had gathered with some of the men. Cole caught her eye across the flames and smiled at her.

"Aw, woman," Clytie said, "I know you'll be ruttin' with that man of yours tonight." Lydia laughed and Clytie kissed her on the forehead, and then left to talk with the circle of wives who stood together close to the fire.

Clytie was right. Lydia was thinking of Cole.

Again, a desire had welled up in her, something more than physical, though. She wanted Cole that way, yes, but the feeling had to do with what once was. She thought about the time when Cole had courted her, when they had walked to the ledge and seen the devastation the timber Company had wreaked, and when he had touched her at the river. She went back in her mind, to the times when they had hiked together, and kissed, and then way back to the time she had asked Cole if he could do something with the lucky bobcat's paw. Her heart had nearly burst from her chest back then, for her nervousness in asking. And now it beat heavy once more as she looked at Cole, her husband, now returned. She thought also about her father and about Inez, about how they loved each other. She remembered the day of the bear killing, years ago. She had wondered back then, when she was just a girl, about the animal's nobility, its greatness above other animals, and how it provided for the hungry people of Black Boar who even then were finding it difficult to provide for themselves. She remembered how her father and mother had lain together that night, and how she had listened to it, and how it fascinated her and confused her at the same time. She would lay with Cole soon, though she realized then that the mystery of life and death, of coupling and birthing children, of the great cycle of things, was still in many ways just as much a mystery to her. She rose and made her way over to Cole, who slung his arm around her as he talked to Cornelius and the others about the bear and his brave wife. She pulled herself into his chest and wrapped her arms around his waist. Soon they would walk off to their cabin, as would the others. She would take Cole again on the bed tick with the fire stoked high. And Cole would forswear heavy drinking as he had promised. Lydia would, too, but for different reasons.

She felt that she was carrying Cole's child inside of her.

Long, Long Ago

BLACK BOAR MOUNTAIN

The woman never could conceive a child. Still, the couple tried. Some said she was not right, that she was too much a man to get with child. If she would remain in the home, if she would tend to things as women did there, she might have better luck. Others offered her roots and leaves that would do the trick, they said. She tried these, and she continued to lay with her man, but nothing happened. For a long time, she was disappointed. She felt that she had failed as a member of the clan. But the husband never made her feel this way. He didn't believe that going out in hunting parties was the cause of things. He knew that he'd rather have her with him in the woods, tracking, hunting, and just walking under the trees and through the brush and briars. Once, when she told him how badly she felt about things, he told her how he felt about it. She smiled and felt relief. He said that maybe *he* should be the one eating the roots and leaves. And when she laughed, he did, too.

BLACK BOAR MOUNTAIN

(Lydia, age 20)

Lydia hadn't seen Cole in several weeks. Two days after the burgoo feast, he had left for work at the mill in Queen's Tooth. He stayed at the boarding house now, owned by the Company, and though part of his pay went for rent there, he figured he'd have enough in a about a year to rent his own place, or to go in with some others and buy a plot where he could put up a few modest little cabins. That was the plan, he said. In the meanwhile, he'd visit Lydia as often as possible, on the weekends. Even then, though, it wouldn't always be possible, especially not in these first few weeks where he was just getting settled into a routine at the mill.

Lydia wasn't at all bothered by it. She had her Cole back, and she trusted in his judgment. She would get along just fine with Clytie, Cornelius, and Inez. And Cole promised to bring flour, sugar and other such items the first time he visited. For now, there was still smoked bear meat, and Lydia had gone out with Clytie everyday looking for food. Between the two of them, they had taken some hares and squirrels. Cornelius, too, went along with them a few times. He shot a dove with Clytie's .22 single shot. And when the women expressed mock surprise that he had killed something, he was good natured about it. "How come you two are the only ones to know about how to hunt?" he said. But this only made Clytie and Lydia laugh even harder. He shook his head and said, "You two, by God."

Lydia was delighted to be back alongside her dear friend but saddened that she would be leaving Queen's Tooth. She promised to visit Clytie often, and she meant it. But Clytie knew that it wouldn't happen that way. Those who left Black Boar didn't come back, not even for visits. It seemed like every few weeks someone else would leave for town, for work at the mill or the Railroad. When Corny learned about Cole's job, even he asked Clytie about whether he should think about a job at the mill. But she simply wouldn't have it. "I'm gonna die on Black Boar, Corny. You are, too, because if you try to leave me up here, I'll kill you." She laughed when she had said it, but Corny knew he had no say in the matter. They would stick it out on the mountain, for better or ill. He had thought of some improvements for the land, too, and he had begun to remove some trees to expand the little fields he worked now. A friend on Black Boar who had taken a job at the Railroad passed on his many animal traps to Cornelius. The man said he wouldn't need them in town. And so there was that, too. They would make do, at least that's what Clytie said.

For her part, Lydia still sensed that she was pregnant, and she was late in her cycle, but she wouldn't know for certain without talking to someone. There was no granny woman up on Black Boar anymore. The last one had died, and since no young girls were interested in learning the ways of childbirth and womanhood, Lydia had to walk all the way into Queen's Tooth to see someone. The woman herself had moved down from Rusty Mountain when the timbering began. Her son worked at the sawmill and her daughter-in-law earned a little money cleaning at the bunkhouse where Cole and many of the men lived. Lydia felt a physical release when the granny woman told her she was pregnant. "You're with child," the woman said flatly. "I thought I seen it in your face when you come in here." She told Lydia she could get up from the bed and put on her dress. "But now I'm certain of it," she added. Lydia was on shaky legs and she resisted the urge to steady herself on the woman's shoulder. But the granny woman saw it. "Just set there for now," she said. Lydia felt the strength in the old woman's hands when she helped her back to the bed. "This is your first one, I can tell."

Lydia felt like she had been freed, spared from some dire fate. She tried to rest on the bed as the woman cleaned her hands and busied herself about the little Company house her son had rented. But she couldn't suppress the emotion. Soon the tears came, hard and with a deep heaving for air. Before she made the long hike down into town, Lydia thought about how she might receive the good news she hoped for, and about how she would guard against over-reaction, against crying carrying on.

But here she was, helpless in the wake of learning it was true.

She cried on, and couldn't stop, though she tried. The granny woman had seen it all before, time and again, and made nothing of it. When Lydia finally began to get a hold of herself, it occurred to her that she hadn't cried like that since her father was killed, nor during her darkest moments with Cole. When she thought about it later she wondered how such different emotions could produce the same effect on the body. They were raw emotions, she thought, irresistible feelings that could not be countered by will. They were so wildly different—one bad and one good—but maybe they related to one another in some deeper way if the reaction to them was the same. She couldn't figure it out for absolute certain, though. What she felt over the murder of her father was a terrible sadness, something impossible to quantify, but grief in its fullest measure, absolutely. But the news of the pregnancy, of the possibility of a child after trying for so long, was something triumphant, something glorious. And yet, it occurred to her that maybe there was an element of loss even in this. As a mother she knew she would forever be changed. Everyone said so, changed for the better, they said. Motherhood was a *gift* for women, for all of its hardships. Still, Lydia wondered if she were losing a part of herself. Not like the loss of her father, but not completely unlike it either.

The granny woman had sense enough not to interrupt the thoughts of a woman just told she was with child. But she needed to ask something before Lydia was on her way. She said, "There's something I need to know, Lydia. And you need to understand that I ask this of every woman I see. So I'll tell it straight. Do you want this child? And are you sure of who's the father?" Lydia answered yes to both.

"Most women cry some, with their first. But you can't always tell why. Mostly it's good cryin'. Sometimes it ain't, though. And it's best if I talk to them right away if that's so." She set a cup of coffee on the little table next to the bed and tipped a bottle of whiskey over it. "Just a touch," she said. "For this is to celebrate, and to bring good luck to you and your child."

Lydia drank the coffee. "Thank you," she said.

Before she left for Black Boar, Lydia asked the granny woman some questions about pregnancy. The woman explained cures for the ailments common to expecting mothers. Queen Anne's lace or sassafras root tea for stomach pain and the bark of slippery elm for the lungs. The granny woman served Lydia a second cup of coffee and added another touch of whiskey. "That's enough for you," she said. "The next time you can touch a drop is when that baby is born. Not until then. But by then your life will be forever changed. You won't have much chance to do any carryin' on with liquor."

Lydia felt the warmth of the liquor rising in her by the time she left, and in her gleeful state she decided she would go see Cole at the sawmill. She would seek him out when the workers broke for their noon dinner, she figured. Then she'd be on her way. She didn't think the visit would embarrass Cole, but she would leave if she felt that Cole was uneasy. The sawmill was a man's affair, she knew, and she didn't want to tarry where she wasn't wanted. Still, she was carrying his baby, and she felt she had rights now, rights she hadn't had before today. She was Mrs. Cole Clemmons, soon to be the mother of Cole's child.

The mill was on the other side of town and Lydia figured that she'd arrive around the time the men stopped to eat. She would wait to hear the whistle that announced the stoppage, and only then would she look for her husband. She headed off, but still well away from the sawmill, she could hear the fearsome whine of the giant saw as it bit into the lumber. She had never been to the mill, and when it finally came in view she was surprised at the scale of it. The log pond itself was massive, a man-made reservoir nearly black from the debris that came off the logs as they buckled down the packed, earthen ramp from the rail cars above. Lydia watched the huge trunks race down the incline, gaining speed as they neared the water. They seemed a terrible force to her, like an unstoppable mass once they began moving. Yet the men worked right alongside these careening giants. To get in the way would be certain death, she thought. The heavy trunks hit the water and caused wakes that tossed about the little boats and the men who piloted them. Fighting the wake, they worked furiously to get the floating logs secured to heavy chains that rattled and then stretched taut as the logs were pulled up the jack ladder onto the deck of the mill. The engine Lydia heard reminded her of the loader she watched years ago at the mountain ledge. There was the metallic grinding again, and the grey smoke that rose in thick clouds from the steam pipes on the mill rooftop.

It took her longer than she thought to walk around to the entrance, and even then she wasn't sure if she were in the right place, or if she should go any further. Men leaving the mill, their galluses and shirts wet with sweat and their faces covered in dust, paid her little heed. They were from the shift that began before Cole's, bent now on getting home, on eating, on rubbing lineament into their sore arms and legs. Not a single one touched his hat as he passed her by. Eventually Lydia got up the nerve to ask one of them about the work stoppage and about where she might find Cole Clemmons. The man said that he didn't know when the men would resume work, that he only knew about his own break times. He added curtly that "hundreds of men" worked at the mill and that he didn't know any Cole Clemmons. He walked on without another word.

More men passed her by, one after the other. Some walked in clusters, though Lydia noticed that few of them spoke to one another. Others walked on with long strides, by themselves, their shoulders hunched forward as if hastening a retreat from something dire. A man passed by her with a thick grey bandage on his forearm, dark with sawdust that clung to the blood that had soaked through. Lydia figured he must have worked on after an injury, unable to go without the day's wages. She made her way toward the mill deck, which opened directly to the outside in places in order to let air pass through the fiery structure.

Here she could see it all, a frenzy of furious activity. And all of a sudden, she was overcome with fear. She worried about her husband, the father of the child she carried, about the deadly saws in the mill and the potential for injury, or worse. Was Cole to work here forever, she wondered? The high-pitched whine from the saw wore on her nerves. It never stopped. There was a terrifying rhythm to it and Lydia braced herself for the moments when the spinning teeth bit into the logs. The shriek of metal against wood was like a recurring scream that tortured her ears. And the saw itself was a kind of monster, a spinning wheel, four feet in diameter, with sharp curved teeth blackened from eating wood all day long, without stop, its appetite never slaked. She imagined an arm or a leg getting caught in there, the bone giving way to the powerful teeth that would throw a severed limb across the mill floor. And who would hear a man's screams above the sound of the saw?

Never had she seen such a frightening spectacle.

She watched as heavy chains pulled the massive logs onto the carriage, a huge piece of iron that sat on rails and drew the log through the dreadful saw. For all the sound of the saw, though, the din of the enormous logs being hauled, lifted, and dropped on the carriage was fearsome. She braced herself each time a log was about to drop onto the carriage, but the sound was still deafening. Lydia felt the vibration travel up her ankles and legs. And then there was the dust that shot out from the saw teeth. It covered everything: men, engines, tools, the entire floor. A team of young boys, covered head to toe in the shavings, desperately worked their brooms toward a steam boiler in the center of the mill deck. She watched one of the boys use an iron rod to open the furnace door. Instantly a raging orange flame threw out light and heat across the mill floor. The boy turned his face from the flame and shoveled the shavings into the red-hot mouth of the boiler, without looking, as if he had done it a thousand times before. He threw the door shut with the shovel and mopped the sweat from his face with his sleeve. Lydia noticed that another boy had soon taken his place at the boiler with yet another pile of shavings. On and on it went, log after log, shovelful after shovelful. The men never stopped moving. The noise wore on.

It occurred to her that the whole enterprise was unstoppable—not merely the mill, but the clearcutting, the hauling of the timber, and the spread of the rail line that made it all possible. There was a frightening momentum in every phase of the work. From the sawyers at the trees, to the powerful loader, to the rail cars one after the other, and to the mill where the logs buckled with such speed and power into the pond, only to be hauled out and pushed through the mill at breakneck pace. At every phase, she thought, there were men who hurried about to keep up with the speed of the work. There was a force behind it all, she sensed, something ungovernable once set into motion, and it scared her. In her panic, it dawned on her that maybe the mill was a danger to the life inside her, unformed as it was then. She turned and practically ran from it all, her nerves a jangled mess and her ears ringing.

She had forgotten altogether about the visit with Cole.

1909

BLACK BOAR MOUNTAIN

(Lydia, age 21)

By summertime the timbermen had arrived at the farthest reaches of Black Boar. Bertie had left for Queen's Tooth by then, her cabin soon swallowed up by the tree crowns and debris the sawyers had left behind. The rail line had climbed even higher in order to extract the felled logs, and the sound of the loaders, the engines, and the sawyers were a part of daily life for Lydia and those few who remained in the little mountain community. Game was almost impossible to come by now, and Lydia, four months pregnant, wondered what life would be like for Clytie and the few others who would remain. She told Clytie that she and Cornelius would always have a place with her and Inez and Cole, down in Queen's Tooth, come what would. But Clytie seemed to think she could hold out against the timber Company, that she and Corny would stay in their cabin even if every tree around them were taken. She would laugh when she told Lydia such things, but Lydia thought maybe Clytie was fooling herself that she could out-duel the Company.

Cole had visited in the first months after he got on at the mill, but the work tired him, and more and more he stayed in town on the weekends to recuperate. He was saving for a spot of land outside town, something to build on, but the plots were more costly than he had hoped, and he would need more time before he could bring Lydia and Inez down. He had lost weight and he looked drawn in the face, gaunt and tired, Lydia told him. Cole didn't counter her, either. Work at the mill was hellish, he said, grueling and unending. Lydia recalled her visit there when she first learned she was pregnant, and the memory made her uneasy. She tried hard to put it out of her mind, and she longed to get off of Black Boar now, to join Cole in town. She told herself that things would be better for Cole when she could be with him. She would restore him, she thought.

And then things got worse.

Fire had broken out amongst the tree crowns and debris left by the Company. It ripped across the hillside and came close to taking Clytie's cabin before rains halted its progress just in time. The Company took the attitude that the "such things happen," and that anyone who decided to remain on the hillside, where the timber work was lawfully enacted, was taking a risk. They washed their hands of any responsibility. For days wood smoke hung oppressively in the air all across Black Boar. It burned the eyes just to go out and about.

But that was just the beginning of things.

Clytie was delirious. She would awaken long enough to ramble senselessly, and then swoon again. In and out of consciousness she went, with Cornelius, Lydia and Inez by her side. Her entire calf was black and distended to three times normal size. The slash from the clear cutting had made a nice home for timber rattlers. But the fire forced them from their warm nests. Clytie was not twenty feet from her cabin door when she was bit on the leg. Cornelius drained pus and blood from the wound almost hourly.

For a long while it seemed like maybe she wouldn't make it, but Cornelius and Lydia would rally her. Inez made a poultice from comfrey leaves and applied it to the wound again and again.

"It's that goddamn timbering!" Cornelius raved. "Goddamn woodhicks. I will kill all of you!" Clytie's hair was matted to her forehead with sweat, and Inez drew a cool, wet cloth across her neck and shoulders.

Cornelius cursed and paced the little cabin floor, back and forth, back and forth.

"Cornelius, you need to go get some air. Go outside now and let us tend to your Clytie," Lydia said.

"Goddamn woodhicks," he spat out. "I will kill you one and all, by God."

"Go on, now, Corny. Let us care for her."

Cornelius huffed and said, "Call for me if she takes a turn for the worse. I'll be nearby." But before he walked out Inez said, "Wait!"

Cornelius stood in the doorway of the little cabin, his hand on the latch. "What is it, Inez? What now?" Inez heard the frustration in his voice, and she couldn't fault him.

"Cornelius Noe," Inez said. And Cornelius knew by the way she used his formal name that what she was about to say was serious, that whatever had happened in the past, whatever uneasiness she may have caused in her own deliriums, her own black moods, she intended now to say something urgent, something that would *matter*. "Get the snake," she said. "We need it. Clytie said it bit her at the wood pile. There's likely a nest there. Get it. Kill *any* snake there. Kill one and bring it to me."

Lydia said, "Momma, what?"

And Cornelius said, "Inez, *why*? What good will that do?"

But Inez shouted them down, raising her voice to a level Lydia hadn't heard since before her father had died. "You hush! The both of you. How come you to know more than me? I know what she needs. Now go, and be careful. Last thing we need is *two* people serpent bit!"

Her manner surprised him, and Lydia, too. Cornelius said only, "I'll try to find it."

"Any rattler serpent will do, Corny," Inez hollered.

He left the cabin and went to the barn where he cut a piece of buckskin and wrapped it around each leg from ankle to knee. He put on his boots and grabbed a frog gig he hadn't used in years. The hickory tines were still sharp, though he took his knife across the tips and tested the them with his finger just to be sure. He thought he could use it equally well to pin a snake. At the wood pile he poked around, knocking off logs from the upper most row with the back end of the gig. Soon he heard a rattle below and as he peeked in space between two logs on the bottom row, he saw the flat triangular head. He jammed the gig in the space and out came the serpent. It was mad, and Cornelius watched the rattle vibrate and hiss as the animal slithered its way out. The black, v-shaped chevrons contracted and expanded with the snake's movement, a graceful serpentine motion that Cornelius admired for the briefest of moments. The tongue darted from the head and the snake picked up speed, moving away from Cornelius at a good clip now. But Cornelius shot the gig true and pinned its head to the earth. The animal writhed in agony with two of the sharp wood tines sent right through the head. Cornelius wasted no time now. In a single pass he drew his knife just below the head. The snake continued to writhe and the rattle sang out once more. Cornelius looked into it the snake's dark eyes, the fangs exposed now and the jaws working hard in search of some final strike before death.

He knew better than to reach for the head just then, but he spoke to it. "You won't soon do what you done to my Clytie, not now, you son of a bitch." He lifted the gig from the earth and watched the snake's jaws open and close grotesquely until they finally stopped, the mouth wide open and the fangs exposed. In one hand he held the body of the snake by the tail end, and in the other he held the gig with the head. "You better hope you can serve my Clytie in some way. Or I will find a way to kill you again," he said.

In the cabin, Clytie tossed her head violently on the bed tick. Lydia tried to soothe her and Inez made up more of the poultice. The shiny black skin had ballooned ever further now and had broken in places across Clytie's calf. It oozed pus and blood and Lydia worked to keep it clean. She wondered if Clytie might lose the leg, or even die. There was no time to send for a doctor down in town, nor were they sure anyone would come, even so. The prospect of an amputation began to weigh on Lydia, and she wondered if she had the strength to do it if it came to that. When Cornelius entered the cabin, Inez said, "Go bury that head behind the cabin, Cornelius. Dig a hole straight down, like for a fence post. Drop it in there and spit on it three times. Then fill up that hole and mark it with a rock on top. You hear me? And leave the length of it there on the table. I need the skin. But first go and get me a hammer and some nails, and a sharp knife, for skinning." Again, there was an authority in Inez' voice that neither Lydia nor Cornelius had heard for years. She stayed busy with the poultice, and Cornelius simply left to do as she directed rather than ask questions.

Inez gave the poultice over to Lydia and said, "You know what to do." Lydia applied the mixture to the leg but it was tough going with Clytie wailing out every time Lydia's fingers touched the calf. Cornelius soon returned with the hammer, nails and knife, and then left to bury the snake head and perform the ritual Inez had directed. Whether it was foolishness or not, he didn't know. But desperation trumped everything now, and there was nothing he could do for Clytie. Once he had left again, Inez cleared the table with a sweep of her arm, knocking bowls and mugs to the floor. She drew on the skinning knife to separate a fold of skin from the end of the snake's body. Then she set a nail in the corner of the skin and slammed the hammer down with a force Lydia didn't know the woman possessed. The head of the tool hit its mark and the heavy iron nail sank into the wood table. She then did the same on the other side of the skin, the sound of the hammer on the nail rattled Lydia. She felt it in her joints, and she clenched her teeth before Inez sank the remaining nails to secure the skin. Inez took the knife and removed the meat in slow, deliberate movements, angling the blade carefully and lifting the flesh to get at the place where it met the skin. She cut off the rattle, spit on it, and threw it in the fire at the hearth. Then she coiled up the meat and set it aside. She sliced the knife neatly across the four corners where she had secured the skin to the table, leaving small pieces of skin under the nail. She gathered up the skin and ordered Lydia out of the way.

"Help me wrap this on her leg. You hold it here, like so," she told Lydia.

"Momma, what is this? We need to keep the leg clean. We can't be fooling with old mountain remedies now."

Inez fixed her with a stare that reminded her of when she was just a little girl, of the times she had committed some deception, or hadn't finished a chore. "You will do this, girl, or I will settle you, you hear me? There is more to life than you know. There are things that older folks know that you don't. Like the skin of this is good for a wound."

Like a little girl, Lydia did as she was told. Wrapped around Clytie's calf and shin, the snakeskin produced an eerie sight, like it belonged to a woman who was part snake. The chevrons repeated each other in a parallel pattern now, and the orange line that had run down the snake's back now traveled round and round the calf, like a cinch. Inez left the last bit loose so that she could poke a hole through the snake skin with the tip of the knife and tie it off with some thread.

Cornelius stopped dead when he entered the cabin after burying the rattler head. Clytie stirred fitfully, trying all the while to raise herself from the bed tick. It was all Lydia could do to keep her down. With the ballooned wound beneath, the leg now appeared like a bloated serpent, something that had taken possession of his wife, who struggled to cast it off.

"What in hell, Inez?" Cornelius said.

"You hush! That skin is gonna save that leg," Inez said.

It tortured him to keep quiet, but Cornelius trusted to Inez' judgment in the end. He too saw that she was moving like she hadn't in years. She was alive again, the old Inez, the old capable mountain wife taking care of others. Still, the vision of Clytie struggling and sweating, clawing out at Lydia and speaking nonsense in her delusion—it pained him. She had become a snake-woman, he thought, struggling to cast off the serpent part of her, fighting and cursing to fend it off.

He clenched his jaw.

In time, though, Clytie settled, and hours later Inez removed the skin. The swelling had receded, and though the skin around the calf was black and dead, Inez announced that Clytie would keep her leg. "Lydia," Inez said as she reached under the bed tick, "Go put this up out of my sight." She handed her a heavy cleaver, the edge newly sharpened, Lydia could tell. She never knew Inez had it at the ready.

One thing Lydia knew for certain now. If it had come to an amputation, it would have been Inez, and not Lydia, who would have done the deed.

The little church up on Black Boar had to be neatened up for Preacher Nichols visit. It had not been used in some time. The church that the Company had built him in town kept the reverend busy, but every now and then he'd come to give a sermon in the old church up on the hill. Word would be sent around and those who wanted could come and listen. He knew of the fire and of the snake bite. And he knew that the blaze nearly took out everyone left on the mountain. Clytie, Cornelius, and Lydia attended these sermons not because they trusted in his guidance, but because they sought news of the Company's plans. In fact, it seemed like Isaac Nichols couldn't keep from talking about the Company, whether he liked it or not. As was his wont, though, he often took a roundabout way to get there.

"Snakes!" he hollered. "Snakes! The serpent! The demon!" He walked down the tiny aisle between the pews. "He has arrived on Black Boar, my friends. Would that this were not true … but alas … it is true." He made his way back to the little lectern Cornelius himself had made years ago, making a show of his uneasiness.

Clytie whispered to Lydia, "He could have been a player on the stage."

"Beware the serpent," the preacher said. "The serpent is God's enemy, my mountain friends. *Our* enemy. And he is here. He is among us. One of you has been struck."

Clytie rustled in the pew and pulled the hem of her dress down to hide her scar. Cornelius took her hand in his.

"Clytie Noe," the preacher said. "This good woman has been serpent bit! She nearly lost a leg. The beast is among us, mountaineers." Clytie struggled against the impulse to get up and leave, but she needed to hear what the preacher said about the Company, about its plans for Black Boar. She squeezed Cornelius' hand hard. But she would have to wait.

The reverend held forth: "Now, I saw four timber rattlers on the climb up here this day. Four! They hissed at me, they did, slithering around on the trail, raising their heads and rattlin' those tails. They surrounded me. Quick they were, and I found no means of escape. For a moment I thought I was not long for this world. Thought this would be my last visit to a church. The end of the line, I reckoned."

He stepped down from the little lectern and again walked down the tiny aisle. "But something occurred to me then, friends. It hit me like a flash of lightning. Like God himself reminded me. I had something that maybe would spare me." He fished into his trouser pocket and pulled out a small wood crucifix. "This I bore against them serpents," he said. "I held it like so, and in time they slithered away. The serpent knows the power of God. He fears it. Them snakes slithered off the path, off into the dark wood where they can hide and reproduce to spread their sinister will. I ask you, friends, how much longer can we hold out up here without God's presence?"

He never answered the question, but once back at the lectern he said, "This is my last visit to Black Boar, friends. I'm scared to come here. Scared for my soul. The serpents are here, now! They have struck one of you." He raised his hands and said, "Heavenly Father, help us. Help us find a way to leave." At this, Clytie and Lydia knew he was about to talk about the Company.

"Mountain friends," he said, "there is a way out. There is an escape from the serpent, and from all that threatens you here. Sell your land and come to town. The Company will pay you well. And you will be free. There's plenty of work in town for you men. Work at the sawmill. Work at the Rail. Work at all of the businesses there in town. But there isn't much time." Then, after some invocations to God and some psalms sung by the few in attendance, he surprised everyone and ended the sermon. "Friends," he said, "I won't be back. And today I have no spirits for you. But the Company promises two jugs of fine whiskey to anyone who sells in the next month, and the prices are prime for your plots, as you know. But I must say again, I'll not be back. The serpents have arrived, and this is no place for a man of the cloth. I love you. In God, Amen."

And then the preacher did something that surprised even the devout, like Hez's wife and a few others, people used to communing with him after a service, congregants accustomed to sharing the word of God with the good man. Today it wasn't to be.

Preacher Nichols walked out of the church, mounted his mare, and rode out.

Clytie was furious when the preacher left. She had planned to confront him, to stand up and say her piece right there. She was ready to name it to him and everyone else. It's the Company, the timbermen and the Rail who brought this all on. What *they* did, the cutting and hauling of the trees, well, now that's what brung out the snakes. It had nothing to do with God but with the Company, and with their love of money, no matter the cost to people.

It was too late, though. The preacher was true to his word.

It was all an act, Clytie felt, a piece of theatre, leaving abruptly like that. And it might even fool people into believing that evil had really come to Black Boar. The preacher had deprived her of her moment, and she was angry about it. In the coming days, she wondered about what she could do, about what action she could take.

And then something occurred to her.

"Corny," she said. "Did you ever do anything with that snake skin?"

"It's in the barn. I tanned it, but I haven't done anything with it."

"Well, why not?"

Cornelius shrugged. Clytie could tell he was working up an answer. "I guess I don't like to look at it," he said. But I hate to waste a thing. What do want with snake leather anyway?"

"I want you to make a covering for my scars. The skin is awful, and I can't stand to look on it. Reminds me of what happened."

"What? With the snake skin?" he said. "That doesn't make any sense. You'll be reminded of it even more so if you go around wearing the skin. Let me use some buckskin, or some muslin, some linsey wool, maybe, that can be properly washed. Maybe Inez can make something like that for you."

But Clytie wouldn't have it. "No, Corny. I want the snake skin."

Cornelius shook his head. And then a thought occurred to him. It wasn't exactly a lie either. He said, "Snake leather is too thin to do something like that. It won't last. Let me use buckskin, or muslin or some such thing."

"Corny," Clytie said, "that snake ain't a serpent like that preacher wants us to think. It's just a snake, and it does what it does, protects itself. You told me you were gonna go kill every snake around here after I got bit, but I told you not to. You remember why?"

"Yes, because they're good to have around. Keep pests away. That's what you said. And I never killed another one, though it was hard for me not to."

"That's true," Clytie said. "And I want to show that preacher I ain't afraid of a snake. It's just an animal. We use animals up here. I'm gonna show him what I think of his story, that Black Boar is infested with demon serpents. It's foolishness."

"But, Clytie, it will look more foolish to have a wrap made of snakeskin, now, won't it?"

But Clytie had said her piece. She would discuss it no more. "Corny, can you make a thong that sews it all together from the skin itself? Can you cut a piece from the skin to make the thong itself, I mean?"

"That snake leather is too thin," he said again. But she heard the weakness in his voice.

"Can't you sew it onto some buckskin, then?"

He thought to say no, but that would have been an out-and-out lie. He knew he was beaten. He shook his head. "I suppose I could do that."

"Thank you, Dear," Clytie said.

He rose wearily and headed to the barn.

Clytie touched Lydia's belly. "I think you're gonna have a baby girl."

Lydia laughed. "Now just how do you know that?"

"Mountain woman's instinct," Clytie said. She tried to keep a straight face about it but she couldn't, and her broad smile told Lydia she was only teasing. They were still laughing when Cornelius came through the door of the cabin. "What's so funny, you two?"

"You," Clytie said, and the two of them fell into laughing again.

"By God," Cornelius said with a smile. "You two." He poked around the hearth and then headed up into the loft.

"Clytie," Lydia said. "There's something I want to ask you about. That fire. I've been thinking on it. Now, Cole thinks I'm crazy, but I wonder, do you think it's possible the Company started that fire to get rid of us, to burn us out, I mean? Would they do something like that?"

"It doesn't matter," Clytie said. "The point is that they *would* do it. They're not interested in people. They use the preacher, that Isaac Nichols, to tell us God wants us to leave. Now that's pretty low down. They want us out, one way or the other. Whether or not it's legal, or righteous, ain't their concern." She shook her head and laughed. "The funny thing is that it's a preacher doing their evil work for them." She took a sip of her coffee, spread her legs out in front of her and crossed them at the ankles. Lydia reached out then and touched the snake skin wrap Cornelius had made for Clytie's lower leg. Clytie could slip it on like a boot, and then tighten it just below the knee with the thong Cornelius had made from the same skin. He threaded it through a casing he sewed together with another long strip of skin he carefully cut with a razor. The covering was entirely made of snake skin.

"You like it?" Clytie asked.

"It's lovely," Lydia said. "It's softer than I thought and the pattern is beautiful. Cornelius is good. I tell you. When I first saw it, I thought it looked wicked, like you were part snake, Clytie. But I come to like it now."

Clytie laughed. She took a little jug from a mantle above the hearth and poured a splash of whiskey into her coffee. "Hey Corny," she hollered. "Lydia's admiring your handiwork on my snake leg."

"Oh, lord," Cornelius said from up in the loft.

The two women smiled and Clytie said, "He thinks it looks wicked, too, but *only* wicked. Still, he knows why I did this. It's me saying, *I don't hold with the preacher's ruse*, that there's serpents up here, that some demon is up here on Black Boar. I'm sayin', *look here, I don't believe it. I know it's a trick.*" She sipped from her mug and said, "And more than that, I *know* you don't believe these rattlers are serpents in that way. They come from the fact that the tree crowns and such leftover wood was burned up. They have no home and so they leave, look for places to live, like a barn. Me wearing this snake skin says to that preacher and to the Company, *Go to Hell. I don't hold with any of that foolishness.*"

Lydia ran her finger along the shiny skin once more and marveled. "It's just lovely. It's not wicked at all, Clytie. And it's more than lovely, too. It's just what you say it is. Like a way to say, 'I'm not buying what you're selling, mister.'"

"Damn right," Clytie said. She took hold of Lydia's leather cinch for her prosthetic. "You know, this here is getting worn out. You might have Corny make you one from that skin. That was a big snake, almost five foot. Corny has more hide from it."

"Well …" Lydia said.

Clytie winked at Lydia. "Hey Corny," she hollered, "Get on down here. Lydia needs a new cinch for her thumb. And she wants one made of rattler skin. Will you oblige her, dear?"

There was a long pause, and then Cornelius' voice came from the loft above. "Law, now there's gonna be two serpent women on Black Boar."

The women howled.

The body had been found by two fishermen down in Georgia. It was that of a log runner from a camp up in North Carolina, they later learned. He had traveled a long way, through some rough water, and ended up in a snag near the river's edge. The anglers had pulled the corpse onto the bank in the shade of the same elm that had snagged him. It was bloated grotesquely, ghostly white, the face and torso a mess of gashes and contusions. He wore only pants, no shoes or shirt, and those were torn to shreds. Bloated as he was, the men could tell that the man was already large before he became so distended. Beneath the damage caused by the rapids, beneath the gaping cuts where the skin was pulled taut around the gashes, the men saw other scars, proof of a life hard fought. This was no yeoman. And though they weren't police detectives, this fact, coupled with another, told the men that it wasn't the river that killed him. But one didn't really have to be a detective to figure that out.

There was a buck knife plunged to the hilt in the side of the big man's neck.

1909

BLACK BOAR MOUNTAIN

(Lydia, age 21)

hen it was nearly time for the baby to come, Clytie told Lydia, "You'll have that young'un before you move down to the valley, which is best, I think."

"Why do you think that, Clytie? I think I should be with Cole when the baby's born."

"You'll get down there soon enough, but the baby should be born up here, Cole or no Cole. He can come visit when it comes, but you're close now, maybe only a few weeks away. That's what Hez's Emma told us. You heard her."

Clytie took a pull off her bottle and sat it on the table in Lydia's cabin. "The main thing is that the baby be born here, on Black Boar," Clytie said. "The first breath he takes ought to be of mountain air, not valley air. Now you know that as well as anyone. After that, well, the baby will be able to live anywhere. Mountain air makes a baby strong. Everyone knows this much. But it's bad luck to have a birth down there in town." She took another sip and plugged the bottle.

"Oh, Clytie, that's all mountain nonsense and you know it," Lydia said.

"Like hell it's mountain nonsense, woman!" Clytie hollered. But she couldn't keep from laughing. And then Lydia joined her. "Anyhow," Clytie said, "I want to be there for the birthing, and I ain't going into town for it. It's going to happen right here, on Black Boar."

"I thought I'd be in Queen's Tooth by now," Lydia said. "Cole's been working like a demon, putting in hours as much as they allow. He's tired, Clytie, but he's putting money aside. Still, it's more money than I thought it would be to rent a little place."

"Of course, it is," Clytie said. "It's town greed is what it is."

"Oh, Clytie. Stop now."

"Well, I plan to catch that baby, me and Inez. Hez' Emma likely, too. I'm no granny woman but I been there enough times to know what I'm doing. That girl's going to be a native of Black Boar, Lyddie. Maybe she'll be the last one, or one of the last. The way it's going with the Company. Corny and me might be the last folks up here. But one way or another, we will die here, the both of us. It's been decided." Lydia saw the water in her eyes and reached across the table to take her friend's hand. Clytie smiled. "Then you and Cole can take that baby down to Queen's Tooth. I know I tease, but it will be nice for you there. You and Cole and the baby. The truth is that there's not much up here anymore, and there won't be anything soon. But you can make a life down there, Lyddie. The three of you, and Inez."

Burr had borne the indignities of working as the new man pretty well. The way he saw it, he had no choice. Since he and Simms had walked out of the woods years ago, he had bounced around doing mill work and timbering under assumed names. Few of the companies cared about official documents anyway. It was all about profit. If you could work long and hard without giving out, you could stay on. If this meant taking on some rogues, well then, so be it. Such was company logic. Burr knew how important it was to stay out of trouble, but even so, it was hard for a man accustomed to the rule of the roost to take orders from anyone. He fled a paper mill in Tennessee after a fight left a man without an eye, and in Georgia, he ran off an orange grove after a boss had short changed him. Burr raked a buck knife down the man's back, taking to the woods and leaving behind his few belongings.

Now he was at a log runners' camp in North Carolina. As the new man, he accepted the worst bunk, the worst duties, and the worst treatment generally. But he was tired of running, and he told himself that this time he would have to make it work out if he didn't want to run forever. He went by Albert Cooley, or just "Cooley." So far, he had earned some decent pay and had kept out of trouble.

There was a big man in charge, Mackenzie, a strapping tough with bushy sideburns and a wide moustache that ran to the edge of his chin. He had worked long as a log runner in other places. He knew his business. On his second day on the job, he delivered an open-handed slap to a long timer, a man named Phillips, who had decided to take an unauthorized break. Phillips was stunned and instinctively went at the big man. Tough as he was, Phillips was tossed aside like a rag doll and then kicked viciously in the ribs. At the bunkhouse that night, Mackenzie told everyone that things had changed, that the owners had hired him to shape up the crew, to increase productivity, and that he intended to do just that. He wasn't around to make friends, he said.

"You ain't got to worry about that," someone chimed out from a bunk. Mackenzie walked to the man's bunk, grabbed him by the hair, and yanked him to the ground. "You will heed me," he said. And then again, "You will heed, *or else*." The man was stunned, but looking up at Mackenzie, he knew better than to make a move. The big man seemed as much animal as human, and Burr checked his every instinct against a confrontation with him. He told himself he would steer clear, and that he would work especially hard to avoid even the outside *possibility* of a conflict. He told himself, yes, he too would "heed."

But it wasn't to be.

On the river bank near the bunk house the men were cleaning up after sending a raft down river. The work was grueling, and the pace had slowed. Mackenzie felt the need to assert himself. "Let's pick up the pace, girls," he said. "Company ain't paying you to goldbrick it."

Mackenzie chuckled when he noticed that Burr had added a little step to his pace, tired as he was. "That's right, Cooley," he said. "That's a good boy, right there. You all need to take a page from Cooley's manual. Does what's he told. Knows how to heed, that Cooley."

Burr had been moving some iron tools to the shed, and they clanged when he dropped them, echoing off the hillside across the river. Everyone turned to see what had happened. Was there an accident?

"Don't speak to me that way, Mackenzie," Burr said evenly.

There was maybe twenty feet between the men. "Cooley," Makenzie said, "pick up them tools and get your fuckin' ass over to the bunk house. You're docked a day for insubordination. Do you know what that word means, you dumb hayseed? I guess you don't know how to accept a compliment. You ain't got any breeding, I can tell." He laughed. "Anyone want to stand up for Cooley? Anyone want to tell the boss how to talk to the workers?"

The men continued about their labors, eyes to the ground.

"That's what I thought," Mackenzie said. "And as for you, Cooley, I thought I told you to go pick up them tools you dropped and likely damaged. That too will come out of your pay. Step lively now! Unless you got something to say about it."

"I do," Burr said. "I do have something to say about it."

Makenzie sighed, but readied to do what he had done dozens of times before. "Cooley, I'm gonna teach you a lesson before I throw you out of this camp for good. Now set that knife on the ground. Knife fightin' is for nancies." Burr unsheathed his work knife from his belt and tossed it to the earth."

When Mackenzie began to narrow the distance between them, Burr said, "How about your knife? Ain't you going to put it down?" he said.

"I don't need a knife to deal with the likes of you. Just you watch. This will be over before it begins," Mackenzie said.

It was what Burr had hoped for.

The woodhicks quickly circled the two. Mackenzie feinted only once and when Burr moved to duck, Mackenzie grabbed him by the shirt and delivered a right-hand punch to the side of Burr's face. It came fast and nearly knocked him out. But Burr was focused on one thing only, and he rallied. He broke Mackenzie's grasp with his forearm and attacked the man's leg with both arms, wheeling himself around so that Mackenzie's backside pushed up against his face. Blood streamed from a cut beneath Burr's eye, but he had secured the leg. Mackenzie stood strong and laughed. "Well, Cooley, I knew you wasn't much, but I didn't expect you to fight like a youngin.'" Burr looked ridiculous, his face in Mackenzie's ass and his arms thrown tightly around the leg like a tiny child clung to his mother. Some of the men laughed. But then Burr released his hold on the leg and moved around to face the big man. His breath was coming hard, and the wide gash Mackenzie had made poured blood down the front of his shirt. Mackenzie shook his head. "This is sad, Cooley. Unfair, it is."

Burr crouched low, almost to his haunches, his arms tight to his sides like he were playing some child's game. And again, Mackenzie let out a laugh. "You haven't done this before, have you?" he said. "This is men's play, Cooley. I can tell you ain't accustomed to it." He shook his head and said, "Let's get this over with." He moved on Burr with a speed that surprised the men. When he let go a ferocious kick to Burr's crouched body, Burr seized the leg and thrashed out near the knee with the big man's knife. No one had seen Burr take it from the sheath, nor had they seen it as he crouched and waited for Mackenzie. But now it flashed silver in the high sun, and Burr buried it in the leg again, and then again. The men were aghast, but before anyone had thought to do anything, Mackenzie lay on the ground, the knife sunk to the hilt in the side of his neck. Blood pulsed out in a stream and Mackenzie clawed at the knife grip, his eyes wide and his mouth open and pouring blood.

Burr picked his own knife from the ground and leaned over Mackenzie. "Now what do you think of that?" he said. "Guess there's one of us here ain't willing to heed you." He laughed.

The last thing Mackenzie saw before he closed his eyes forever was Burr's silver cuspid.

The ring of men that had closed in around the fighters had widened now that Burr held the blade. There were plenty of men there to disarm him, but no one did. Like a herd of animals in the face of a single, greater predator, they retreated. Burr recognized it instantly. He had seen it before, time and again. "No need for worry, friends," he said as he sheathed his knife. "It's all over. You should be pleased to know you won't have Mackenzie to bully you any longer. Nor will you have to worry about me. I'll just be on my way." But as he walked through some men on the perimeter, he made fast for a young worker and took hold of the boy. Before anyone knew what had happened, Burr had the kid in a choke hold, his knife at the neck.

"Friends," he said, "I have one last request of you, I'm sorry to say. I need every last one of you to go and dump that foul corpse in the water. All the way out in the middle of that river. In the current, you hear? All of you. Not a one can stay here on the bank. The water will carry you off, but I know every man among you is a good swimmer, and every man will make one bank or the other without much trouble. Let that wretched corpse float down the water. I don't want to see anyone try and rescue it for the grave. Let it get tossed among the rocks and rapids. Let it be borne by the white water. The river's Mackenzie's grave now."

The men stood stock still.

"Go on now," Burr said, "or this young one gets the same treatment. You can take off them boots, but do it quick like." He poked the knife tip into the space above the boy's collar bone. The boy winced. But it was fear that the men saw in the boy's wide eyes, not pain. They all moved to the water then, again like a herd, and Burr had to remind them to take Mackenzie's body with them.

The boy began to whimper. "Easy now, son. It will be ok," Burr whispered in his ear. Soon all the men had made their way into the river and released Mackenzie's body. Burr watched it float away, the knife briefly visible above the surface of the water. The men had begun to drift themselves, every which way, the herd separating. Some stroked hard and made their way toward the far bank, doing their best to put distance between Burr and themselves. Others allowed themselves to drift alongside the body, their wary eyes on Burr and his hostage, back on the receding bank.

When Burr had judged the men to be far enough away, he said to the young log runner, "You ain't done me any wrong, boy, but that don't really matter. I need a head start, and you're in my way. There really ain't no right or wrong in all of this. There's just stuff people do." Burr slit the woodhick's throat from ear to ear.

He was three steps running toward the woods before the boy hit the ground.

I nez said it was the bog woman that done it.

Clytie hushed her. "Inez, dear, please do not say that again, not while Lydia's around. You and me can talk about that some other time. Just don't say any more about it with Lyddie near."

"Alright, Clytie," Inez said, "but it was that bog woman sure as hell. Preston and Lydia let loose a curse back then."

Clytie clenched her teeth. She felt an impulse to grab her old friend by the hair and slap her hard across the face. Cornelius saw it all. He tugged on Clytie's arm and said, "Clytie, go sit with Lydia. I'll talk with Inez now. Go on."

For three days Lydia had been at Clytie's cabin. She hadn't eaten anything until Clytie forced her, screamed at her finally, telling her that the baby's health was at risk, that Lydia was acting the fool. But this was after hours upon hours of consoling, then of gentle suggestion, and then of more urgent requests, flat demands, and then finally the screaming at her friend. Lydia eventually took down some soup that Clytie fed to her by hand. But she remained like a catatonic.

No one had slept hardly at all, not even Cornelius.

Only Inez was talking, and then all she had to say was the same thing. "It was that bog woman that done it. She's the one who brung it all on." It was maddening, and here and there Cornelius forced Inez outside to help him with some task or other. Clytie was surprised that Lydia hadn't screamed at her mother, told her to hush. She reasoned that Lydia couldn't hear her, that she was deaf to everything around her. She looked that way. Pale, with dark splotches under eyes red from hours of crying.

At length, though, it occurred to Clytie that maybe Lydia hadn't said anything to silence Inez because she may have believed that what her mother said was true. That it *was* the doing of the bog woman, that it was the defilement of the grave, years ago, that set loose a curse.

Whether it was or wasn't, this is what happened.

It wasn't the first time someone had gotten hurt, not by a long-shot. Hands and limbs were injured regularly, and the bands that pulled wheels and cogs had also drawn many a man into their fearsome motion. Some of the worst injuries eventually caused death, and a few men had even drowned in the log pond. Still, the blade itself, the circular saw, had never cut anyone, not until now.

Cole was exhausted at the end of a twelve-hour shift. He wasn't as alert as she should have been, or could have been, depending on who you asked. The way it really happened Lydia didn't know. She was told that Cole stuck his hand where he shouldn't have. It wasn't exactly a lie. But it wasn't the truth either. Not the full truth, anyway.

What happened was this.

Cole got his hand caught under a log on the moving carriage. Had he gotten free, he'd never work another day in the mill. Likely he'd not have a hand anymore. The bones were pulverized instantly, and it was probably true that Cole felt this pain more than he felt what came next. On it its heavy iron rails, the carriage wheels rolled on toward the spinning saw. Cole cried out louder than he ever had in his life, but the man who operated the carriage couldn't hear him for the whine of the saw and for the general din that never stopped. Nor could he even see Cole because of the girth of the log that lie between the two of them. The carriage moved on, unstoppable, like every other machine and like every other phase of the timber work. Like the loader with its continually moving arm, and like the cables that hauled logs from the pond up the jack ladder. Like the steam furnace that ate, and ate, and ate sawdust fuel, and the saw that never stopped spinning. Cole saw it coming at low speed, watched it moving toward him second by terrible second. When his shoulder hit the blade, blood shot out across the mill deck. Men nearest the saw felt the warm liquid on their faces.

But the saw never slowed.

When he realized what had happened, the operator threw the lever to stop the carriage. Cole had fallen between the blade and the large wheel and band that pulled it. The log was so huge that it was easier to run it all the way through the blade so that the men could access Cole's body more easily.

He was dead by the time the log had passed by.

The noise of the mill suddenly ceased when work was stopped to get Cole out. His body was removed, and the men were asked about what happened. It was quickly determined that it was all Cole's fault, a lapse in attention. Everyone agreed. But Cole would never be asked about what happened or why. The floor was mopped and a half an hour later the saw was spinning again. The first few rotations left concentric red arcs on the cut lumber. A millhand asked if the bloody blade should be removed and properly cleaned before cutting again. But a floor boss said that removing the blade took time and care, special tools and a practiced hand. It was much easier just to keep running lumber. The end result would be the same, he said. The blade would run itself clean.

Early the following day, a boy who worked at the mill was sent up to Black Boar to deliver the news. He saw two women boiling clothes outside of Clytie's cabin and he hoped it wasn't the pregnant one who was the widow.

But it was Lydia who recognized the boy first. He was one of those who had stoked the steam boiler with sawdust the day she learned she was with child and had gone to deliver the good news to Cole at the mill. The boy's face was free of grime now, but his presence re-awakened a terror in her. Instantly she recalled the infernal mill deck with its fearsome sound and movement, and this boy who stoked the hungry, fiery maw that kept it all going. A hell on earth. As he walked toward her, she felt instinctively that something was wrong, and she touched her belly without realizing it. The memory of the mill—the ferocious pace of the machines and the workers yoked to them—it caused her to feel the vibrations in her ankles and up her calves again. She remembered the man with the injured arm, the bloodied bandage filthy with sawdust, and she felt the full measure of the fear she had felt that day almost nine months ago—that Cole would be killed there in that hell. Her mouth became dry and she looked to Clytie in desperation.

"Ma'am," the boy said.

And now Lydia saw in his dull eyes how the work had removed the life from the poor boy. Up close, she saw a red lesion on his neck, something that hadn't healed. A burn? And there was a wide scar that ran along his jawline, at one time the site of a deep wound, she could tell. She figured it must have been caused by the mill work. Her heart raced. From the corner of her eye, she saw Clytie moving toward her, and she heard Cornelius from over near the corn plot call out, "Who's that now?"

"Ma'am," the boy said, "are you Mrs. Cole Clemmons?" He hoped against hope that she would say no.

But when she fell to her knees without answering, he knew it was she.

Somewhere in
Western Tennessee

Simms could count on one hand the number of times anyone knocked on his door in the rooming house. He kept to
himself. He had to. But it was also true that he wanted it that way.
Nowadays he felt little desire for human company, not because
he didn't want it. He did. But because he thought he wasn't wor-
thy of it, and because it was a risk. Most of the time, Simms felt
that the prison escape was the worst decision of his life, worse
than what put him in prison in the first place. What happened on
Black Boar and afterward, running the hills with Burr, haunted
him daily. There were only two taps on the door, soft ones, but
they reverberated in Simms' chest, and he was gripped with an
immediate fear. He sat at the tiny table in the only room there
was, absolutely unable to move. His mind raced with the *rational*
possibilities—a child at the door, a drunk border, a confused old
man, or maybe someone looking for a friend at this late hour.

But the truth of it overwhelmed him even as he tried to deny
it.

It was the double tap of the prison. The convict's signal. Same
in every jail Simms ever ended up in. Tap-tap on the cell door.

Tap-tap on the long wood tables of the cafeteria. Tap-tap with a stick on the yard wall fence. It said: A message is about to be delivered, a guard is coming, someone is "gonna shine boots" on someone. Whatever it was, the message itself was always grim. Never was there a double tap that signaled welcome news. As a prisoner, you came to hate the sound, and you only hoped that whatever befell whomever, you could somehow hope to avoid involvement.

And there it was, on Simms' door in the rooming house, miles away from any prison he ever spent any time at. He didn't know who it could be ... but he did know, too, deep down. Who else *could* it be? With a muffled curse he rose and opened the door. And there his fears were confirmed.

Burr Hollis stood across the threshold.

"Well, well, look at the swell," Burr smiled and revealed the silver cuspid.

Simms moved aside to let Burr in, and peeked out into the hallway to see if any residents noticed the unwanted guest. His gut was already knotted, and he wasn't sure that he could talk evenly yet. Though Burr had asked nothing of him, Simms mentally cycled through a list of excuses as to why he couldn't meet with Burr now, why he couldn't host him for very long, and finally, why he couldn't put him up for any period of time.

Burr caught it all in an instant. "Not to worry, convict," he laughed, "I won't stay here for any too long. You'll be shut of me in a few days." Burr looked around and smiled. "Looks like you're a bachelor, boy."

"Yes ... what are you doing here, Burr? This ain't the best idea you've ever had," Simms said.

He gestured to the one other chair at the tiny table and Burr took it. Simms moved to sit down. But Burr didn't miss a beat. As if the men had never been apart since the escape, he said, "Ain't you got any spirits to offer your old friend?"

Simms sighed, "Yes." He opened a cabinet and pulled down a bottle of corn liquor. "How's this?" he said.

Burr unplugged the jug and sniffed the liquid inside. "Oh, this is fine stuff, I can tell," he said. He took a pull off the bottle and slid it over to Simms. Simms wasn't sure if this was a slight or if Burr were genuine. Who ever knew for sure with Burr? But it was like Burr to put you on your guard for no reason at all, just so that he would gain the upper hand. If Simms had countered Burr in either direction, the man would surely act offended. Whether or not he was genuinely offended didn't matter because the next step for Burr would be anger. And that, Simms knew, he most surely did not want.

"Help yourself," Simms said.

"That's kindly of you. Now, as to why I'm here. Well, let's get reacquainted first and I'll tell you. But like I said, I won't stay long, friend."

Simms hoped it wasn't a lie, but he knew there was at best half a chance of it. Likely the odds were much longer.

"What are you doing with yourself?" Burr asked. "Hope to God you've been staying out of trouble." Burr smiled and the look took Simms back to the old hermit on the mountain, and then back to Black Boar, and from there back to the prison guard and the bloodied convict in the tunnel. The images flipped rapid fire across Simms' memory and he felt the nausea again, the feeling in his gut that only the presence of Burr could summon.

He reached for the bottle and took a pull. "I've been staying out of trouble. No one knows me here, and no one ever will if all goes well."

"Praise God," Burr said taking up the bottle. "Let's hope it stays that way."

Like everything Burr said, the remark came off as a mixture of insincerity, guile, and threat. Simms knew he needed to know more before he told Burr anything else. "How'd you find me, convict," he said, hoping to use Burr's own levity to advantage.

Burr smiled and winked. He tipped the mouth of the bottle toward Simms. "I wondered when you was gonna ask that," he said. "I'm surprised you don't know how. And I'll tell you directly. But tell me this first. Are you working here? How are you getting any money?"

To lie to Burr, Simms knew, would be to pay, one way or the other. He didn't like the question, but he didn't like Burr sitting inside his home in the first place. Now that he was here, it was as if Burr were in charge again. He had to cut his losses and hope for the best. "I lay low as much as possible, as you can see," he said, sweeping his arm to indicate the tiny room. "Odd jobs and whatnot. There's little things I do depending on the season. Bail hay. Set fence post. Run a mule and harrow. You know. I go by Harper out here."

"By God I do know," Burr said. "It's what I've been up to these years, too. Same as you. That and layin' low otherwise. Cooley's the name I last used," he laughed.

Simms did his best to smile, and hoped Burr didn't sense that it was false. He reached for the bottle again. The best way to deal with Burr, he knew, was to follow him, to drink if Burr drank and to let go, be a part of it all, as much as it was possible. To allow Burr *into you* and hope for the best. If you opposed him, he would see it. The worst was possible then.

"Here's to you, Burr," he said.

Burr took the bottle and said, "And to you."

There was a quiet that followed. And Simms knew that Burr wanted it that way. He fed on fear, on the unspoken things in moments like this. Those seconds said, *Yes, you know I'm here. I surprised you, didn't I? Well, there's not much you can do about it now, is there?*

Finally, Simms broke. "So, how'd you find me?" he said.

"Oh, hell," Burr laughed. "I almost forgot. Well, remember what you told me back when we were in Kentucky, in Hellerville?"

"No," Simms said.

"You told me about this place, about western Tennessee and this tiny town. You said how when you were little there was an aunt here. That you used to visit her and your uncle before they died. And that this place was better than anywhere you'd been because it was simple times back then, before you got on to women, and booze, and thieving and such. You told me you would come back here if you could. That this would be the place you'd be if ever you could, if ever you got out."

Simms face flushed beat red. The story was true, but he knew for a fact he had never told it to Burr. He laughed and took a pull off the bottle to mask his uneasiness. "Oh, yes," he said. "I should have remembered that."

It was a lie and Burr knew it.

And Simms knew that Burr knew it was a lie. In a matter of less than ten minutes, Simms also knew that Burr was back in his life.

The taste of bile filled his mouth. It was all he could do to keep the whiskey down.

Fear rose up in the boy the instant Lydia collapsed. He knelt and touched her shoulder with his hand, though he surprised himself in doing so. Lydia lay on her side, oblivious to the boy, to the damp ground, to Clytie and Cornelius, to everything. The boy swept her hair from her face and reached his arm under her neck and shoulders. He lifted her dead weight until she was sitting. It was the first time the shy boy had ever touched a woman besides his mother. But there was something desperate in Lydia's wailing, something human that he responded to, as if her arm were pinned under a rock, as if she were drowning in a river. That she was pregnant somehow made things more urgent. It seemed as if he tended to her forever, but it was really only a matter of a seconds before Clytie was on them. She pushed the boy aside roughly and took Lydia in her arms. She didn't ask the boy what had happened. She already knew. And then, from out of nowhere it seemed, Inez was there. Clytie hadn't even known where she was until now. The woman would just disappear, everyone knew. But this trauma eclipsed her own, and she was there, on the ground with Lydia, the girl's head on her breast, the three women cleaving to one another. Lydia's screaming tore through the forest, sending birds from limbs and animals rustling over the ground like they were begin hunted.

The boy was relieved when Cornelius pulled him aside. "What happened, son?" Cornelius asked.

"His hand got trapped under a log and the carriage run him through the saw. Tore his arm clean off. He bled to death."

"Whose hand?"

"Cole Clemmons."

Cornelius winced. "Jesus God." He sunk to his knees and then sat himself on the ground, his face in his hands. Something between a cry and cough came from him. At length he began to hiss curses into his hands.

Terrified, the boy said, "I'm sorry, sir. Are you kin to him?"

Cornelius didn't respond at first, and the boy waited. When the boy placed his hand on Cornelius' shoulder, Cornelius answered him. "Not exactly," he said, his voice unsteady. "But we're all sort of kin to one another up here. Tell me, boy, how in hell did this happen?"

But Lydia's wailing was like a wind storm that raged through the trees and across the hillside. Cornelius got up and walked the boy away from the cluster of women. "I don't know, sir," the boy said. "Company said to tell the family it was his fault, the man who died. His fault, Cole Clemmons' fault, not the Company's. A *lapse in concentration* was what they said. I don't know."

"A lapse in concentration?" Cornelius said, rising to his feet. "What in hell does that mean? There wasn't no safety precautions? No one there to watch out for that kind of thing?"

"I don't know. I wasn't there." The boy began to cry, though he tried hard not to.

"Holy Jesus."

Wiping his eyes, the boy looked over at the women on the wet earth. It was an image that would be with him forever, the women clustered together, wailing, keening, their skirts fouled with mud.

He would quit his job when he got back to the mill later that night. "I quit." This was all he would say to the man in the office, to the man who had told him that the blame fell squarely on Cole Clemmons himself, to the man who told the boy to inform Cole's kin of that fact in no uncertain terms. He had coached him about what to say, in fact, insisting that the boy repeat the line about the lapse in attention. He also told the boy to be sure to tell Cole's kin that the Company would provide a casket, and that they could bury him nearby, in Queen's Tooth, but that they would not be responsible for ferrying a body up a mountain, up to Black Boar, or whatever it was called. The boy hadn't known he intended to quit until he had seen the women together on the ground.

Cornelius fumed, but he didn't curse the boy.

Still, the boy thought he needed to tell Cornelius what he had just then decided. "I didn't know this man, this Cole, sir. I'm not gonna work that mill a day longer. I won't do it. I'm sorry." He looked on the trio of keening women once more, and then he ran from them all, speeding toward the rutted Company road that now ran well above Black Boar, winding high onto the mountain and into the areas where the timber was begin harvested.

Cornelius knelt with the women, his arms about all of them. But he alone turned his head when the boy hollered out, "I'm sorry."

Cornelius watched him disappear.

Somewhere in
Western Tennessee

Simms had sheltered Burr for too long. A *single day* was too long in Simms' thinking, and the visit had now stretched out a few weeks. Simms worked as little as possible then. He had to beg the landlord for a reprieve on his already cheap room. To feed Burr and himself wasn't easy with no money coming in. Still, he kept Burr distant from those who normally offered him work. Anything was better than having Burr ask him about the possibility of a job. What trouble that would bring him was untelling, Simms thought. He acted instead as if he were looking for work, when in fact he had to tell some of the people who found odd jobs for him that he was busy with other work, and that he would be unable to help them right now.

He prayed Burr didn't discover the deception.

For his part, though, Burr seemed only to want to eat and drink, and to lay about in Simms' tiny quarters. When he finally told Simms one day that he would be leaving, going to Chicago to work in a slaughterhouse, Simms felt relief wash over him, though he tried to act as if he would miss Burr's Company. Burr knew this was false. And again, Simms knew that Burr knew this, too. Still, Sims asked Burr about the job up in Chicago.

"There was a flyer hanging up in town," Burr said. "They need men up in Chicago to work on the killing floor up there."

"Is that so?" Simms asked.

Burr laughed and said, "Now that's the kind of work I think I can do. Killing … but not the kind they throw you in prison for!"

Simms did his best to laugh.

When Burr had left the next day, Simms walked into town and found one of the flyers on a post at the general store. He tore it down, folded it, and stuffed it in his pocket. Then he went around to the people who sometimes had odd jobs for him to perform. Normally, begging people would have shamed him, would have left a sour taste in his mouth.

But Simms felt relief instead. Burr was gone.

There were four of them who went to Queen's Tooth to retrieve Cole's body: Lydia, Clytie, Cornelius, and Hez. It was the hardest thing Lydia had done in her life, harder than anything with her father even. None of the others wanted Lydia on the duty. They rightly believed that she wouldn't be able to handle it, seeing the casket and the men from the mill, and she a woman big with child. What would that mean for her health? And for the baby's, they said? But she insisted on going. After a long argument, it was Hez's wife, Emma, who said she would stay back on Black Boar and watch over Inez so that Lydia could go. Hez countered her, as did the others, but she quieted them all at once. "Are you gonna tell this young wife that she can't see her husband," she said, "that she can't bring him back with her, to bury him right and proper? You all say she oughn't to go because she's with child. What in hell do any of you know about being with child anyway? Not a one of you knows a thing. Hellfire. Women been doing the same things with child as without for centuries. Cook, clean, take care of menfolk. And now you tell her she ain't up to doing this? You all hush." She looked Lydia in the eye when she had finished. "I'll stay here with Inez," she said. Emma kissed Lydia on the forehead and whispered something in her ear.

And then the party were off.

From the start it had gone badly, and Hez worried that he let himself be henpecked into the worst of situations. Earlier he had yoked his mule to a tree nearest the two rut road, well away from the cabins. When she saw it, Lydia fell to the ground and began to howl. It was the same wagon from years ago, from the day of the killed bear and the burgoo feast. The day she watched the eagle kill the screech owl. It was also the day she had met Cole. She remembered his fine smile, the sight of him across the fire that Clytie tended with her tobacco stake. Cornelius suggested that Lydia go back to Hez's wife and Inez, but Lydia swore she wouldn't. Instead she continued to cry and to fall to her knees as the rest of the party walked silently behind Hez and his wagon. Finally, Clytie and Cornelius lifted Lydia onto the bed of the wagon where she lay on her back, her stomach rounded high on top of her. It would have been a funny scene if it weren't so tragic. The only sound was Lydia's occasional wailing.

For hours no one said a word.

The casket sat out behind the sheriff's office in the center of town. Some deputies and a man from the mill had set it under a lean-to where tools and harnesses were stored. The company had paid the ice man to wrap the casket in a sheet of muslin and pack it with ice. The sheriff was out, and Cornelius announced that he felt they should walk to the mill to have a word with the operators. It was the first time Lydia spoke out. "No, Cornelius. There's no reason to. Nothing will come of it. That place is a curse. I regret my own visit to that hell." Cornelius began to explain his intentions but Clytie shushed him. Hez made a quick visit to the

Rail office to telegraph a message for Cole's parents. With the casket on the bed of the wagon now, they set out for Black Boar.

There was nothing in town for them.

Hez giddy-upped his mule and the wagon creaked its way ahead. It was a forlorn sight to the people walking about the main road. A party of poor mountain folk leading a broken-down wagon out of town, a pregnant, bereaved wife lying prone on her side in the bed of the wagon, her hand on the side of her husband's casket. Most of the townsfolk turned away at the sight, but some were compelled by the spectacle of it, by the sheer sadness of the slow-moving cortege. But just as they headed out toward the two-rut road, a sound came from off in the distance. Heads turned and people stopped. The sound, a long, high whistle, then gathered in strength. Soon the object came into view around a long bend far off in the distance.

The Shay.

A few years back the town added tracks right down the middle of Main Street so that the Shay could make stops outside of the mill. The locomotive ran on a regular schedule, but occasionally it made unexpected runs, and the novelty of this still thrilled the locals, and not only the children and young folk. At the sound of the whistle, men and women drifted out of storefronts and from around the back of the livery. The arrival of the giant locomotive was still a notable event.

Hez's mule halted and then began to buck when Hez gave him a tap with his switch. The mule was going nowhere. The sound terrified him, though the town horses, hitched and unhitched, made nothing of the Shay's arrival. Hez could see the giant cargo of logs on the rail beds as the locomotive neared, and though the arrival of the Shay might normally interest him, he wanted no further reminders of the Company. And he knew the very sight of the giant logs might send Lydia into another crying spell. Hez slashed the mule now, but again the animal only bucked and resisted. There was a danger of upsetting the casket on the wagon bed, Hez realized, and he decided he would have to wait for the Shay to come to a stop. "He's not wanting to pull," Hez announced. "We'll have to wait 'til the engine stops. All this noise has got him worked up."

No one said a word in protest, though they all wanted to be on their way.

Children pulled away from the hands of their mothers, and men walked right up to the tracks to look at the impressive engine that breathed and hissed even at rest. The flatbed cars, loaded with the massive logs, stretched well beyond the curve in the distance. Who knew where it ended? Each bed was stacked high with giant hardwoods, massive trunks that once raised a tall canopy in the forest, now laid low, ready to be processed into boards.

The engine itself was a marvel. Young children peeled with laughter at the sound of its high whistle and the stack that belched a thick cloud of steam into the air. An engineer sat in the cab along with another man, but just what they were doing was unclear. No workers made to ready the engine for water, nor did anyone disembark.

"Why are they stopping?" Cornelius asked. "Don't it just go on to the mill?"

"Not sure," Hez said. He spat on the ground and packed tobacco in his pipe.

"Hell," Clytie said. "How long 'til it moves out?" But no one had an answer, and no one was willing to engage the spectators with such a question, fearing questions in return about the wagon and its sad cargo, something no one wanted to talk about.

Lydia got down from the wagon bed and moved toward the engine. "Lyddie, dear," Hez said. But she nodded to him, as if to say, "I'm alright." She walked alongside the engine, from the dangerous-looking drawhead past the cab and back to the first car that held the massive logs. Like the loader she remembered from before she was married, the Shay seemed alive. Even at rest it seemed to breathe, to seethe. Noises came from in and around the cab and she could see heat rise in blurry waves at the smoke-box. And like the loader, one color dominated, an impression as much as a color: black. She didn't know if it were a real word, but "blackness" came to mind, a blackness that was further thrown into relief by the clean red paint on the cab that identified the engine, #3, and the name of the Company painted in sharp, bold letters, outlined in gold trim. Even the shafts and sleeve couplings at the wheels were painted black. Lydia looked down the line of cars with their timber piled high, and she thought of the sheer force required to haul it all. The loader hauled massive logs onto the beds of the locomotive, but here was the engine that carried all those massive logs at once, not one, but hundreds at a time.

She wasn't aware of how long she had stood there, in a trance of sorts. But she gave a little start when the whistle blew and the shafts and rods beneath the huge cylinders began to turn and spin. Like a monster awakened, the Shay had decided to move. It pulled the heavy cargo yoked to it, slowly at first, but without strain.

The stop in the center of town remained mysterious to Lydia and the party.

Now the Shay was rolling again, up to pace and intent on some other task it had performed thousands of times--dumping its load in the mill pond before it headed off to collect more tim-ber. It never stopped, the engines, the fuel, the men. It just kept going. To the mill, to the water tank, and back to the hills again. This momentum, this force … it was what had killed Cole, she felt. Now the cars sailed by with their massive loads, the giant timbers that lay neatly horizontal in rail bed after rail bed. Never would they rise skyward again, Lydia thought. She turned and made her way back to the wagon where Clytie consoled her, but Lydia quickly broke free from the woman's embrace, not out of anger, but ready to move on. She slid herself onto the wagon bed unaided, unconcerned for any decorum.

Hez would need to wait until the sound of the engine and the hundreds of wheels had ceased before he could set his mule to moving. But when the last car had passed by, Hez realized he couldn't leave just yet. On the other side of the tracks stood the sheriff and the reverend. The groups were surprised to see one another. Lydia thought she saw some uneasiness on the face of the Sheriff, as if maybe he had hoped the party had already collected the casket and headed back up the mountain. Maybe he had seen them moving that way before the train arrived, she thought, and had intended to wait them out without a greeting.

For a moment it was unclear what would happen. The Sheriff and the reverend simply stood still, staring at the party across the tracks. No one said a word. The only sound was that of the Shay and its whistle as it disappeared up ahead. Hez was about to giddy-up his mule when Clytie's voice rang out. "We come to get our loved one, his body. That woman there, in the wagon." She pointed at Lydia who now leaned against the casket, her heaviness braced by Cole's weight and that of the box. "She's with child as you can see. You remember her, don't you? Lydia King was her name. Now it's Clemmons, the name of the man in the casket. Her father was killed by them prisoners you failed to hunt down. Her mother violated. And now her husband's been killed by your sawmill."

"Clytie," Cornelius said, "let's move on."

But Clytie ignored him. "Sheriff, I just want to know when you came to be a lackey for the Company. And how come you never did anything to find them rogues?"

The Sheriff made to respond, but it was Reverend Nichols who spoke out first. "I want you to know that I am aggrieved by the death of that fine man, Cole Clemmons." He spoke formally, as if he were delivering a sermon, confident of the support of his parishioners. "I shall preside over the funeral, if you wish. I want to do so, please. I was on my way just now toward Black Boar, hoping to see you there or to find you on the way."

Clytie felt it was just more of the preacher's ruse, the theatre he used to sway folks to his arguments. She was about to answer him, but Lydia had let herself down from the wagon bed and walked toward the preacher and the sheriff. She spoke over Clytie, "I'll not have you at the funeral, Mr. Isaacs. It would be a black spot on my dead husband's name."

Cornelius and Hez shifted uneasily, their heads bowed. But Clytie felt the force of Lydia's words. It was a stance that she herself had assumed all along, one against the reverend and against the Company he represented. It may have taken the death of Cole to do so, but Lydia understood things now, Clytie felt. She moved to stand by Lydia's side.

It was the Sheriff, not Reverend Isaacs, who answered. "Mrs. Clemmons," he said, "I am deeply sorry for the death of your husband, but you need to understand--"

Now it was Clytie who interrupted and surprised everyone. "Neither of you are welcome on Black Boar," she said, "and you might come to harm if you come up there." Clytie reached low to grab the hem of her day dress. She lifted it, revealing the snakeskin wrap over her scars. For a long moment, she said nothing, just smiled at the pair of men on the other side of the tracks. She pushed her snake leg out in front of her. Both the reverend and the sheriff were stunned.

Clytie said, "You said some time ago, reverend, that Black Boar was under threat of the devil, the serpent you called it." Clytie held her head high, her chest thrust forward and her bloomers in view. "Look for yourself. The serpent has come and taken me."

"And me," Lydia said as she held out the snake leather cinch that fixed her prosthetic thumb. She made to walk across the tracks, toward the men, and Clytie moved to follow her, but the preacher raised his arms, his palms out in a halting gesture. Backing away toward the shops and people behind him, he cried out, "God protect us! Get back!" He dashed off then, back into the crowd that mulled about the storefronts. The sheriff was unnerved, but more embarrassed than fearful of the serpent women of Black Boar. It got worse when Hez burst out laughing, with Cornelius following. Then the two women, together, fell into a laughter utterly inappropriate to their mournful purpose.

But they couldn't stop. They laughed even as the Sheriff walked past them and into his office. The women laughed until they exhausted themselves. Then Hez and Cornelius had to help them up onto the bed of the wagon.

The mule finally began a slow pace toward Black Boar. In the bed of the wagon, the women clung to one another, their laughter turned to tears now.

It was true, what Clytie said, that the Sheriff had long ago given up on solving the King rape and murder. But she was wrong to think that the case was dead. As the town had grown, the Sheriff needed more deputies to keep peace and to do whatever bidding the Company and the Railroad required. A young man was hired on, a local, and a graduate of the Pinkerton Detective school. He was better than the Sheriff and the other few deputies at solving crimes, at ferreting out labor agitators, and at general police work. He knew it would only be a matter of time until the Sheriff retired. Until then he kept his head down and did what he was told. But unlike the Sheriff and the other deputies, the Pinkerton was not given to long sessions at the saloon or to gossiping with the locals. Instead, when things got slow he worked on the King case and on tracking down the escaped convicts. He remembered it from years ago, before he went off to the Academy. It itched at him that the men seemed to make off so easily, and that the sheriff seemed unaffected by it all. The Pinkerton considered detective work a noble calling, and thought the sheriff's office had embarrassed itself—though he never said this openly.

A few months after Cole's funeral, he caught a break in the case.

It was true that Simms had told someone about the little town in western Tennessee. The Pinkerton had interviewed dozens of convicts who were still in Hellerville, men who knew Simms, Burr, and the man Lydia had killed, Henry Byrd. But it was a convict who had been released, the Pinkerton discovered, who would hold the key to the case. Nestor Fugate was a drunk--before, during, and after his incarceration. He knew how to make a potent brew from fermented fruits, which he stole regularly from the mess hall where he worked at Hellerville. The Pinkerton learned about Fugate months into his investigation. A prisoner told him that Fugate had been a friend of Simms, and that he, too, had worked on the rail crew. Maybe Fugate would know about where to look for Simms.

"What can you tell me about this Fugate?" the Pinkerton asked the convict.

"Not much," he said, "beyond that he has a mournful taste for alcohol."

The Pinkerton took two days off, unpaid, to track down Fugate where he was living now, up near Lexington. It didn't take him long to get what he needed, either--the name of the town in western Tennessee where Fugate suspected Simms might be found ... maybe. Fugate himself was living in a cheap rooming house in the meanest part of town. The Pinkerton could smell the alcohol coming off the man as he pushed his way inside the tiny room after knocking politely. "Does anyone but you live here, Nestor?" he asked him as he shut and chained the door behind him.

"No, but what does a deputy from the hills want with me. I done my sentence. Been released and ain't been in any trouble. Why did you chain that door?" It was predator and prey, Fugate could feel it, but there wasn't much he could do about it.

The Pinkerton said, "I'm trying to find out about an escaped convict named Simms Jackson. You two were friends. Where do you think he might have gone to when he escaped?"

"How should I know? If someone is gonna escape, they don't tell others where they're running off to. That's not good sense." But the Pinkerton already knew the man was lying. He saw it in the way he blinked, shifted his eyes. Little things he had learned from the Agency. On the rough wood table against the wall sat a full bottle of corn whiskey and one with a few snorts left in it, something the Pinkerton had noticed when he entered. He smashed the full bottle against the wall, the glass shards and booze flying everywhere. The room quickly filled with the smell of liquor. "Now that smells good," the Pinkerton said. Fugate was terrified, but tried not to show it.

The Pinkerton told the man to sit down at the little table. He sat down across from him then. Shards of glass covered the table, and whiskey dripped in rivulets onto the floor where it continued to pool. He pulled the plug from the other bottle and took a short pull. "I like whiskey," he said. "So do you."

"So what?"

"Well, it's just that you might not get to drink any of this. I intend to keep you from it. At least until I get some answers about where you think this Simms might be living, or where he *might* have fled to when he escaped."

"Like hell I will."

"Settle in, pardner," the Pinkerton laughed. "It's gonna be a long night."

In time, Fugate began to squirm and whine. "You can't keep me here like this, a prisoner in my own home."

"You were a prisoner in your own home long before I got here. You want to drink some of this? There's a few snorts left, and I intend to take them if you don't. You want a sup? Then talk." The Pinkerton drew on the bottle. "Tastes good," he said.

Fugate managed to make it almost two hours. Eventually, the sweat poured from him and the close room began to stink. The

Pinkerton knew he was close to getting what he came for when Fugate sat on his hands to stop them from shaking. Finally, the drunk caved. When he gave up the name of the town in western Tennessee and swore that he knew nothing more, the Pinkerton slid the bottle across the table to him. Fugate drew from it hungrily, the amber liquid spilling down his chin and onto his shirt.

"If I find out any of this isn't true. I'll be back to settle you."

Fugate knew this was true. He nodded and said, "I ain't lied to you." He gulped the last bit from the bottle. "If you find him, don't tell him it was me who told you."

"If I find him in the morning, he'll hang before sundown. He won't know a thing."

Fugate hoped that was true.

Little was said on the return trip to Black Boar. Lydia and Clytie rode in the wagon bed with the casket, arms around one another. At one point Lydia pulled some black hairs from between the old wood slats in the wagon bed and commenced to wailing.

"What is it, Lyddie, dear?" Clytie asked.

Lydia held the coarse hairs out to Clytie. It's the bear, Clytie," she cried, "from way back when. When I saw Cole for the first time." Clytie only clung to Lydia the harder, not feeling it necessary to point out that the hairs could be from any number of animals Hez had killed over the years.

For their part, Cornelius and Hez said almost nothing beyond directing the mule.

Inez and Emma had heard the wagon approaching and were outside to meet the party. When the sad carriage rolled into view around the bend Inez bolted. "Whoa! Whoa!" Hez commanded his mule as Inez jumped in the slow-moving wagon with Clytie and Lydia. She lifted herself up onto the bed without aid, surprising Hez and Cornelius, and then it was the three of them who huddled together. Then Emma walked around to the rear of the wagon and climbed in, joining the others, a cluster of crying, cleaving women, the casket crowding them to one side of the bed. Hez and Cornelius exchanged glances but said nothing.

They waited.

A few families attended the little funeral behind the King cabin, but there weren't many people left on Black Boar. That Cole's parents only knew of the event after he was in the ground most people figured was a blessing. It would have been a burden on them to travel so far, and the burying simply couldn't wait. They understood, they said later, in answer to the message Hez had telegraphed. And they wished Lydia and the others the best. They had known that Cole was working for the Company sawmill, and that Lydia was with child, but little else. In time, they would visit the grave. For now, though, they would endure. Soon enough, a real letter followed. Lydia could barely get through it. Cole's mother's hand was jagged and halted. There was none of the clean cursive lines Lydia remembered, the same clean lines she had taught her son to write, a script Lydia would never see again, in neither mother nor son. The ink had blotted in places where Lydia imagined Cole's mother didn't know what to say, or how to say it. There were crossed out letters where her hand betrayed her, and in places entire lines were roughly scratched out. The mother-in-law she knew would never have sent such a letter. That she did was testament to her state of mind. It was as if to begin again, to write it all down properly, in the clean style she prided herself on, would have been too much for her.

She sent the ugly letter, which spoke to Lydia beyond the words themselves.

The sparsely attended funeral was made worse for some because of Lydia, because of the especially sad figure she cut in her black dress, the hem raised high on the shin because of her swollen belly. Such dresses had been worn by young wives many times in the hills, for funerals come about in all sorts of different ways. But a woman with child cut a different figure in such a dress. It looked odd, and sad, a fact that added to the general sense of tragedy that hung over the funeral. Clytie supported Lydia while one of the old men read a verse form the Bible, something Cornelius had chosen because Lydia was unable to face the question, and because Clytie needed to attend to her in this latest of crises. Clytie told Cornelius to choose a passage, and when he worried her about not knowing which one to choose, she snapped at him, "Just choose one, goddamnit."

He did.

A wind gusted through the trees and shook the dry leaves as the old man read the somber words. The pages of his bible blew at the corners, and he had to stop here and there to find his place. Lydia wailed and Clytie clung to her. The others hoped the passage was short, not because they wanted to go home, but because no one wanted to prolong the agony that had begun before the actual service. Those who witnessed it would never forget it.

The nails of the coffin lid had not been driven flush to the wood, and Lydia had asked Cornelius to open it once before she set Cole in the ground. For Cornelius' part, he generally found it wisest simply to do the bidding of Clytie and Lydia, even of Inez, when he was asked. It caused less trouble in the end, he realized. But he asserted himself this time. "Lyddie, dear," he said, "you don't want to see this. Believe me, please."

"I want to say goodbye, Cornelius."

"But, Dearheart, you will have to live with whatever you see in there. Likely it ain't pretty."

Even Clytie tried to dissuade her. "Lyddie, Corny is right. That's not how you want to remember Cole."

"And by God that *is* how you will think of him, Lydia," Hez said. "There ain't no way around it."

But Lydia held firm.

Cornelius removed the nails with the hammer claw and Lydia looked in. From the waist up Cole's body was covered by a hemp sack. Lydia could read the name of the mill in reverse through the fabric. His legs were uncovered, though, the blood still visible on his pants. Lydia set her hand on Cole's chest, through the hemp sack, and after a minute Cornelius asked if he could nail the lid back.

Lydia shook her head no. She said, "I need to look on his face, Cornelius."

It was what Cornelius hoped she wouldn't say. He knew there was a reason the Company had used the long sack. But Cornelius was as much surprised as Lydia and Hez when Cole's arm fell out as the sack was pulled off. Lydia keened high and Cornelius and Hez immediately worked to get the sack back onto the body. But it was too late now, for all of them. They had seen the carnage, the severed arm and the flash of blood, now turned black, that ran across Cole's shirt and galluses, that ran onto his face and across the bridge of his nose in lines that tapered out on his cheek bone. Another thing, Cole's eyes were open, lifeless and grey.

The image would live with all of them.

Cornelius drove the nails in hard, creating deep indentations in the wood from the force. Birds cawed and flew off, and something scattered off in the brush behind the gravesite. Clytie held Lydia, the two of them on their knees, but she saw Cornelius' rage, saw him shake and swear under his breath as he drove one nail after the other furiously into the soft pine. Inez and a few others in the background looked on, but no one said a word. The only sounds were Lydia's wailing and the fierce strokes of hammer on nail, again and again, until Cornelius had driven them all back down.

By the time the old man had begun the reading, everyone simply wanted it over. But it wasn't to be.

There was more to come.

Somewhere in
Western Tennessee

I n his prison photograph, Simms held a plate at his waist bearing his convict information. The Pinkerton had carefully cut it with a sharp blade, removing the number plate, and then cut the image out in a rough oval. He mounted it on a piece of painted board, and then set it in a cameo portrait frame. The ride to western Tennessee took a few days, and again the Pinkerton suffered the loss of pay.

But it didn't take him long once he got to town.

The Pinkerton didn't want to involve the local sheriff's office, but he needed their help. He walked in unannounced, showed his star and introduced himself as a deputy from Queen's Tooth, "up in Kaintuck." He said he was looking for the man in the photograph, that he was wanted up in Kentucky, and that he may be living here in the little town in western Tennessee, maybe under an assumed name. He never got around to the rest of the story he had cooked up. The deputy took one glance at the photo and said, "That's Raymond Harper. He sometimes sets fence post and grubs weeds and such around here. I think he lives at the rooming house." The deputy was all ready to walk the Pinkerton over to the rooming house himself, but the Pinkerton lied and said he knew where it was, and thank you kindly for the offer. It wasn't anything horrible that the man had done, he said, but it involved a theft from an old person in the Pinkerton's family, supposedly anyway, and he just figured it'd be best to handle it himself, a family grudge and all. The Pinkerton confessed that he wasn't absolutely sure the man had committed the theft after all, but he was there to figure it all out. The deputy stared at the star on the man's suitcoat. The Pinkerton said, "Of course, if you want to come along with me, that's fine, but it's really only talk I want to do. I don't mind if you sit and talk with us."

The deputy looked once more at the Pinkerton's star and said, "No, that's ok. Thank you. Good luck."

The Pinkerton watched the rooming house for Simms' return, and around dusk the man showed up, his work shirt covered in red dust and spotted with horse muck. The Pinkerton took note. He waited for five minutes and then made his way to Simms' door.

It would be the second worst visitor Simms had ever received.

When Simms opened the door, shirtless now, the Pinkerton held out a small leather suitcase full of neatly arranged shaving supplies and men's toiletries. A salesman, Simms thought. But by the time the convict's instincts took over, telling Simms that no salesman would work such a place as the rooming house, it was too late. The Pinkerton had already shoved the suitcase into Simms' gut and taken him to the floor. Simms reached for the hawkbill knife he had in his pants pocket, but it wasn't there.

"This what you're looking for?" The Pinkerton held the knife in his hand.

Simms shifted to his side and reached out to take the Pinkerton's leg and reverse positions. But the Pinkerton was no common lawman. Before Simms could gain any leverage, he felt his own hawkbill rake the length of his back, from ass to shoulder.

It was the worst pain he had ever felt, and his scream hurt the Pinkerton's ears.

"You open your mouth like that again, convict, and I'll cut your ears off," the Pinkerton said. He drew the blade across Simms' ear diagonally. Simms wailed and clamped his hand to his ear, but the blood poured thick through his fingers and down his neck.

"Not to worry," the Pinkerton said. "It's just a cut." He raised his voice, "You can still hear me, right?" Then he laughed. "You convicts make are funny. What? You think that being in the penitentiary makes you tough? Tough is only as good as smart allows. And mister, smart you ain't." Simms' face and neck were a sheet of crimson. He saw where the gap between two floorboards had filled with his own blood, and he knew it was over. The Pinkerton would not be bested, or at least not by Simms alone. For the briefest of moments, Simms wondered what would have happened had Burr still been there. Burr might have gotten the better of this man, he thought. Just as quickly, though, he realized that this would also mean he and Burr would be on the run again.

Simms decided he was better off with the Pinkerton.

The Pinkerton allowed Simms to get to his knees and then to his feet. "You're gonna need some clean pants, I think," he said with another laugh. He punched Simms in the ribs viciously, dropping the man to his knees again.

When it was all over and done, the Pinkerton patched up the cut with bandages he had the foresight to bring along. Within thirty minutes they were headed out of town in the wagon, with one of Simms' hands clasped in irons and secured to a metal ring the lawman had screwed beneath the seat of the vehicle.

Simms was a convict again.

C ornelius, Hez, and some of the other men tamped down the
earth with their spades. Hez's wife, Emma, had arranged
bunches of wildflowers, neatly tied together with vines she has
stripped of their green and worked in water to make pliable. Each
one was a little different than the next. Now she set them around
the grave, placing them at evenly spaced distances. Cornelius
tamped down a spot of earth that didn't need it, and the other
men shifted their feet and drew their wives to them. One of the
last cows on Black Boar lowed its miserable sound and a sudden
wind shook leaves above. Finally, one of the wives kissed Lydia
and told her to seek her out if she needed for anything. The others followed suit, and after the old man who read the Bible passage had taken leave, it was over, mercifully.

Or so everyone thought.

The last of the visitors was just out of sight when Lydia collapsed on the mounded earth of the grave. Again, Clytie and
Inez kneeled to comfort her, to lift her once more from the earth
and to get her into the cabin. They cooed her sweetly, "Come on
now, dear, we're gonna get you inside. Come on now." But a low,

guttural sound emerged from Lydia's throat, rising as it gained intensity. This was no longer the keening widow, or at least it was *more* than just that. The women hushed and petted her, but the agony was too great to be borne. The scream became something primal, and it was Emma who first noticed. "Oh, Lord. That baby's coming."

The Sheriff was smart enough to know that the Pinkerton had more chance of getting information from Simms than he did. He was also smart enough to know that the Pinkerton would become Sheriff the minute he retired, and he didn't want any trouble once the time came. Best to be on good terms with one's replacement, he thought. And so the Pinkerton was asked to find out what Simms knew about Burr Hollis, before they hung the man. After all, it was the Pinkerton who had captured him in the first place. It was his prisoner, in a manner of speaking.

Queen's Tooth had grown since the trouble up on Black Boar, years ago. There was a holding cell for criminals and drunks who blew into town to gamble or fight at one of the two saloons. Sometimes a prostitute, or one of the johns from Miss Laura's house, was locked up if there had been a dust-up. As the town had grown, its vices had expanded, but so had its economy. It was a double-edged sword. To deal with changing times, the town had to build a larger holding cell, several cells now, in fact. They were whitewashed and clean, the walls painted with the same white that covered both the Rail and timber Company buildings.

When Simms' was taken for a bathroom break, the Pinkerton had set a three-legged stool inside the cell. As he was let back in, Simms noticed it right away, set only a few feet away from the narrow cot that sat against the whitewashed wall. Something in him told him that the Pinkerton was behind this, whatever it was. And something also told him that to move it away was a bad idea. He simply lay down on his cot and waited. But the Pinkerton never showed. When Simms had gotten so impatient that he couldn't take it anymore, he called out for a deputy.

"What's this stool doing in here?" he asked the man.

"I don't know, you sunuvabitch," the deputy said. "Go to bed. And don't bother me no more."

Simms slept restlessly, and when he awoke, the stool still sat there. He asked again when he was taken to use the toilet the next morning. "Why's that goddamn stool in my cell?"

It was a different deputy this time. "Shut your fuckin' mouth," he said, "you rapin', murderin' sunuvabitch."

The stool was there when he returned, and it sat there all day. It wasn't until Simms returned to his cell from the toilet the next morning that the Pinkerton sat there, rigid and formal-like. He had moved the stool even closer to the cot, and Simms had to squeeze around the man in order to get onto it, the only other place to sit in the cell. Simms sensed what was about to happen, and he thought he'd maybe gain some advantage from a salvo of his own. "What in the hell do you want?" he said. "You already got your man, haven't you? What do you want now?" The Pinkerton laughed through his nose and looked at Simms. But he said nothing. He simply looked at him, neither with malice nor pleasure.

Eventually Simms said, "Well?"

The lawman up and removed his jacket, placing it neatly between the bars of the cell so that it lay folded over the cross bar. He pulled down his galluses and stretched his arms behind his back and up in the air. He looked straight into Simms' eyes and flexed his neck from side to side. Simms figured he knew what he was in for, and he readied himself.

But the Pinkerton sat down on the stool again. "I need to know where is Burr Hollis," he said.

Simms had guessed correctly. It was information on Burr the man wanted, something Simms had figured they'd ask him about. But in the two days he had sat in the cell, no one had said a word about Burr. Simms had been thinking on it, though. His situation, his imprisonment. It had all been Burr's doing, in one sense at least. Yes, Simms had agreed to the escape years ago, and to what happened on Black Boar. But Burr had made things worse with the old hermit on the mountain. For the last several years, Simms had been living a life in fear, hiding and running. He regretted the whole thing. It was the singular emotion he had felt over the last many years: regret. He'd have been better off in Hellerville, he figured, better off had he simply served his time. He'd have been out by now, maybe.

But one doesn't say no to Burr Hollis.

And Simms had agreed to the escape when Burr proposed it. What choice did he have? And now look at him. In a cell, soon to walk the gallows. For his part, Simms decided that he owed nothing to Burr. He would tell the Pinkerton about Burr working the killing floor in Chicago. He hoped they would catch him. To hell with the convicts' code, he figured. More than that, to hell with Burr. He had told himself that if he was asked about Burr, he'd tell them what he knew.

But his resolution didn't last long.

Something happened when the Pinkerton had said the name out loud. "I need to know where is *Burr Hollis*." It was this, the name spoken aloud, that changed it all for Simms. Outside of using Burr's name himself when the man came uninvited to see him, Simms hadn't heard Burr's name for years, hadn't heard it actually *spoken* aloud. It shook him.

And it was worse the second time the Pinkerton said it: "I said

I need to know where is *Burr Hollis*." Simms realized then that his will had left him. He thought about it later on, after the Pinkerton had left his cell. The best he could figure was that it would be better to die on the gallows than to die at Burr's hands. It would be better to be beaten by the Pinkerton, perhaps even to be beaten to death. Rationally this made little sense. If Burr were captured, he'd be placed in another cell, surely. He'd have no chance to do harm to Simms. So why not tell the Pinkerton what he knew, tell him about Burr working the killing floor in Chicago? But Simms couldn't answer this. He only knew he couldn't give the man up. He feared him ... still. For now, though, Simms knew what was in store for him.

The Pinkerton stood from the stool and rolled up his sleeves.

C lytie and Inez turned Lydia on her back and then realized that what Emma said was true. Lydia held her stomach in both hands, her teeth clenched. Sweat matted her hair to her forehead, and her face became a mottled, red mass of agony.

Clytie said, "Let's get her inside, Corny!"

"It's too late for that," Inez said. "The worry of all this has brung it on. You men, go make a fire and put water on the fire."

Emma pulled off Lydia's bloomers and placed a hand on her abdomen. "You need to push now, Lyddie," she said. She held Lydia's good hand and Clytie swept the wet tresses from her brow.

"I can see the head," Inez said. "You're doing good, Lyddie. We're gonna catch this one soon. Keep pushing."

In a moment the baby was in Inez' arms. "Go get some whiskey," Inez said. This cord has got to be cut." She drew a blade from her dress, one neither Clytie nor Emma knew she carried.

When Clytie got back from the cabin with the jug, Inez poured the liquid over the knife blade and onto the cord where it entered the baby. In one swift thrust she drew the knife through the cord and then poured more of the whiskey over the baby and onto her own hands. She tied off the cord and then swaddled the baby in Lydia's bloomers.

It was a girl.

The Pinkerton lifted his galluses and pulled on his coat. Patches of blood covered his shirt and a splotch was spread across one cheek. "I don't think he knows where Burr is," he told the Sheriff.

The Sheriff shook his head. "Well, what do you want to do? We can hang him tomorrow. But a day or two later might be better. Could be good for everyone if we can get a story in the paper. Anyhow, we can't keep this quiet much longer. People are gettin' curious who we got in here, and why we ain't saying anything about it."

"I'd like to have one more chance with him," the Pinkerton said. "Say a couple days from now. Let him think it's all over. Then I'll go work him again. You can call that newsman now if you want. Just make it plain the prisoner doesn't know anything about the other one."

"Do you want to talk to the newsman yourself? I mean, you're the one's caught him? You did well."

"No," the Pinkerton said. "I don't mind if you tell him I was the one who tracked him down. But I don't want to talk to no newsman."

"Ok, son. We'll set the execution for Saturday, four days from now. Will be nice for people to come and see. Do this town good to have it resolved."

The Pinkerton set his derby on his head and said, "Well, half-resolved, I guess."

"You did well, son. Better than anyone could have."

The Pinkerton shrugged and said, "Anyhow, I'll be on patrol tonight. Likely have to break up a fight over at Creely's or at the saloon. You know how they are over there. If you need me, send someone."

"Ain't you going to change your shirt?" the Sheriff asked.

"Why? They know it ain't my blood."

I t was the young boy who had worked at the mill who again delivered the news.

The story in the *Mountain Sentinel* had announced Simms' capture. Few of the new residents in Queen's Tooth knew of the incident from years ago, but the mill boy's mother remembered. She read the story to her son, and his eyes went wide when she said Lydia's name: *Lydia Clemmons, formerly Lydia King*.

"I know her, Momma," he said. "Her husband was that man who got killed at the mill. I took the news up to her, remember?"

"Oh, Lord," his mother said. "That was Lydia King? You didn't tell me that. She's still up there? Lydia King?"

"Her name is Clemmons now. I told you, Lydia Clemmons. She had a baby in her when I brung the news about her husband."

"Law, it's been years since all that. I don't know her as Clemmons, just as King. And her pregnant and the husband dead?"

"Yes."

The article hadn't said much about the King family, only that Preston King had been killed eight years ago, along with one of the escaped convicts. Lydia and Inez were mentioned, but there was nothing about the violation or about Cole's recent death."

In his mind, the boy saw Lydia again. He saw her face and heard the cries that rent the air and tortured his ears. He saw Clytie now, too, and Cornelius. The sense of alarm, that fear that gripped him when he first saw the pregnant woman fall to her knees, surged through him once again. He felt his heartbeat in his neck and ears. It all rushed back on him, the feel of his arms under Lydia's shoulders and his fingers on the warm skin of her throat as he reached underneath her armpits.

"How will she get word of this, way up there?" the boy asked his mother.

"Who, son?"

"Lydia Clemmons."

"Lord, I don't know."

"The story says there will be an execution. Do you think she might want to know that?" he asked her.

"I don't know. Maybe. Yes, I suppose. Might give her some comfort."

The boy reached for his boots and said, "I'm going to deliver the news to her. Can I take that newspaper?"

"Son … I don't know as to you doing this," she said.

He stared at her and said, "I need to do this, Momma."

She handed him the newspaper. "You best get going if you plan to return by nightfall," she said.

"I'm going now," he said.

"Son, there's something else to think about. It says something else here, at the end. And I don't know how it will be to tell her this."

"What's that?"

"It says the other one is still out there somewhere, if he ain't dead, that is."

"The other one?" the boy asked.

"Yes. One of them is still running free somewhere. The

captured one don't know where that other one is. Or he ain't saying."

"Who? What other one?"

"Says here his name is Burr Hollis."

The mill boy walked a long arc around the spot where Lydia had collapsed the last time he was up on Black Boar, though in his head he saw it all again, heard it all again. He winced even now. It was only then that he wondered about the baby, and he stopped dead in his tracks to consider things. Babies died all the time, especially up on little settlements like Black Boar, he thought. What if she, too, had lost the baby, in the stress of her husband's death. Would the news of a convict's capture mean anything different? Or would it only be more hell to bear? And what if she hadn't had the baby? What would the news do to her, a pregnant woman near birth? For a moment, he considered turning around. It might be better to avoid the whole thing, like his mother had suggested. But there was also part of him that needed to tell Lydia he had quit the mill, that he was not a part of it any longer. In the end, he decided to soldier on, to tell the woman that one of the marauders had been captured and was set to hang. As he neared the cabin, he heard a baby crying. Something in the sound heartened him.

He had hoped someone would be out and about, but there was no one, and he knocked on the cabin door. It was Inez who answered. She recognized him.

The boy said, "I was here not long ago. I brung the news about Cole Clemmons, the man I worked with in the mill who died … who was *killed*." Inez looked over her shoulder, stepped outside and closed the door behind her. She asked the boy what he wanted.

"There's news that Mrs. Clemmons might want to hear. It's

in the newspaper here, from today." He handed Inez the paper which he had turned open to the article about Simms' capture. "They caught one of them marauders from way back when, one of them convicts. I thought Mrs. Clemmons might want to know. It's in the paper here." He pointed to the article.

Now it was Inez who almost fell to the ground as she read the report. Her cheeks reddened and tears brimmed in her eyes. The boy saw it, and again he wondered if he had made the right decision in coming up on Black Boar. But what could he do now but stay the course?

Finally, Inez said, "Come in."

The boy saw Lydia near the hearth at the back of the cabin, sitting on one of Cornelius' chairs feeding the baby. He watched the infant's little hand lift to grab Lydia's breast, and he listened to the soft sounds she made as Lydia shifted her about in her arms. Again, he wondered if he had made the right choice in coming up to Black Boar, and again he told himself it was too late to reconsider. Lydia looked at the boy and for an instant he saw a fear register in her eyes. But just as quickly he saw it disappear. Her husband was already dead and buried, the boy realized. He could bring no worse news than that. Inez asked the boy if he could wait a few minutes until the baby had been fed.

"Yes ma'am," he said.

In time the baby released its grip and fell asleep in Lydia's arms. She set her down in the little crib Cornelius had put together quickly from wood he had around.

"Let's go outside," Inez said.

Lydia looked back at her sleeping daughter before she closed the cabin door on her. Clytie had been working around the back of the cabin, and when she saw the group, she joined them. Inez delivered the news: "This young boy come up here to tell us about what came out in the newspaper today." She handed the paper to Clytie. "They captured one of them marauders. Not the one that killed my Preston, but the other one." She looked at the boy for an instant. "You know, the one that done me that way."

Clytie and Lydia stood stock still. "Hellfire," Clytie said. "Do you mean it?"

"It's all right there," Inez said as she pulled Lydia into a hug. She turned to the boy. "How come you come up here, anyway? Who sent you?"

"My momma read the story to me this morning. I recognized your name, Cole's name." He looked at Lydia. "I brought bad news the last time. I had to do it then. The Company made me. I hope this news is better. Either way, I thought you should know this."

Lydia pulled away from Inez and stared at the boy.

He looked at his feet and said, "Anyway, I thought you should know. And I also thought you should know that I quit my job at the mill. After what happened and all. Just wanted you to know, is all."

Tears wet Lydia's face but she didn't speak. She looked at the boy as he told his story, and then she smiled at him. Suddenly, she moved toward him and took him in her arms.

Then it was he who broke down in tears.

The Pinkerton never got anything more from Simms, try as he did. His knuckles were raw and his shoulders pained him. "He don't know anything," the Pinkerton said to the Sheriff.

"Well, hell then."

"Yeah. Goddamnit, though."

The sheriff sighed and said, "You done well. Let's not forget that."

"I suppose so," the Pinkerton said.

The Sheriff set his hat on his head and said, "Well, Saturday will be the day. I'll get them boys to build the gallows. It won't be much, but it'll do the job."

"Ok, then."

Simms didn't bother to clean up. He sat on his cot, dejected and in pain. The bowl of water and cotton cloth a deputy had sat just outside the bars of his cell sat there untouched. Part of him wished he had told the Pinkerton what he knew about Burr's whereabouts. His ear and back still pained him terribly from the Pinkerton's first assault. And the second beating nearly killed him. He thought about it still, wondering why he hadn't come clean about Burr's whereabouts. But in his mind's eye he saw Burr's silver cuspid smile.

And then he figured maybe he had done the right thing after all.

I wonder if he knows where the other one is at," Clytie said. She had taken up her gun, and she paced the floor of the little cabin now, back and forth.

"Clytie," Cornelius said, "can you set that back on the wall, kindly. It makes me nervous, a loaded gun in a room, and a baby in here with us."

"I know how to handle a gun, Corny. Don't you worry on it."

"Lord," Cornelius said. "I don't even know why you're carrying it around. They already caught the man, didn't they?" He shook his head.

Clytie snapped back, "They caught *one* of them, Corny. That means there's one still out there." The baby began to cry at Clytie's outburst.

"Hell," Cornelius said, "just look at what we have now. Just listen to it. Three women and a tiny little girl. All worried to death because of that gun. Hell, Clytie."

"By God, Corny," Clytie said. She put the gun on its rack above the mantle. "There, I put it up. Will that do?" But Cornelius didn't answer. "Will that do!" Clytie hollered.

The baby was screaming now, and Lydia began to coo her softly. She tried to feed her, but the baby wasn't interested.

"Yes, dear," Cornelius said. "Yes, yes, yes." He sat down heavily at the table and removed a piece of wood and his hawkbill knife from a pocket.

"We need to settle down," Inez said. "Why are we gettin' on each other?" She turned to her daughter. "Lyddie, dear, what do you think of all this?"

But Lydia didn't know what to think. "Well …" she said.

For a moment no one said a word. The only sound came from Cornelius' whittling.

Hoping to break the spell of the news and to end the little quarrel with her husband, Clytie asked, "What is that, Corny?"

Cornelius took his time in answering. "A little play pretty, for Colette," he said as he held the piece up. A tiny horse was forming in his hand.

"It's lovely," Clytie said. She reached out and touched Cornelius' forearm.

"Yes, Corny, it is," Lydia said.

"Lydia!" Inez demanded.

"What, Momma?" Lydia said.

"What do you think of all that in the newspaper? And what about you, Clytie. And you, Cornelius?"

Lydia shifted Colette around and stroked her chubby cheeks with her fingertips. The baby wrapped her tiny hand around Lydia's snakeskin prosthetic. Cornelius saw it and shook his head. "Lord," he said. "That snake leather you two wear."

Clytie smiled and Lydia and Inez laughed through her nose so as not to agitate the baby.

"Well," Lydia finally said. "I'm pleased they caught that one. That Pinkerton. We'll need to talk to him, Momma."

"Yes," Inez said. "A determined man, according to that story."

"But not that goddamn Sheriff," Clytie hissed.

"Clytie," Cornelius said. "Hush. The baby."

Clytie nodded. "Yes, yes. I know," she said. She took a few deep breaths and said evenly, "It's just that … well, I think if it wasn't for that Pinkerton, they wouldn't have caught the man."

"Likely that's so," Inez said. She sighed and added, "Well, I guess I need to tell you that I want to see him hang. Not for what he done to me. But for Preston."

Now it was Clytie and Cornelius whose eyes welled with tears. The baby had begun to cry again, and Lydia gave her over to Cornelius. She wrapped her arms around her mother and Clytie together, a cluster of aggrieved women huddled together once again.

It was pain and succor, once again.

Finally, Lydia pulled away and said, "I've not decided on going to that hanging. I'm not sure about it, but I guess I can do it, if Momma can."

"We can get Hez and his wagon," Cornelius said as he shifted the baby around in his arms. "He'll take us into town."

"Wish they could find that other one," Clytie said. "Wish that Pinkerton had a line on that one."

"The paper said they interrogated the one they got, and he don't know," Inez said.

"Maybe he's lying, though," Clytie said. "Them convicts cover up for one another." Cornelius saw Clytie's eyes rest on the gun on the mantle again, though she didn't reach for it.

"I'm gonna go and see if I can find Hez," Cornelius said. He handed the baby off to Lydia.

"Hold on, Cornelius," Inez said. "I want to look for some bloodwort over by Hez' cabin. Let me come with you." The two walked out together.

The baby still fussed but this time she settled down to feeding. When it got quiet Lydia asked Clytie, "Do you still have that tintype? The one that marauder left behind?"

"Yes. Why do you ask, Lyddie?"

Lydia shifted the baby around and said, "I studied some about that raider. Maybe we could use it, the tintype. Maybe."

Clytie rose from the table and took down the gun. "She walked the floor of the cabin, back and forth, and asked, "What are you thinking, Lyddie?"

"Clytie, why do you have that gun down again?"

"I don't know. I just do. You sound like Corny. Hellfire. Tell me what you're thinking."

Lydia smiled and laughed. And then Clytie did, too. She put up the gun.

Lydia told her the plan.

The following day they mounted two mares and rode down into Queen's Tooth one more time. Cornelius badgered the women to tell them why they needed to go, to tell him what devilment they were up to, and to answer him, whatever it was, what good it would do. He worried about Clytie's temper with the Sheriff and he was determined this time to let himself be heard. "You will *not* take that rifle with you. I *forbid* it," he said.

But it was Lydia who answered him. She told Cornelius that she needed to talk to the Sheriff before the execution. It was important. She wanted Clytie with her, a woman friend, she said. That, too, was important."

"But *why*?" Cornelius said.

"Cornelius," Lydia said, "will you deny me this? A widow with a baby?"

Cornelius knew he was defeated again. He shook his head and dug his hawkbill into a piece of whittling wood. Finally, he said, "Be careful on them mares, especially that grey, Clytie. She can spook sometimes."

The Sheriff told Lydia "No, absolutely not."

She could not talk to the prisoner. Whether it was an issue of Christian forgiveness or personal peace of mind or solace or whatever, it simply didn't matter. It wasn't part of any protocol to allow a victim to talk to a prisoner before an execution, or anytime, anywhere, no matter what. Lydia could come to the execution, naturally, and hopefully she'd feel avenged afterward, the Sheriff said. But she would not go in there and talk to the man.

Clytie let the Sheriff have it, railing at him for years of inefficiency, for being a Company toadie, and for being a second-rate lawman.

But it didn't matter. The Sheriff wasn't going to budge. He set the women on their way, wishing them well. He said he hoped to see them at the execution. Clytie slammed the office door so hard she was surprised the glass didn't break.

On their way out of town, though, they ran into the Pinkerton. Though he had never met either one of them, he knew who they were. Lydia thought this was just what a detective did, used his instincts to reveal identities. But Clytie later told her it must've been easy to know the two women. Who else came down from the hills with a prosthetic thumb and half a leg covered in snake leather? When they ran into him, right there on Main Street, he greeted them kindly by name and tipped his bowler. The women said that they read the story in the paper. They thanked him for all he had done. And then Clytie named it to him, right then and there, Lydia's plan, hoping that maybe the Pinkerton would be able to sway the Sheriff to it.

The man smiled and said, "I had several interviews with that devil, ladies. He's not talking about his accomplice. I don't think he knows a damn thing, in fact. I tried hard to get him to talk to me." He rubbed his raw knuckles, sure that they would understand. Clytie began to rehearse the story again. "Lydia was the victim here, a Christian woman who wanted to forgive her tormentor. She needs the peace that comes with offering forgiveness. The fact that she wasn't allowed this decency is only more punishment she will suffer."

The Pinkerton made to answer, but it was Lydia who spoke out, "Look at this, sir." She held out the tintype. That Simms, the prisoner, he dropped this on the night he violated my mother. There's a girl he's posed with. I can tell she means something to him by the way he's looking at her. And how she stands there, too. Her head on his shoulder and all. I think maybe I can get him to tell me something about the other one, that Hollis, if I show him this."

The Pinkerton took the tintype and looked at it. It was Simms, he realized. He smiled at Lydia and said, "How did you get this?"

"It turned up after that raid," Lydia said. "A boy come across it in a laurel patch nearby. That rogue must've lost it trying to get away. By that time, the Sheriff had given up trying to catch those men, I reckoned. I set it in a drawer, buried underneath things. Then I remembered it when I read about the execution. I think I can use it." It wasn't a complete lie, but Lydia thought it would work best.

The Pinkerton knew as much instinctively, but he said only, "How are you gonna do that, ma'am?"

"I'm gonna offer to give him the tintype, so he can have it with him when he dies. But only if he tells me what he knows about that other one."

The Pinkerton laughed and said, "Well, how do you know he'll want this with him when he hangs?"

"He had it with him when he escaped, didn't he?" Lydia said. "Of all things, he took this with him. It must *mean* something to him."

The Pinkerton stared hard at the tintype, turning it every which way. "Why don't you let me ask him. I'm a detective. I know about such things. I was the one who caught him, you know?"

Lydia took a deep breath and said, "But if he wants to be forgiven for what he's done, and he just might, you ain't the one can do it. I am." The Pinkerton considered this. He sensed she had more to say, too, and he waited. Lydia said, "And I'm a woman. It's harder for a man to refuse a woman." Her voice caught when she said the next part. "Especially a man like this one."

The Pinkerton looked once more at the tintype. It wasn't the way he wanted it to go, but it tortured him to think that he might never get the other raider. He sighed and shook his head. A little smile appeared at the corner of his mouth. "I don't know as I like it," he said. "But you might be right. Let me talk to the Sheriff."

He handed her the tintype. "You're a clever one, aren't you?" he said. It was how a man who knew he was bested by a woman would talk. But Lydia sensed something genuine in it, too.

She took the tintype and lowered her eyes. "Thank you."

The Pinkerton explained to the Sheriff that there was no need for anyone to know that Lydia would have spoken with the prisoner, and that maybe, just *maybe*, the idea would work. He said that the sheriff could right a wrong here--and more importantly for the Sheriff, though he didn't say this openly, the Sheriff could retire without the shadow of the case forever hanging over him, the tale of the convict never captured.

It was then that the Sheriff saw the light.

He finally agreed that Lydia could talk to the prisoner, but only with the Pinkerton just around the corner, out of sight but ready to act should something happen. Lydia would need to sit on a stool against the wall that faced the cell. She'd be well out of reach there, the sheriff and the Pinkerton agreed. She would give the tintype to Simms if he delivered the information about Burr's whereabouts. She would slide it across the floor at the cell door and leave.

"What if he lies about it, just to get a hold of the picture?" the Sheriff said.

"That's when we beat hell out of him again," the Pinkerton

said. "Take the tintype and hang him high. What difference will it make then?"

The wood nymph looked different, but Simms recognized her. He felt the shame, yes, but he had long ago accepted who he was. He figured Lydia was there to confirm what he already knew about himself, that he was hell-bound, for certain. But after she told him who she was, she didn't say anything. Just looked at him. Just waited. Simms didn't know what to say.

"Miss, I'm going to burn in eternal fire," he finally managed. "I guess you already know. I don't know what to say to you except that. I hope it brings you some comfort, my death, my damnation." He stood with his hands on the iron bars and lowered his head. "I am sorry for what I done. You can watch me hang. I hope you do." When Lydia didn't reply after some time, he lifted his head to look at her. She stood next to the stool and looked at Simms. Finally, she smiled thinly and said, "Looks like someone busted you up some. I bet it was that Pinkerton. I'm sorry for that. It's not what I asked for, you know."

Simms was at a loss. "That's ok," he said. "I deserved it."

Lydia returned nothing but the closed smile. She gave him

nowhere to go. Finally, Simms said, "Is there something I can do for you?"

She shook her head.

Simms sighed and lowered his head against the bars again. He knew he couldn't ask her to leave, knew it wasn't right even to ask why she was there. The Sheriff must have given her permission. But he didn't know what she wanted. He felt trapped, imprisoned beyond the cell. "Well ..." he said.

"Well?" Lydia said.

Simms nearly asked her, *What do you want?* But he didn't. He felt the moisture on his palms against the iron bars and he began to feel nauseous, not exactly like how Burr made him feel, but uneasy, scared in a way different from what he felt daily because of what he knew awaited him. He was going to die, and that he feared. But this woman, standing across from him. He couldn't make her leave. Her presence was maddening. And there was something else. The snake skin cinch. It recalled for him the bloody floor of the little cabin, years ago, and the young girl's thumb that lay there, the white bone visible against the flesh and blood. He felt the nausea rising in him. Again, he asked, "Is there anything I can say to you?"

"No," Lydia said. "I just come to see you."

Simms felt a bead of sweat run over his rib cage. He wanted to sit on his cot but thought that would be an affront somehow. Still, he felt his legs weakening and he weighed the consequences of it. He shuffled his feet and said, "Well, I don't know then."

Lydia said nothing, and at length Simms decided to ask about something he felt he probably shouldn't ask about. He needed an escape, though, and he gambled on it. "Is your mother alive?" he asked.

"Yes," Lydia said. "She's poorly though. Ever since ... well, you know."

Simms regretted the remark even before Lydia began to answer. It would have been better if the mother were dead, he thought, rather than ill and suffering. But it was too late now. Simms chest welled up. He struggled to get air. "Oh, hell!" he finally blurted out. "I'm hell-bound, woman. What else do you want from me? I can't take it back, but I'll burn. You can know it. You and your momma can know it. Every day I'll burn!"

Down the hall and around the corner the Pinkerton took a step in the direction of the cell, but he checked himself when he heard Lydia's voice.

"Maybe not," she said.

There was a long pause, and again Simms was the one to break it. "What do you want from me, then? I've asked you now more than once."

"It's me that needs something from you," Lydia said. "Not the other way around."

"How do you mean?" Simms said, flopping down on the cot, his face in his hands. Eventually he looked up at Lydia, who still stood bolt upright. "Why don't you take that stool there," Simms said. "That's for you."

"I'll stand, but thank you," Lydia said.

"Well," Simms said after yet another pause. "What is it I can do for you, then?"

"You can allow me to forgive you. That's what I need more than anything."

"Go ahead and forgive me, then. You have my permission, though you don't really need that, do you?"

"I need you to *accept* my forgiveness, and my mother's forgiveness, which she's asked me to get from you. She's poorly, like I said, and can't come here."

Around the corner and out of sight, the Pinkerton smiled wide at the lie.

Simms said, "Ok, you've got it. And I thank you. And I'm grateful for your forgiveness."

Lydia breathed a sigh of relief and tears welled up in her eyes. She took the stool and worked to catch her breath. "I'm sorry," she said between the tears. "It's just something I needed, and my mother, too. You will *not* burn in hell, Mr. Jackson." Her body began to shake now, and she covered her face with her hands. "God will accept you. I thank him. I do. Oh, Lord God above, thank you."

Simms felt it then. It washed over him all at once. A state of Grace. He had heard of this, from other cons in the prison, those who had devoted their lives to God, men who had committed unspeakable sins. They claimed to have been saved, to have been offered God's grace. And now Simms felt it, too. His heart raced, but there was a warmth that ran though him, and a sense of peace he hadn't felt since before prison. He tried to speak to Lydia, but his voice caught in his throat.

Lydia saw it all through her fingers and tears. When she thought she had waited long enough, she said, "That other one. We want to forgive him, too. My mother and me. And I know my father wants it, too, though he can't say so, naturally."

"What?" Simms said.

"That other raider, that Burr Hollis. He needs to be forgiven, too."

Simms lifted himself from the cot and moved to the bars of the cell. "That one, ma'am, he's not righteous. I mean, none of us are, none of my kind, I mean. But he won't want your forgiveness. He's a different kind, ma'am."

"He needs to have the *offer* of it. He can decline, but he needs to have the offer. You don't know what people want or need. We're talking about eternal salvation, about hellfire or grace, one or the other. None of us can decide that for someone else. He needs the chance to say yes or no to me, to my mother, and to my dead father, who he killed like an animal."

"Ma'am, I don't know where he is …"

Lydia closed her eyes and breathed in deeply through her nose. Her chest rose and fell and rose and fell again. Finally, she raised only her eyes and whispered, "Now, I know that ain't true. You and I both know that ain't true."

Simms held firm, "By God, I don't know." But Lydia could hear it in his voice, could see it in him. He knew.

Now was the time, she thought. "I have something that belongs to you," she said.

Simms shook his head. "Ma'am?"

"You must have lost it that night, the night of the raid," she said. She reached into the pocket of her dress and held out the tintype. He knew what it was, though he couldn't really see it. He knew the shape of it, the thick black lines that framed the image, the cut corners. He saw the image itself only for an instant, but that, too, he knew. It was the solution of an old mystery. He never knew what had happened to it for sure, only that he had lost it sometime between the escape and the day after the raid. He had often wondered if it had fallen out when he and Burr changed clothes in the King cabin after the violation and murder. What if they had found it, the King family. This, too, he had wondered over the years. How would they have reacted? A happy image of the man who had helped destroy their family, who had violated the mother, an accomplice in the father's murder.

The memory had made him cringe, and yet he had always mourned the loss of the tintype. Surely he deserved it, the loss. But now here it was, magically. And from the woman who would forgive him his greatest sins. A part of him thought maybe it was meant to be. In exchange for his life he could possess the tintype, the singular moment of bliss in his life. He and his sister, happy, for the moment at least. That was before his life turned. Before the horrors of his mother, the abuse of his father, and of everything else that bedeviled him, that led him astray. For her part, though, Lydia only knew he wanted it. She saw it now in his eyes, in his fingers that uncurled so slightly on the bars of the jail cell.

He wanted the tintype.

But he wouldn't get it for nothing. Lydia held the image out in front of her. "Who is this pretty girl?" she asked.

Simms nearly reached out for it. He couldn't help himself. Lydia caught it, too, a little movement in the shoulder and upper arm, stifled almost as quickly as it started.

"Who is she to you?" Lydia asked when Simms hadn't answered.

"My sister," Simms whispered.

"Oh," Lydia said. She smiled now, but with her lips closed. "She has lovely hair. And her face … She's a true beauty."

"Yes," Simms said. He took a deep breath before he continued. "She's dead now. My mother … she killed her. She made her die, I mean."

"Oh, lord. I didn't know. I'm sorry." Lydia turned the tintype this way and that but kept the image out of Simms' sight. "She's passed on, you say?"

Simms' eyes glossed over and he said, "She killed herself. She took her own life. My mother … she was a witch. She's the one made my sister do it."

Lydia lowered her eyes and then placed the tintype in the pocket of her dress. She romse and moved close to the cell door. Simms shrunk back. Lydia whispered, "No, come here. I want to give it to you." She reached out and took Simms' hand. He felt the snakeskin leather now, and the prosthetic thumb. But he also felt Lydia's hand, her long fingers and her warm skin on his own. He felt the heavy thrum of his heartbeat in his temples, and in his throat and chest.

Around the corner, it was all the Pinkerton could do to remain out of sight. It was torture to him. And yet, he knew something was happening. He tilted his head back and stared at the ceiling. He waited.

"I need to know," Lydia said. She looked Simms dead in the eyes.

"But, I … I can't," Simms said.

Lydia ran her fingers across the back of his hand. "Yes, you can. Your sister needs to see you before you go. The *real* you. The good one ... before things with your mother, I mean. Now you know that. Do it for her. For her memory." She reached into her pocket with her good hand as if to draw out the tintype. But she waited.

Simms could almost feel the tintype in his hand. The cut corners he liked to run his fingers across in his cell at Hellerville. The image of his sister he would stare at. The only human who had ever treated him decently. Long gone now, but still there in the picture, just out of reach. It would take only one remark. About where they could find Burr. He felt she would honor her part of the bargain. She would give him the tintype. That's why she was here, he figured. To trade. Simms did his best to get a look down the hall. He wondered if that Pinkerton was behind all of this.

Lydia saw it working in him. She drew out the tintype and held it in her good hand. She placed it on the iron cross piece that ran horizontally across the heavy iron bars of the cell. Simms could simply snatch it away if he wanted. But he knew that would do no good. And he knew that Lydia knew as much, too. That Pinkerton would break Simms' teeth on the spot. It warred inside of him, all of it. In his mind, the image of Burr loomed. Simms saw his cuspid smile, and a wave of fear ripped over him. But he also saw the tintype sitting there.

"You can have it now," Lydia said.

Simms took the tintype and squeezed Lydia's hand. Tears ran down his cheek and he kissed the image he finally held. He hollered, "Hey Pink! I know you're there. Come down here. There's something I got to tell you."

The Sheriff saw the benefit in a dual hanging, and hopefully a way to correct the greatest shortcoming of his career. He delayed the execution to see what the Pinkerton could discover in Chicago, though he knew it would raise some eyebrows in town.

Simms had remembered the name of the packing plant where Burr once said he was going to look for a job, the one from the flyer in Tennessee. He named it to the Pinkerton and that's all it took, that and a phone call from Queen's Tooth's very own phone, brand new and hanging on the wall in the Railroad office. The Pinkerton laid it all out to a fast-talking cop up in the Chicago precinct: Burr's description, the name of the plant, everything Simms gave him. But he felt the Chicago cop was short with him, as if he thought the Pinkerton was some sort of country bumpkin.

"I am a Pinkerton, sir," the deputy told the cop. But when the call ended, he wasn't at all confident that the Chicago police were interested in Burr Hollis, or in anything that happened in the back country of eastern Kentucky.

But the Pinkerton was wrong.

The Killing Floor
Chicago

This time it was different, and Burr knew it.

There were two entrances to the killing floor room, and both were covered by large uniformed police. And then there were the three walking toward him, big men with clubs. Burr could tell just by looking at them. If these men weren't police officers, they'd be convicts, toughs, or killers like him. They *wanted* to use the clubs, he could see that much right away. Even if he could get by them, the floor was slick with blood. It was enough just to walk around in the room without falling, let alone run somewhere. "Son of a bitch," Burr said to himself. "Simms."

"Put down that knife, hillbilly, or I'll gut you with it," the bigger of the policemen said to him. Burr might have gotten through one of them, or maybe even two, but the others would be ready to pounce. The *wanted* to pounce, they were *used* to it. He'd seen them in town, drinking freely, carousing with prostitutes freely, using their clubs freely. *What a job,* he had often thought. Too bad he couldn't apply for a position.

Burr dropped the knife and allowed them to take him away.

The Pinkerton's train arrived, and he walked to the station house downtown. The cops at the receiving desk were busy, and again he thought they treated him like a hayseed. But when they directed him to a burly detective with a scar that ran down his face and into his shirt collar, he learned that they hadn't dismissed his inquiry, not at all. The Pinkerton thought he misheard the cop when he was told, "We got your man, Kentucky. He's in the holding cell. You can take him back to the hills."

"What? What did you say?"

The detective rose from behind his desk and set his bowler on his head. He was on his way out, he told the Pinkerton. "Burr Hollis, right?"

"Yes. Yes! Burr Hollis," the Pinkerton said.

The cop pulled the Pinkerton alongside of him as he headed out. "Go see Officer Quinn," he said. "Walk across the street to the jail. Quinn will release your man to you. He'll give you some shackles. You can take him back to Kentucky tonight. Just head on back to the train station and look at the schedule. You can manage that, right? I'll send an officer with you."

"Yes, I can. But tell me, how did you find him."

The detective slapped a hand on the Pinkerton's shoulder as he moved beyond him, headed toward the door. He said, "You found him, Kentucky. We just picked him up for you. Take care, fella." The Pinkerton didn't really believe it was true until he saw Burr in the holding cell.

Burr gave the Pinkerton a look up and down, and then acted as if he couldn't care less about the man. The Pinkerton knew it was best to wait until they had boarded the train to ask Burr the questions he wanted answered. For now, though, he was content just to get his man.

A rookie cop was sent with the Pinkerton to the station as a security measure. He wasn't pleased about the assignment, but then again, he didn't complain openly about it. They walked on either side of Burr all the way to the station. When they got there, the cop shackled Burr's legs and waited until the Pinkerton and the prisoner had boarded the train. The Pinkerton used every trick he learned at the Academy, but Burr simply refused to talk. And he said only one thing during the entire train ride. Just before they arrived at the station in Queen's Tooth, he asked, "Will I be in the same cell as Simms Jackson?"

It wasn't the kind of news that would make the Chicago papers, and the Pinkerton wondered how Burr knew that Simms had even been caught.

"Well, will I?" Burr said.

All the way home, Clytie asked Lydia how she had done it, how had she gotten the rogue to give up what he knew. Lydia explained it again and again, but it wasn't enough for Clytie. "But Lyddie, what did you *say* to him? What were your words, woman? Tell me *exactly* what you said."

"Clytie, I told you as much as I can remember. I just studied on him the whole time. I watched what he said and how he said it. Lots of times I just kept quiet. Let him feel unnatural for a bit."

"Just kept *quiet*? What in hell, Lydia?"

"Like when we hunt, Clytie. Sometimes you need to be quiet, just set and listen. Set and watch. You know this as much as I do."

"But it's *man*, Lyddie, not a hare or a buck!"

Lydia laughed along with Clytie.

Holding the reins in one hand, Clytie took a bottle from a pocket in her dress and sipped hard on it. "Eye-God!" she screamed. "Whoooo—weee!" She passed the bottle over to Lydia who tipped it back and laughed. Soon enough, Clytie started with her questions again. "Now, Lyddie dear, how did he answer you when you told him about the tintype?"

And so it went until they finally arrived at Black Boar.

For a full week, things were nice. There was hope up on Black Boar again. After Clytie made the rounds to the few remaining families on the mountain, telling of Lydia's great feat and generally ramping up the details of the grand detective story, people began to feel that maybe there would be some peace for Lydia and Inez, and for Cornelius, too. Clytie related the great skills of the handsome Pinkerton, the one who single-handedly caught that raider, that violator, Simms Jackson. "Ain't no two ways about it, the way I see it. That Pinkerton is likely to bring in that other one soon enough. Anyway, the Sheriff is confident enough to wait and see. He sent that Pinkerton to Chicago. Now I know that's a big city, but Lydia found out where that rogue is working. Some factory up there."

"Law, Clytie," Hez's wife said. "Now tell it again, and don't leave anything out."

"Woman, I didn't leave anything out the first time I told it," Clytie said, but she added details that might or might not have been in Lydia's story. Who knew with Clytie Noe? Mountain forthrightness and honesty were values much esteemed on Black Boar, but most everyone loved the way Clytie told a tale.

"That country Sheriff was too dumb to know what was best," Clytie told one neighbor. "He flat refused Lydia a chance to talk with that rogue. But me and Lyddie stood right up to that Pinkerton. Told him what we were thinking. And being an intelligent man, a *trained detective*, I mean. Well, he knew what we said made sense." Clytie always winked when she told this part.

The neighbor woman and her husband were spellbound. "Well, what happened then, Clytie?"

"Hold on, now," Clytie said. She pulled her bottle from her

dress and pulled on it. "Have you a sup of this if you want to hear the rest now."

The man took a sip and passed it to his wife.

"Oh, Clytie Noe," the woman said. "You know I don't want any of this right now."

"Well, then I guess you don't want to hear the story of how Lydia Clemmons got that prisoner to give up his partner in crime."

The woman shook her head and took a sip of Clytie's whiskey, coughing violently with the effort. Clytie said, "Oh my, how you carry on, like you don't never have yourself a sup. Lord, woman. You ain't foolin' anyone."

"Clytie Noe. You stop that, now!" the woman protested.

Clytie shook her head and said, "Alright then. I'm gonna tell all of it now." She took another sip off the bottle, made a show of replacing the plug, and then told it, yet again.

In the days after Lydia's talk with Simms, the neighbors made it a point to stop by and talk with Lydia and Inez, and with Cornelius and Clytie. Lydia could never forget about Cole, nor could Inez forget about Preston, they knew. But there was a feeling on Black Boar, in the wake of Clytie's telling of things, a hopefulness, a sense that maybe something good would happen, or if not good, then something righteous, something just.

Lydia knew she had done something remarkable, but said little about it when people asked her, though Clytie still hounded her for details of her interview with Simms. She knew Lydia didn't want to go over it again and again, like she already had, but the story was too great, Clytie thought. She needed every detail. This was partly because she simply *had* to narrate it for others. But another part of it was pride in Lydia's savvy, in her skills and in her fearlessness. It was love for Lydia that kept her asking about it, even if Lydia had finished with it.

For her part, Lydia took a few days to break from her usual duties. Between Clytie and Inez, and with Cornelius' help, the work got done one way or the other. And it wasn't as if Lydia was shirking. She had simply decided to take Colette out into the woods with her, to look for the game that had become more and more scarce every year. She had cut two holes in a feed sack for the baby's legs and threaded buckskin thongs through the top of it. It was a sling, and it sat right beside Lydia's quiver of arrows. As they walked under the pignuts and sugar maples, she felt baby's hand touch the arrows now and again. Inwardly, this lifted her. She knew that someday she would show the girl how to nock an arrow, how to set a trap, and eventually how to shoot. She would tell her of how her own father had taught her such things. And of how the *little girl's* own father had gone out hunting with the little girl's mother when they courted. She would show her those places where they hunted, all of them, and the girl would hunt, too.

If there were anything left to hunt by that time.

They were well away from the cabins now, but Lydia knew where she was. She wanted to get far enough from even the few homesteaders remaining. She wanted to bring Colette into the woods where only the birds and the wind that gusted through the leaves could be heard, where only the riffles of the stream made noise. Lydia undid the ties on the sling when she reached the tiny waterfall she and Cole used to stop at. She took Colette under the arms and turned her so that she could feel the water course over the limestone rocks. The baby laughed when her hand touched the running water and she pulled her tiny fingers from it. But then Lydia placed Colette's hand beneath her own and set in on the stone over which the water flowed. It was a little riffle. The two of them, together, touched the stone and felt the water run over their hands. The baby squealed with laughter and slapped the water when Lydia had released her tiny hand. Lydia touched the baby's cheek with her wet hand, and then kissed the wet spot.

The baby howled with delight, but the sound startled something wild upstream.

Quickly Lydia swaddled the baby's legs in the feed sack sling and set her up against a beech tree, away from the water. She grabbed her bow, a single arrow, and moved upstream, looking for whatever it was on the other stream bank. She waited for several minutes, hearing only the little sounds of Colette, still in her line of sight when she looked back. Up above a red tail landed roughly on a branch and somewhere far off a jay sounded. A little breeze rustled some leaves but Lydia could hear nothing else. Her instinct told her to cross the stream, but she wasn't about to put the baby out of sight. For a second, she thought maybe she should have left Colette with Inez.

But then she saw it.

Across the stream a fat brown hare bounced out from behind some brush. It stopped and sniffed the air. Lydia waited. She knew she'd get a good shot if she could just wait. She nocked an arrow, but the hare drew back inside the brush. She heard it moving, but she couldn't see it. Then it popped out downstream, directly across from where Colette sat swaddled at the beech tree. The hare moved toward the water and Lydia saw it lift its nose and sniff the air again. She could see Colette, who had rolled onto her side and pointed her tiny hand at the hare.

Lydia watched the arrow pierce the soft fur of the animal, which shuddered and died on the spot. Colette chirped out and shook her little arms. Lydia took off her boots and waded across the stream. She drew the arrow fast through the animal, washed it in the stream, and then crossed over to Colette. She dried her feet on the hem of her dress and pulled her socks and boots back on.

She let Colette stroke the hare's soft fur and feel its warmth. The baby pulled on the hairs and squealed. Lydia laughed and kissed her. She dressed the animal there, leaving the entrails for the turkey vultures, and washed her hands in the stream. Then she cinched up Colette and headed back to the cabins. On the return it seemed to Lydia that Colette sounded out every time a bird chirped or the wind rustled the leaves. Lydia had stowed the hare in the bottom of the feed sack sling thinking Colette might like the feel of the animal's fur on her bare feet. Now she felt the baby's warmth on her back and the warmth of the hare just below that.

In time Colette began to whine and Lydia stopped to feed her. The baby's fingers clawed at Lydia's breast, and she suckled hard for much longer than normal. Lydia kept Colette in the feed sack sling, and she could feel the hare there in the bottom of the sack, against her stomach. She was glad that it could be done this way. It would be something she would tell the girl later on, she thought, a story about the hare in the feed sack, the hare her mother had killed along the stream, not long after her father had been killed by the Company. A story for someday, years from now.

Up above some sparrows sang their sharp notes and Lydia breathed in the smell of the wet earth and the thin, clean mountain air. She shifted Colette to her other breast, cupped her head and fingered the downy hair as she watched her nurse. And then Lydia noticed a small spot of blood on Colette's forehead, a smudge right where the hair met forehead. She hadn't noticed it before. Maybe the baby had reached down and touched the hare in the bottom of the feed sack sling, or maybe a trace of blood came off Lydia's hands earlier. Lydia could have cleaned off the smudge, wiped it away with a wet thumb. But she didn't. "That's a good sign," she said to Colette. "I think you're going to be woman of the woods someday." When the baby had finished feeding, Lydia cinched up the sling again and headed back to Clytie, Inez, and the others.

The train from Chicago was delayed in Louisville and didn't

arrive in Queen's Tooth until the middle of the night. Even so, the sheriff and two deputies were there waiting. The Sheriff insisted that the men wear their stars and that they clean up before the prisoner's arrival. But the deputies were tired now and not much concerned about how they looked with no one around to see them. They slouched on the railings of the train station deck.

"Seems like we're waiting on a pretty bride, Sheriff," the young deputy said. "Having to get all gussied up and such." Both of the deputies laughed. "Or maybe someone from the royal family," the other one joked.

The Sheriff shook his head. "Burr Hollis has killed many-a-man," he said. "Killed women, too, according to his prison record."

The young deputy said, "I understand that, but it seems like---"

The Sheriff clapped him hard across the face with an open hand. Then he slapped the other one. The men were stunned. "Pick up your hats and fix yourselves," the Sheriff said. "And don't open your fuckin' mouths again. Not tonight."

When the train arrived, the Pinkerton and Burr were the only passengers to depart. "Burr Hollis," the Sheriff said. "I'm Sheriff here. Come with me." The little party moved toward the jail house. No one said a word, and the only sound was the chains rattling on Burr's ankles.

When they arrived at the jailhouse, the Sheriff said, "You will be treated rightly here, so long as you treat others the same."

Burr spat near the Sheriff's boots. "Do you consider hanging proper treatment?" he asked.

But it was the Pinkerton who answered. "Hanging is much better than you deserve."

Burr laughed and said, "OK, then. Where's my cell?"

With both the Rail and the sawmill in town, the jail saw its fair share of trouble—saloon brawls, drunkenness, and the general vice brought about in a place where most of the male workers felt cheated and overworked. The two saloons in Queen's Tooth were places that saw fights almost nightly. But the Sheriff made certain no one was jailed on this night. It was just Simms and Burr, in separate cells. He made sure of it beforehand.

A gas lamp had been turned low, but Burr heard Simms' snoring the moment he entered the hallway. The Pinkerton removed Burr's shackles just outside his cell while the other deputies trained their revolvers on the convict. The door was closed, and the party left with no parting words to Burr. Only the sheriff said, "I'll see you in the morning."

Burr said nothing in reply.

Simms snored away down the hall. A few minutes after Burr's arrival, though, he awoke violently, gasping for breath and reaching at the air. Something was there. He could feel it. He just couldn't see it. Then he heard Burr's soft laughter down the hall, and he had to will himself to breathe again.

And Simms wasn't the only one. Way up on Black Boar, on her bed tick with Colette beside her, Lydia, too, awoke in a blind terror, though she could find nothing out of the ordinary in the cabin.

Still, she pulled Colette close to her.

The day after Burr arrived, the Sheriff had scheduled the double hanging for the coming Saturday, three days hence. He wanted to make sure Lydia and Inez knew this, but he wasn't looking forward to delivering the news himself. He thought about sending one of his deputies, but someone reminded him about the boy who used to work at the mill, how he had made a friend of Lydia and her mother, and of Clytie and Cornelius. So the Sheriff sent for the boy and asked him to deliver the news, and to take the newspapers up to the families on Black Boar.

"I was fixin' to do that anyway," the boy told him.

"Well, OK, then" the sheriff said. "Go on, now."

Lydia and Clytie were busy boiling clothes at a fire when the boy appeared on the two-rut road. Colette tried to roll herself over on the quilt that set nearby on the ground. Lydia made for the little baby quick-like, though she wasn't sure why. She only knew that she felt something like that cold terror that had awakened her the other night. "Go see what he wants, Clytie."

"Maybe it's good news," Clytie said. She hailed the boy. "C'mon here, son. What is it this time?"

The boy looked at Lydia, who held Colette close, both arms wrapped around her. "How's that baby doing, ma'am?"

"Fine," Lydia said, though her guard was still up. "Thank you."

"Well," the boy said, "I brung good news this time. They caught that other raider, that Burr Hollis. It was that Pinkerton detective who found him. It's all right here in the paper." He handed the newspaper to Clytie, who looked over the article.

"Hellfire, Lyddie. They got him!" she said.

Lydia pulled Colette's face up into her neck and kissed her.

"Lyddie?" Clytie said. "Are you hearing this?"

"Yes, yes, I am," she said, though she seemed far away someplace.

"I was glad to do it, Mrs. Clemmons," the boy said. "There's gonna be a double hanging come Saturday. Right in town. Out in front of the Sheriff's office, the Railroad office."

Clytie jumped in, "We'll be there. Tell that Pinkerton We'll be there." Clytie pulled her bottle from her dress pocket and took a sip of whiskey. "Eye-God!" she screamed. She handed the bottle to Lydia, who took a small sip so as not to spoil Clytie's celebration. But Lydia didn't tell her about what she had been feeling ever since she awoke in a terror the other night, about the ever-present dread, that sense of sick unease that she didn't have a word for. "Fear" was the closest she could come up with.

It was with her all the while now.

The Sheriff had given strict instructions to the overnight jailers: Do not allow Burr Hollis out of his cell. He has a bucket in there, and his food will be brought to him. If he's dying somehow, let him die. Do not call a doctor. Better that than give him an inch. Burr figured as much himself. He knew he'd have to go about things differently this time, without any confederates and without a real plan.

Still, he had a notion.

At around four in the morning Burr removed all of his clothes, stuck his finger down his throat, and vomited on the floor at the cell door. He dumped his waste from the bucket on top of the vomitus. Then he began to bang on the cell door with the bucket. When he heard the quick steps of the jailer coming down the hall, he lay face down in the mess, one arm through the cell door posts.

Down the hall, Simms curled himself into a ball on his cot.

"By God, what's going on here?" The jailer was unnerved at the mess and didn't know exactly what to do. He knew one thing, though: He wasn't about to open the cell door. Burr could only moan in answer to the jailer's demands.

"What in hell is going on here? I ain't calling no doctor, Hollis. You'll die here if you don't tell me what in hell is happening. It stinks like hell. What have you done to yourself?"

Burr said nothing now. He held his breath.

Eventually, the jailer kicked Burr's arm, but Burr didn't react. He did it again and then hollered out to Simms down the little hallway, "Do you know what happened here, Jackson? What's happened to Hollis?"

Simms curled himself even tighter on his cot.

"What happened here, Jackson, goddamnit?" There was a real urgency now in the jailer's voice, a blind terror spreading.

"I don't know," Simms choked out. Something in him told him to warn the jailer, but he was afraid to do so. It was just like up on the mountain in the days after the escape.

The jailer nudged Burr's head with his boot. Nothing. And then again he poked him in the ribs. Again, no reaction. But when he bent down to look in Burr's face, Burr's arm shot out. He caught the jailer's ankle and yanked it toward him. The man fell and let out a scream. But Burr had already managed to draw the leg inside the bars on the jail door. He sat on the man's knee and pulled up on the ankle. When the knee snapped, the jailer let out a scream that ripped down the small corridor and carried into Simms' cell. Bound tightly into a knot on his bed, his arms around his knees, Simms let out a low groan.

"Hush now," Burr told the deputy.

He reached through the bars and grabbed the jailer's shirt collar, drawing him to the base of the door where he gouged out an eye with his thumb and then crushed the man's windpipe. In a few seconds he had the key ring and was out of the cell. He did his best to wipe his face clean with his jail clothes, but he didn't spend much time at it. In a minute he was in the jailer's clothes, a little big for him, but they'd have to do. The man had had no gun.

When Simms heard Burr's laugh and his slow footsteps coming toward his cell, he swooned and went out.

Burr hadn't said a word to Simms since his arrival, and though Simms thought several times of saying something, fear got the better of him and he never opened his mouth. When he came to, Burr was standing at his cell door. He was smiling, and the silver cuspid caught the dim light of the oil lamp on the wall. He shook the ring of keys he held and Simms swooned again.

"Hey you," Burr hissed, "don't you go out on me. I ain't gonna hurt you."

"Burr," Simms said. He tried to say more but he couldn't.

"Yes, it's your old friend Burr. I don't have time to talk, convict. But I need to know why you give me up? Now that ain't like you. That I never would have figured. Talk fast, friend."

"Burr," Simms tried to gather himself, "that Pinkerton. Look at my ear, look at my back." Simms unbuttoned the prisoner's shirt he wore and turned his back to Burr.

"He beat it out of you, huh? He *is* a determined one. That I can tell."

"Yeah, Burr, he beat it out of me."

Burr was about to head out into the night, but he saw something in Simms that told him not to go just yet, something in his eyes.

"Well, hold on there now," Burr said. "Are you sure?"

"Burr, look at me," Simms said. But his voice shook when he said it.

Burr jangled the key ring lightly and said, "I may need to look at them wounds, friend. I'm not sure that's what caused you to give me up, now that I study on it." He raised the ring to eye level and began to finger through the few keys.

"Burr," Simms said. "Don't do it." He knew Burr had sniffed out the lie.

"Don't do what?"

Simms laid out the story, fast. Yes, the Pinkerton had tried, but Simms held tough. It was the girl, the young girl from Black Boar, years ago, the one who was the reason for everything. She had something Simms wanted, the tintype."

Burr shook his head. "That little goddamn wood nymph. One who killed Henry. Cut off her own goddamn thumb. Hell, Simms."

"It's the truth, Burr."

"Give me that tintype," Burr said.

"Burr, please. I'm gonna die anyhow. Let me have it."

Burr lifted the key ring and made to search for the key to the cell. Simms tossed the tintype through the cell door.

Burr picked it up and said, "I've got to go now, convict. Got to get far away from here. Now, I'll take good care of this keepsake. I'll not desecrate it. But just you remember that I have it, and that it makes me think of you." Burr left the key ring at the base of the cell door. "Here," he said, "you can be free, too."

Then he was gone into the night.

Simms' collapsed on the cot. His entire body shook, and then he began a sustained whimpering, a crying like he had never before experienced, even when he learned of the death of his sister, years and years ago.

He never once considered using the keys. They were right there on the floor the next morning when the Sheriff arrived to find the horror that awaited him. To be hanged, Simms knew, was better than to be free in a world with Burr still out there.

Burr knew the Sheriff would send trackers up Rusty Mountain and along the roads and canebreaks into and out of Queen's Tooth. Rightly, he figured they'd not send men looking for him up on Black Boar, where he was headed. But not because he thought it was the best route for escape. No, Burr had something else on his mind.

A reckoning.

The sky had just begun to color when he arrived at the same spot where he had killed Hez's dog years ago. He had no weapon this time, just an old oil lamp he had stolen on his way out of town. But a weapon didn't matter much, he figured. He still had his hands, weapons enough against a one-thumbed mountain girl. He envisioned it now, his eyes closed, how proper it would be. Every bit as just and good as the others who had crossed him over the years, maybe even more so. Soon the gray light began to seep through the tree canopy, with its little hints of orange that set the oaks and sycamore leaves into relief. Hill people rose early, in all seasons, Burr knew. It wouldn't be long.

And then he saw her.

The cabin door opened, and a woman was framed by the doorway, the orange glow from the hearth outlining her form. He would need to get up close to see if it was her, though. The thumb. That would tell him. She moved down a little path that disappeared into the tall trees. Burr flanked her, using the trees as cover. He lost sight of her now and again, but he could hear her, he *sensed* her, and he hoped she continued on further away from the cabin. Eventually she stopped and Burr got a fix on her. The sky had lightened some, but what made its way through the canopy was still orange-gray.

Burr moved in, little by little. He peeked out from behind a wide sycamore, and she moved into his line of vision. She just stood there, arms at her sides. Again, Burr moved closer, and he thought he caught the scent of pine tar soap. He watched the woman lift her face to the tree canopy. There was a cardinal up there that sang out. Maybe that was what she was fixed on. Burr crept nearer. He could see her chest expand and sink now. She took in deep breaths. A morning routine, he figured.

Her last.

But just then something in her manner changed. Burr felt it more than he saw it, though her head shifted slightly, and she stiffened. He moved behind a tree not ten feet from her and she wheeled on him. He had pulled behind the wide trunk just in time. Burr listened. He couldn't see her but he felt the fear in the air.

This had to be done now, he knew.

The woman felt it, felt it keenly in all of her senses. Something was there, close. Some animal. Something unafraid. Something hostile. She turned and ran toward the cabin.

But it was too late. Burr darted from behind the tree and took Lydia's wrist in a death grip. Before she could do anything about it, he had swung her around and clapped his hand over her mouth. He saw the snakeskin cinch and the wood thumb. He looked Lydia in the eye and smiled. The last thing she saw, before he punched her square in the mouth, was the shiny silver cuspid.

Long, Long Ago

BLACK BOAR MOUNTAIN

It was a large cat. One of the old men had chased it away from the body. When he told the story later to the others, he said it wasn't the mangled kinsman that affected him as much as the animal itself, with its reddened nose and whiskers. One of its long fangs was covered in blood. It was rage that he felt, he said, not sadness. And the animal looked directly at him before it stalked off, brazenly and without fear. The man was old and the big cat knew it. But the cat knew better than to linger. There would be others if this old one were still alive.

That's what the old man told the others. Years ago, he also said, he would have gathered his weapons and tracked it himself. But he knew he couldn't do such a thing now, not at this point in his life. This was the source of his rage. This and the fact that a man had been killed, a kinsman.

The woman, the wife of the killed man, had already gone out with the hunting party.

1910

BLACK BOAR MOUNTAIN

(Lydia, age 22)

Soft orange light fell through the tree canopy and two wrens communicated with one another in the hickories. Lydia's head throbbed, and for a moment she was unsure where she was or what had happened. She heard water moving over a riffle and she groaned as she tried to rise. But she could only roll onto her side. She recognized the place, the stream and the small riffle. She knew the tree, too, a large beech. It was coming back to her, some pleasant place. But then Burr moved into her vision, both legs astride her body. And she remembered. A wave of terror coursed through her.

"Well, I ain't got time for a long talk, or nothing else," Burr said. "You ought to be glad that I'm gonna make this quick." He took a handful of Lydia's hair and yanked her up. She swooned but she didn't go out. Her head throbbed. She had to work just to get air, to spit out the blood that had filled her mouth. It covered her chin and neck, and a singular, long thread of it dangled grotesquely.

"You are a sight, woman," Burr laughed. "Like a monster, you are."

He yanked her hair again and set the tintype in her field of vision. "You remember this?" Lydia worked hard to focus, and just as it came to her, what it was, Simms' tintype, Burr covered her mouth and raked the sharp metal corner down her cheek, from temple to chin. Lydia's scream was buried in Burr's grip and in the blood that had continued to fill her mouth. She choked and tried to pull away, but Burr had dropped the tintype and now held her head in the crook of his arm, his hand still fast to her mouth. Lydia's eyes bulged and blood shot through her nose. Burr released her and she gasped for air, doubled over.

"Well, now, like I said. This is the end of the line and I ain't got time for much more of this, entertaining as it is. Woman, I am gonna strangle you to death and you're gonna watch me do it."

Lydia's eyes were filled with water, and she wiped at them with her good hand. There was an instant just before Burr moved on her, a moment that lasted more than a moment. Lydia knew then where they were. It was the beech tree where she had set Colette when she stalked and killed the hare. All at once she saw it—the baby by the tree, her tiny hand extended toward the hare across the stream. She heard the sounds Colette had made that day, and she remembered the soft, wet lips she kissed before she set her again into the feed sack sling. She saw the girl's eyes, the wet and dark little orbs that darted toward the sounds of the forest and recognized the mother who swaddled her and kissed her ruddy cheeks.

Burr grabbed a fistful of hair and set a hand to Lydia's throat. He made to say something, but that's as far as he got. Lydia summoned what was left in her. With her good hand she seized Burr's wrist and broke his hold. She sank her teeth down onto two fingers. Burr yelled and tried to wrench his hand free, but Lydia's jaw crushed the hand with feral desperation. Her head and body swung this way and that with Burr's efforts. Burr cursed and hit her brutally on the head, but she held on, her teeth sinking all the way to the bone.

Eventually, she could hang on no longer, though, and Burr

shook free. He cursed and tried to stanch the blood coming from his hand. But his problems were worse than just bleeding. The knuckle of his index finger was collapsed, and his middle finger was set off at a crazy angle. The blood sheathed his hand now and began to run down his forearm and onto the forest floor. Lydia made for the stream, but Burr was right behind her. He took her down at the knees and she fell, half into the water. Burr used his good hand to haul her to her feet by her dress. He made to seize onto her neck again, but he didn't realize that Lydia had grabbed a rock when she fell. It came full force across Burr's cheek and he went down.

Lydia ran off into the woods, running like she had never run before. Soon she realized she was headed away from the cabins, but when she turned to right her course, she saw Burr walking toward her, a bloody mess, like some kind of forest demon. She saw him smile then, at least she thought that's what she saw, silver cuspid and all. She had no choice. She turned and headed on a path over some sandstone boulders higher up the mountain. Her head throbbed but she kept moving, fast as she could. She took routes she thought Burr wouldn't be able to navigate easily, through briar patches and laurel slicks, forcing her way, keeping on, though in time she began to tire. Every now and again she'd gain a vantage point on a boulder or up on a rise where she'd stop just long enough to see if Burr was still on her trail. She was encouraged when she seemed to have lost him, but then she'd hear him, and once she even caught a glimpse of movement below her. He was still there, still moving just as fast as she.

The climb wore heavily on her.

She tried to descend a gulley too quickly and fell, rolling to a stop in the wet earth at the base of the slope. She worked hard to get her breath. She knew she'd have to take the rise that faced her in one march. To stop midway up would be disastrous. When she got her wind, she began the move up the steep incline. But as she neared the top, she began to fade. Her head ached but it was her legs that failed her. She cursed and clawed her way up, barely gaining the top of the rise where she collapsed, wheezing. She could *feel* her heart about to explode, and she knew that if she didn't rest, she'd not be able to go on. She turned onto her back and lay there at the top of the rise.

A sudden terror seized her then and she sat up to look for Burr.

He was nowhere in sight, and she couldn't hear any movement. She lay back down heavily and stared up into the tree canopy. A pair of cardinals tore from a branch above her, the red male following the gray female, and something rustled about behind a fallen chestnut trunk nearby.

Her legs had given out, her head throbbed, and her face stung horribly from temple to chin. She was terribly dizzy, she realized, but she didn't fight it, not just yet. She tried only to take in air and still herself, to recover before she rose and headed out again. A part of her desperately needed to rest, to lie there in the leaves and give over to fatigue. She fought the urge from within, from the same place where she found the strength to use the knife on her own hand years ago. She fought the bouts of dizziness with declarations that she would rise up and continue to run, to move through the woods she knew so well how to navigate. But at the moment she began to rise, her legs would fail her.

It was in this in-between space when things changed for Lydia, when she saw her.

For a second, she didn't recognize her, and then just as quickly it came back to her. The bog woman. The image lasted only an instant, but it was enough. In her mind, she lay just as Lydia had seen her that day with her father, still covered with wet black soil, but with her features visible. She lie there in the shallow grave, her tawny skin taut over her high cheekbones, and her coal black hair pulled back from her forehead.

When the bog woman opened her eyes to look at her, Lydia shot up off the ground.

Long, Long Ago

BLACK BOAR MOUNTAIN

The woman got onto the trail before the others. It was hard for her, though. The blood she followed was not that of a wounded animal this time. It was that of her husband, traces left behind from the animal's paws and face. She followed too fast, guided by rage more than cunning or intelligence. And it surprised her when she came upon it. She barely had time to nock an arrow. Even then, it wasn't a clean shot. She had hit the leg only, and now she had to follow the trail much further. Eventually, the animal tired and faded, just as she did. She hit it properly the next time. The men of the party were far away when she dispatched the animal with her axe. Still, they heard a terrifying sound, a wild cry, a scream that shook the trees, they said.

It was not the sound of the cat she had killed, but the woman herself.

BLACK BOAR MOUNTAIN

(Lydia, age 22)

Lydia knew where she was headed. Her legs carried her there now, almost as if they worked independently of her body. How she arrived there from the base of the gulley, a place she wasn't sure she had even been to, she didn't know. The trek was long and tough, over boulders and through dense briars. She saw Burr only once on the climb, but she knew she would never outpace him, would never be able to hide or escape. She *would* encounter him at some point. This she knew in the deepest depths of her being. Though she didn't know how it would end.

At the farthest edge of the bog, she stopped and caught her breath. She heard movement not too far below her. She would need to find it, quickly. She looked for the rocks, but the bog was full of small ponds and little pools of water. Now it was Burr's voice she heard below. What he said she couldn't decipher, but the tone she knew. That of the predator.

She scanned the space slowly. She took a single step and then stopped. The limbs of an old birch creaked in a strong gust of wind and Lydia watched some leaves swirl and fall to the earth. And there it was, she realized. She ran toward the spot. Just under a small pool of water the stones were visible, the rough outline of the grave. Lydia dropped to her knees and scraped out a trench in the soft earth. The water began to flow away. She heard movement and turned behind her to get a fix on Burr. He had slowed now, knowing his prey wasn't going anywhere.

Lydia figured she had about a minute, but she didn't know if it would be enough. She tore furiously at the earth, hoping she was digging in the right place. Burr hollered something but she didn't have the time to look back, didn't have time to take stock of his position. With both hands she shoveled at the wet soil. Her arms and shoulders ached, and her fingers had stiffened from the effort. Still, she tore at the earth.

And then Burr was upon her. Still, she didn't turn to face him.

"I reckon you're digging your own grave, woman," he said. "But I intend to leave you for the buzzards." Lydia kept at it, sinking her hands and searching for it.

"Well, then, if you've got nothing to say, neither do I," Burr said. He stepped toward her and reached out to take her from behind.

But it was Lydia who reached out first. In a single motion, she rose from the earth and set her bad hand on Burr's chest, the palm flat against his body. The last thing Burr saw before it happened was the snake skin cinch that held her prosthetic, there flat against his chest. Before the strike Burr heard something like nothing he had ever heard before, even in a lifetime of killing things. It was a wild and deafening howl—unholy sounding, something of the forest, untamed and inhuman. It was the collective sound of all the predators that ever lived, that ever stalked prey, throughout time, brought together in one primal sound from out Lydia's bloody mouth.

He saw only the flash of an object, the quick motion of it through the air. But he didn't yet feel that his ear had just been shorn from his head. He felt only fear, then, the absolute terror of the prey, an instinctive sense that his end was near.

Then the motion again. The blade of the stone axe snapped Burr's clavicle and bit deeply into his shoulder. He felt a hot sharp pain this time, beyond anything he had ever felt before. He held his hand up against another blow, but it never came. Lydia had slipped in the wet earth of the bog and Burr ran with the speed and fear of a hunted animal.

Long, Long Ago

BLACK BOAR MOUNTAIN

Something happened to the woman and she died. Her insides had ruptured, or some spirit had killed her. In agony, she had clutched at her abdomen for hours before she left the earth for good. None of the herbs or rituals worked this time around, and they buried her with the others, high on the hill where the ground was soft, where mosses grew alongside strange flowers and plants. A kinswoman set a line of rocks around the body after it was covered up. This was unusual, but the kinswoman wanted to mark the spot in case she ever came back. The clan were leaving soon to find a place where there was more game. The same kinswoman knew the value of the axe for the one now gone. And so before she helped lay her friend in the soft black earth, the kinswoman made sure to sharpen the axe as best she could. Maybe her friend would need it in the next world, she thought.

1910

BLACK BOAR MOUNTAIN

(Lydia, age 22)

Burr stumbled across the bog, unmindful of the pools of water that tripped him and slowed him. When he fell, he scrambled and raced on, without a curse word, without checking to see what damage might have been done. He simply jumped up and ran. He had no destination, no route. His only feeling was to get away. At the edge of the bog some sense began to return to him, and he turned to check on his predator. He couldn't see her. And for an instant he thought maybe she had given up. But then he heard the scream again, the howl, not close, but getting closer. The terror rose up inside and he raced on blindly, heading he knew not where, just away.

It wasn't difficult. Deer and elk trailed far less blood than what Lydia now tracked. But there was the sense of urgency, the feeling that, somehow, her prey might escape. It could happen, Lydia well knew. More than once she or Cole had injured an animal only to lose it somewhere, somehow. It was part of the mystery of the forest. And so Lydia moved fast over the clearing. Her linsey dress dripped water from the bog and mud covered her arms to the elbows. She had gambled on a shortcut through the laurel slick, but it was tough going and now the dress was ripped everywhere.

A spider's web of blood spread across the bridge of her nose and cheek. On her high collar a solitary filament followed the line of buttons that ran down the front of her dress. Nor had she cleared the flow of blood from her nose, and coppery red traces lined the spaces between her teeth. Her chin was a shiny red mass.

When she reached the edge of the clearing, she pulled up short. There was a red tail somewhere above, and for a moment she confused its song for her quarry. She closed her eyes and listened, trying hard to slow her breathing. High up a squirrel darted from a drey and somewhere nearby a woodpecker worked on a tree. Lydia realized then that she had lost her wooden thumb in the chase, though the snake skin cinch that had held it was still fixed to her wrist. But all this had to be put aside now. She would have to listen more deeply. Again, she took in a long breath and closed her eyes.

And then she heard it.

There was movement at the base of the limestone formation a full forty feet below. She clambered down a route more dangerous than one she would have normally followed, and when she hit the boulders, she took off running. She heard him moving, heard the crisp leaves rustle with his uneven stride, and she saw ahead where she thought she might intercept him. She leapt over a crevice and sighted him. Burr was a mess of his own thick gore clotted with the debris from briars and brush. A rhododendron leaf clung to the place where his ear had been. He moved along the path the best he could, with a desperation fueled by the desire to escape a more powerful animal. He looked up when he heard something on the boulders above.

But it was too late.

Lydia flew like a hawk above him, her arms outstretched. And like a hawk she came straight down on him. In her good hand, she extended the stone axe, and from somewhere deep inside her, she released the terrible sound again.

All through the forest birds shrieked and animals scrambled for cover. Trees groaned with a cold wind that gusted leaves and felled smaller branches to the earth. The entire hill roiled with panic and flight. All things living shook with it and Lydia raised the axe for the last time.

It took longer to get back to the bog than she expected. She had traveled much farther than she had thought. She worked the rawhide on the axe under a pool of water, trying hard to wash away the blood. Then she removed the snakeskin cinch on her hand and ran her palm over the stone blade of the axe. She touched the sharp poll that protruded through the hole in the wood handle, like she had done with her father years ago. And she thought of something he had said back then: "Once these hills had everything people needed. Once. It was never easy for them folks, my momma and daddy, and them before. And I ain't sure what will happen with this Railroad. I don't know if life will get easier or harder. But once these hills were enough, Lyddie dear. Once. That much I know." Lydia drew the axe head flat across her forearm and felt the heft of the tool one more time, just as she had done with her father at the bog grave, years ago.

She removed enough dirt to reveal the bog woman's face, and her high cheekbones and black hair. Then she set the axe on the woman's chest along with the snakeskin cinch. She bent forward and kissed her lips.

"Goodbye, sister," she said.

She swept the earth back into the grave.

ACKNOWLEDGMENTS

I am especially grateful to Ron Phillips and all of the fine writers at Shotgun Honey Books for their constant care and aid. Also, I wish to thank Silas House--and those at the Appalachian Writers' Workshop--for some important direction, along with the following writers: Meagan Lucas, Robert Gipe, Karen Salyer-McElmurray, and Dwyer Murphy of CrimeReads. Finally, I'd like to recognize the tireless work of independent book reviewers Brad Proctor, Mark Pelletier, and Kevin Whitten. Of course, I couldn't have the written the book without the support of Julie McGinley.

Chris McGinley's **Coal Black** (Shotgun Honey, 2019) is a collection of crime stories set in the hills of Appalachia. His fiction has appeared in Cutleaf, Reckon Review, Mystery Tribune, Mystery Weekly, Tough, Switchblade, Pulp Modern, and other forums. Non-fiction work--film and literature analysis--has appeared in CrimeReads, Mystery Tribune, Reckon Review, and elsewhere. "The Screech Owl," a short story, was nominated for a Pushcart award, and "Hellbenders" made the "List of Distinguished Stories" in Best American Mystery Stories (2020).

His full-length novel, **Once these Hills** (Shotgun Honey, 2023) is set in late-nineteenth century eastern Kentucky.

McGinley teaches middle school in Lexington, KY where he lives with his wife.

ABOUT
SHOTGUN HONEY BOOKS

Thank you for reading *Once These Hills* by Chris McGinley.

Shotgun Honey began as a crime genre flash fiction webzine in 2011 created as a venue for new and established writers to experiment in the confines of a mere 700 words. More than a decade later, Shotgun Honey still challenges writers with that storytelling task, but also provides opportunities to expand beyond through our book imprint and has since published anthologies, collections, novellas and novels by new and emerging authors.

We hope you have enjoyed this book. That you will share your experience, review and rate this title positively on your favorite book review sites and with your social media family and friends.

Visit ShotgunHoneyBooks.com

FICTION WITH A KICK

shotgunhoneybooks.com

Printed in the USA
CPSIA information can be obtained
at www.ICGtesting.com
JSHW031943161023
50147JS00007B/19